BY ANY OTHER NAME

Forbidden Series
Book One

J.M. DARHOWER

ISBN-10: 1942206135
ISBN-13: 978-1-942206-13-2

"What's in a name? That which we call a rose
By any other name would smell as sweet."
Romeo and Juliet, Act 2 Scene 2

Two families, both alike in reputation,
In the streets of New York, where we lay our scene,
A power struggle gives way to a deadly rivalry,
Where spilled innocent blood makes everyone's hands unclean.

PROLOGUE

The restaurant stood in the southern most section of Little Italy, an upscale brick pizzeria on the corner of a block. Windows spanned the entire front of the building, once giving a clear picture of the fancy red and gold trimmed booths and hanging chandeliers inside, but the glass had since been tinted, blacked out to obscure the view.

The people who frequented the place didn't like to be watched.

Primo Galante stepped out the front door one Friday night in the summer of 1993, followed by his wife, Cara. Once a bona fide beauty queen, Cara had long ago exchanged her crown and sash for diapers and pacifiers, giving up pageants for motherhood and marriage.

She was still the most beautiful woman to ever walk the earth, according to Primo. His love for her had only grown stronger over the years, and standing there, watching her as she held tightly to their youngest, little Genevieve, he felt his heart swell in his chest. His baby girl looked just like her mother, with the same black hair and bright blue eyes. She would be a heartbreaker someday, ripping hearts straight from men's chests with just a simple look, much like Cara had done to him the first time he laid eyes on her years ago.

The boys ran around them, weaving between their legs as they laughed and played, hands held in the shape of guns as they pretend-shot at each other. Cara rolled her eyes at their game, but Primo grinned with satisfaction. His boys. They were his pride and joy, especially his Joey, with so much wit and intelligence at only seven years old. Dante, just barely five, was much more sensitive of the two. Joey was the leader, diving headfirst into everything, so fearless and outgoing, whereas Dante merely followed his brother's every move with a quiet reflection. Deep, that boy was. Maybe even too deep.

Soft-hearted.

"Happy birthday, Primo," Cara said, setting Genevieve down in the gravel lot on her feet. The girl swayed, sleepy and just getting used to her new white dress shoes, the front of her pink fluffy dress covered in pizza sauce. She got her bearings quickly and toddled off after her big brothers.

Primo pulled his wife to him and gently kissed her blood-red lips. His thirtieth birthday. This was the year... the year *everything* changed, the year he made his long-anticipated big moves. He had already set it all in motion. It didn't matter who he had to knock down to succeed. It was only a matter of time before he came out on top.

"I can't wait to get you home," he whispered against her mouth, his hands gripping her hips, fingers brushing against the bare skin beneath the hemline of her shirt. "I want to unwrap my present."

"Hmm," she said, a playful twinkle in her eyes. "What present would that be?"

"You," he said, nipping at her bottom lip. "I want to unwrap it, and play with it all night long."

She laughed, pushing away from him, her eyes scanning the lot for their children. He didn't come first anymore, and he accepted that. These days, he was more like fourth in line for her attention. She stepped over to where Genevieve was bent over, digging rocks out of the ground, her sticky hands covered in filth.

Primo turned to the door of the pizzeria when it opened and some of his business associates stepped out. He struck up conversation with them, finalizing the deal they'd been hashing out over dinner to break into a new territory just south in Chinatown as they finally hedged their way into Little Italy.

But he wouldn't stop there, no. Before it was all over, every block in Manhattan would belong to *him*.

One of the men glanced over Primo's shoulder as they chatted, eyes narrowing suspiciously as he gazed out toward the street. "Hey, Primo, you know that car?"

Primo turned immediately, spotting the black car creeping up, coming to a stop right across the street. "No."

"That's the second time it came by since we've been standing here," the man said. "Stopped both times."

Coldness swept through Primo as he stared at it. The generic black car could belong to anyone, but it wasn't anyone *he* recognized, personally. Two blocks east was the Lower East Side, long-time Galante territory, but to the west, in Soho, the Barsanti family reigned. They were standing on middle ground, arguably the most risky place they could ever be during a time of change.

"Kids!" Primo hollered. They were getting dangerously close to the road, where the car lurked. "Come here."

Joey eagerly ran over with Dante right on his heels. "Yeah, Dad?"

"Why don't you wait in the car?" Primo suggested. "It's getting dark."

"Okay," Joey said obediently, never arguing. His father's word was infallible to the boy. "Can we listen to the radio?"

"Yeah, uh, sure," he said, pulling his keys from his pocket and tossing them to Joey, his eyes never leaving the lingering black car. "Just don't drive away without us, kiddo."

Joey ran off, straight for the black Impala parked along the side of the adjacent lot. Dante started right behind him but stalled after a second, turning to his sister. "Come on, Genna."

The girl looked up when she heard her name, smiling giddily and starting after him, rocks clenched in her small fists.

"What's going on?" Cara asked as she approached, slipping beneath her husband's arm, a look of concern on her face. "Is something wrong?"

"Car by the curb," Primo said. "I think they're watching us."

She tensed slightly but kept her cool, only vaguely casting a look at the street before turning to watch her children. Primo could see the worry in her eyes, the look of apprehension, a million and one questions, none of which he wanted to answer.

Joey climbed into the driver's side to turn on the radio as Dante ambled through the lot, dragging his feet, torn between racing after his big brother, like he wanted to do, and waiting on his tottering little sister, like he knew he should. Primo's eyes remained glued to the car, slowly reaching into his coat and grasping his gun tucked in the holster.

Slowly, the driver's side window rolled down a few inches. Adrenaline pumped through Primo's veins. He expected to see a gun, expected a hail of gunfire, and was preparing to shield his family from a spray of bullets, but it never came.

The second Joey slammed the driver's side door, the tires on the lurking car squealed as it shot away, leaving a cloud of smoke as it hastily sped from the neighborhood.

Primo's heart dropped into his stomach as he spun around to face his Impala. Through the window, he could see Joey sticking the key in the ignition.

Oh, God. No. No.

"No, Joey!" Primo screamed, but it was too late. Joey turned the key as he looked up at his father, his brow furrowing for a fraction of a second before it happened.

BOOM

Primo felt it before he heard it, felt the force of the detonation, shockwaves rolling from the vehicle, vibrating the ground like an earthquake beneath his feet. The car exploded into a raging fireball. Metal flew through the lot as the windows of the pizzeria shattered. The force of the explosion knocked them all off their feet, picking Dante up and blasting him through the air as the fire singed his chest, his shirt engulfed in flames.

Cara screamed, an ear-splitting cry of terror, as Dante let out a horrific shriek of agony. She scrambled to him, frantic to put out the fire burning him, as Genevieve burst into tears, laying flat on her back in the gravel.

Primo sat frozen, the world around him in slow

motion, as he stared through the haze at where the car used to be, seeing nothing but a metal frame, completely gutted, now a ten-foot tall ball of fire with thick black smoke pillowing into the night sky. Joey, his boy, his pride and joy, was nowhere to be found. *Gone.*

Primo's ears rang, blocking out the crying, diluting the screaming as the world around him fell into total anarchy. He faded into a state of shock, one word escaping his lips, barely a murmur of a reaction.

Barsanti.

ONE

They say the night is darkest just before the dawn.

I say if you're gonna break the law, that's the perfect time to do it.

"Hurry up, Jackson!" Genna's vigilant eyes darted around the dilapidated Harlem neighborhood, the streets seeming even shadier through the black tinted windows. "Jesus, what the hell's taking you so long?"

"Relax." His voice was sluggish, thanks to the five shots of tequila he'd downed back-to-back before leaving the party. "It's hard to see in the dark."

Reaching into her purse, Genna dug around and pulled out her cell phone, pressing a button to light it up. A soft white glow surrounded them in the car and illuminated part of the dash, but Jackson still struggled.

Something told her it was the tequila and not the darkness that tripped him up.

Frustrated, she reached over and snatched the screwdriver from his hand, practically climbing over into his lap to shove it into the steering column. It resisted at first when she jammed it in the small key slot, but after wiggling, she managed to get it to turn.

The engine loudly roared to life.

"Ha!" She triumphantly tossed her phone back into her purse as she settled into the passenger seat. "Amateur."

Jackson shot her a playful grin as he flipped on the headlights and threw the car in gear. He pulled away from the curb as his hand darted toward her, grasping the back of her neck to yank her to him for a kiss. It was messy, and reckless, as he sped down the street, eyes closing from lust and not watching out of the windshield.

He clipped a parked car but hardly noticed in the haze.

"You're so hot," he slurred, pulling back from the kiss, but he didn't let go of her. Instead, he yanked her further to him, shoving her head down toward his crotch.

Uh, what?

She pulled from his grasp, shoving him so hard the car veered into the other lane. "What kind of girl do you take me for?"

"Come on, baby," he whined. "I'm so turned on. I need you."

He theatrically frowned, dark eyes flashing toward her in the car. His blond hair was shaggy, pieces curling out around his ears. He was irresistibly cute.

Or maybe I'm just insanely drunk.

Either way, she conceded easily. What kind of girl was she? A girl with a fucked up set of morals. After all, they *did* just steal a car.

A hiss escaped his throat when she went down on him, taking his cock into her mouth. Her eyes drifted closed, blackness surrounding her, and a few short strokes later she felt him tense and gasp, every muscle in his body seizing up.

Coming already?

She prepared herself for the imminent explosion, but instead he slammed the car brakes as his hand grasped the back of her head, forcefully yanking her away from him. "Fuck!"

The moment her eyes flew open, the curse echoed through her mind. *Fuck.*

Red and blue flashing lights illuminated Jackson's terrified face as a siren cut through the quiet night. He fumbled with his shorts, panicked, and tucked himself back away as he swung the car to the nearest free curb. Throwing it in park, he reached for his seatbelt and frantically snapped it into place.

Genna couldn't help it. She burst into laughter. A seatbelt violation was the *least* of their concerns. Who gave a shit if they were wearing one? Jackson shot her a look that said she was no longer appealing, but she thought he was even cuter now.

So naive.

That was why she liked him. To some he seemed ignorant, foolish, even *oblivious*, but Genna appreciated the simplicity. He treated her normal, didn't care about her name or her family, when the rest of Manhattan seemed to gawk at the mere mention.

Genna relaxed in the passenger seat as the NYPD cruiser crookedly pulled right up to their bumper, blocking them in.

Play it cool, she told herself. *Act like you have no idea what's going on.*

Two officers approached, one on Jackson's side and the other on hers. Jackson put down both windows, staring straight ahead. He looked like he wanted to puke.

Really, she worried he might.

An officer attentively shined a flashlight in the car at them. Genna shielded her eyes, wincing, when he aimed it straight at her face.

"Who does the car belong to?" the man asked straightaway.

Jackson stammered, saying nothing coherent, as Genna cleared her throat. "Borrowed it from a friend. Isn't that right, Jackson?"

He stammered some more, of absolutely no help.

"A friend," the officer repeated, moving the flashlight away. Genna was relieved to have the spotlight off of her until he pointed it straight at the dash, highlighting the screwdriver sticking out of the ignition. "You couldn't just borrow the key, too, while you were at it?"

Jackson opened his mouth to respond, and that was when it happened.

He puked.

Right there, right then, all over the steering wheel and his lap.

Cringing, Genna looked away from the mess. *Busted.*

Genna had been wearing the same clothes for almost 48 hours. The stench of stale liquor and old sweat clung to the fabric, making her gag with each shaky breath she took. The black dress hugged her hourglass curves, revealing more skin than it covered. She felt extremely indecent—extremely *filthy*—standing under the bright lights in the lobby of the Criminal Court Building in Chinatown, clutching her stiletto heels instead of wearing them.

She had just been arraigned and promptly bailed out before they even had a chance to transfer her to jail—although, at that moment, she would have rather been locked in a grimy cell somewhere.

It was probably safer.

Her blurry eyes focused on her red polished toes and studied the shiny white linoleum floor around her bare feet, anything to avoid looking at the man in front of her. She could feel his gaze stabbing through her like sharp knives, piercing her insides as shame oozed out from the tiny wounds.

It didn't help that she was hung-over. Every noise seemed magnified to her foggy ears and her head pounded in harmony to the sound of footsteps as people strode around the busy building. The beeping of the x-ray machine, the clattering of keys, the chattering of people... ugh, it was too much to take.

Make it stop.

"Genevieve."

The way he said her name with such calmness made her involuntarily flinch. She would rather him yell or make a scene, *something*. Anger at least meant passion, but this was indifference. This was a man not at all surprised to be here.

Her voice was meek as she responded, "Yes?"

"Look at me."

Her eyes obediently shifted upward at the command, meeting his stern gaze. Primo Galante, mid-forties, sturdy build, and a Brooklyn accent with a slight Italian twist, went by many names on the streets of New York, but he was only one thing to her: *Dad*.

He stared at her, raising a single eyebrow in assessment. She said nothing, and neither did he. After a moment he motioned with his head, silently telling her to follow him as he walked away.

The black town car idled right along the curb out front. Her father slid into the backseat, and Genna tugged on her dress, trying to cover more skin before joining him. He clasped his hands in his lap and stared out the window as they drove through Manhattan, just north of the city to their estate near Harrison, New York.

She hadn't called him. He was the last person she would've ever called. But she wasn't the least bit surprised he had been the one to show up. Her father knew everything criminal that happened on the streets, even more so than the police did.

Probably because he orchestrated most of it.

As soon as they made it home, Genna bolted out of the car, shoving the front door open and sprinting for the stairs. She only made it halfway up when her father walked in and shouted her name.

"Genevieve Elisa Galante!"

Her footsteps stalled. *There* was the emotion. There was the anger, the passion. She was entirely convinced the sole reason people had a middle name was so they could tell when their parents were pissed. "Yes?"

"Join me in my office."

He didn't wait for her to follow him, but he knew she would. He didn't really give her much of a choice. Sighing, she dropped her shoes and her purse, discarding it all on the stairs, and grudgingly made the trek back down to face him.

His office wasn't so much an office as it was a man-cave. Where a desk would be was a massive black leather couch, flanked by matching chairs, a plaque on the wall behind them with *Exodus 21:24* written on it, nothing else.

Bible scripture. Genna wasn't sure which it was, but she was pretty sure it wasn't *thou shalt let your daughter run wild*. A bar lined the far wall with dozens of bottles of alcohol on a shelf surrounding it. Her stomach churned at the sight of them.

Ugh, I'm never drinking again.

Primo took a seat dead center of the couch, stretching his arms out along the back of it as he relaxed in his fitted gray suit. For a middle-aged man, he had a certain swagger about him that she usually admired. *Usually.* She paused right in the doorway, not wanting to go any closer, hoping the lecture would be quick and painless, but his expression showed no sign of urgency.

He knew she was hung-over. He was going to drag it out intentionally.

"Grand theft auto," he said finally, getting right to the point.

"That's a total exaggeration."

His eyes narrowed. "You stole an Accord."

"Well, technically I—"

"An Accord, Genevieve," he said, cutting her off. "Not a Ferrari. Not a Lamborghini. Not even a Mercedes. A Honda Accord."

"It was a nice car." Her voice turned defensive as if an explanation would actually make it any better of a decision in his eyes. "It was custom painted and had a new spoiler. The guy even had an NO2 tank installed."

"It's a *Honda*," he said again, his anger seeping into his words. "I don't care how customized it is. You aren't auditioning for Fast & the Furious 3."

"I think they're up to part seven now."

His posture shifted as he leaned forward, glaring at

her. "Does it look like I care about a movie, Genevieve? Huh? You think that's what matters to me?"

She knew this voice. He rarely used this voice on her, but she overheard him resort to it many times to intimidate and terrorize others right there in that room. Men who worked for him. Men like *him*. There was something about the chilling tone that could make even the hardest man go weak and beg for mercy. "No, sir."

"Then keep it to yourself," he said. "All I care to hear is a damn good explanation of what possessed you to steal a fucking Honda!"

"I didn't," she muttered. "Not really. I was just the passenger."

"An accomplice is no better," he said. "Might even be worse. All of the punishment and none of the glory. At least Jason had the balls to drive the wretched thing."

"Jackson."

"Excuse me?"

She cleared her throat, trying to get her voice to steady. "You called him Jason. His name's actually Jackson."

"I don't care what his name is," he countered, scoffing as he waved the thought away dismissively. "You aren't seeing that Johnson boy anymore."

"What? Why?"

His eyes bore into her, like she should automatically know the answer. "You have *terrible* taste. The worst! You need to find a good Italian boy."

She was rolling her eyes before he even finished. *Not this argument again.* "But I like Jackson."

"He's a car thief!"

"You can't blame him... not completely. We were drunk."

22

"You're only eighteen!"

Okay. He had a point there. "It was a mistake."

"A mistake?"

"Yeah, no big deal."

"No big deal? Did you miss the part where I said you're *eighteen*? This isn't like those stunts you pulled before. I got you out of those because you were just a stupid kid, doing stupid things, but this isn't juvenile court anymore. This is the big time."

Her stomach sunk as she stared at him. She hadn't given anything much thought in her drunken haze. She'd landed in the backseat of police cars a few times since her fourteenth birthday, for everything from underage drinking to trespassing to vandalism, but each time they'd delivered her straight home to her father with a stern warning aimed at him. *Keep your daughter under control.* This time, though, they'd taken her straight in. This time, they'd booked her.

And this was a *felony*.

"I wasn't thinking."

His expression softened at her admission. "You're an adult now. You need to start acting like it. You can't go off running the streets, getting drunk and stealing cars with these little hoodlums. You didn't even wear your seatbelt! What's wrong with you? How stupid could you be? You could've died, Genevieve! Do you know what would happen to me if you died? Do you know what I would do if I lost you?"

Coldness swept through her. They were questions she didn't want to address, but she knew the answers. Knew them, and lived them. They all had.

Primo went on a *warpath* when he lost his family.

"I'm sorry."

"Yeah, I know you are," he muttered. "Just keep

yourself out of trouble, will you?"

"I will," she vowed. *Try, anyway.*

"Good. Now go." He waved her away. "Clean yourself up and put on something decent. I'm sick to my stomach looking at you in that dress."

"Yes, sir."

Stalking over, she leaned down and kissed his rough cheek before scurrying from the room. That wasn't as bad as she expected it to be. She took the stairs two at a time, grabbing her discarded things as she went, and headed straight for her second story bedroom, at the very end of the hallway in the back of the house. It was bigger than most apartments in the city.

Striding inside, she sighed, surveying the mess that greeted her. Clothes were strewn everywhere, most of them clean, from her frantic *'I-have-nothing-to-wear'* tantrum the last time she had been home. She stepped over the discarded piles, having no energy to clean any of it up, and strode over to her walk-in closet. After flicking on the light, she slid her stilettos into their spot on the shelf.

She took a long, hot shower in her adjoining bathroom, soaking under the spray, before strolling back into the bedroom, a fluffy white towel wrapped around her. Grabbing some fresh clothes—yoga pants and a tank top—she nearly dropped the towel to get dressed when someone banged on her door. Wincing, her head still viciously throbbing, she turned around, clutching the towel tightly to herself. "What?"

The door flung open, crashing into the wall. "Hey, sis."

She cringed, glaring at her brother in the doorway. "Dante."

Dante seemed to be the complete opposite of her at first glance. Everything about him glowed warm tan, with his chocolate-colored hair and matching eyes, while Genna always appeared cold like porcelain. It didn't help that image when her father treated her like she'd been delicately chiseled from a block of ice and set up on a pedestal, hovered over in case she ever started to thaw. Where Dante was soft, embraceable, she was sharp, with her steely blue eyes and dark hair, skin paler than anyone else in her family. Growing up, Dante teased her for it, saying she was adopted, that she wasn't *really* a Galante.

Some days, she almost wished she wasn't.

But deeper, below the surface, her and her brother were a lot alike.

"So, spent the night incarcerated, did you?" Dante teased, fighting a smile that tugged the corner of his lips. "How was the ass-pounding penitentiary?"

She rolled her eyes. "It was just a few hours in lockup, which you know, since I called *you* to come get me. Foul, by the way. Did you really have to send him instead?"

Dante held his hands up defensively as he casually leaned against the doorframe. "Not my fault. He saw the number and wanted to know who it was calling."

"And you had to tell him?"

The question was stupid, because yes, he had to tell him. Dante was bound by rules she only vaguely knew about, rules her father tried to shield her from, but she wasn't stupid. Anyone with half a brain and access to the Internet could find out everything they wanted to know about her father's life. In fact, just the week before, the Discovery Channel aired a special on it.

Inside the Mafia.

25

It was a fucked up way to live, she thought, learning all about your family's darkest secrets on a primetime crime show on TV.

"I owe you one," Dante offered instead of answering. "You need a favor, just name it, and I'm there for you, no matter how bad you fuck up."

His response made her smile, although those words were unnecessary. Family meant everything to Dante, and Genna knew, any time she needed him, he would be there with no questions asked. He might not like her decisions, but unlike their father, Dante never judged her for making them.

"So you just come up here to pick on me?" she asked. "Because if you're done now, I'd like to get dressed."

"No, Dad sent me up here to get whatever you were wearing when he sprung you from the slammer." Genna's brow furrowed as she glanced around, spotting the black dress lying in a heap on the floor. Noticing where her attention went, Dante snatched it up, holding it away from him as he dangled it from his fingers. "Is this it?"

"Yes."

"Thanks."

He turned to leave when she caught his arm, stopping him. "Wait, what are you doing with my dress?"

"Burning it."

She gaped at him, wide-eyed. "Burning it? *Why?*"

"So you can never wear it again."

"Because it's some bad luck symbol now or something?" She *loved* that dress. Sure, it needed a good soaking to get the jailhouse stench out of it, but it was practically brand new. "Is it because I got arrested? Because that's not the dress's fault."

"No, it's because you look like a cheap hooker in it."

"I do *not*."

Dante shrugged. "The old man thinks so, and what he says goes."

She glowered at her brother as he strode down the hallway, dragging the dress on the floor behind him. After he was gone, she slammed her door and walked over to her bed, plopping down in it as she closed her eyes.

To hell with getting dressed.

Dinner had always been the one time when the Galantes came together as a family. For one hour a day, seven days a week, everything else was put aside as they gathered in the dining room, enjoying an elaborate meal prepared by the staff. Primo spared no expense at home, keeping trustworthy maids and cooks on his payroll.

Nothing was too good for his family, he'd said.

Rarely did any of them skip dinner, going out of their way to make sure they were home at eight o'clock to eat. Although it had never been mandatory, per se, it was more of an understanding, a matter of respect.

But sleeping off her lingering hangover, Genna damn near missed it.

Something startled her awake, darkness creeping through her bedroom as the sun set outside. Groggy, she blinked a few times, her eyes drifting toward the alarm clock across the room.

8:12 PM

"Shit!" She jumped to her feet, swaying a bit as her vision went hazy from the sudden movement. Discarding the towel, she quickly pulled on her clothes—wrinkled from her sleeping on top of them—and ran her fingers through her long knotted hair, sloppily pulling it back as she scurried from the room. She was breathing heavily by the time she made it downstairs, bursting into the dining room at exactly a quarter after. Her head was still throbbing, pounding to the beat of her heart, as her gaze sought out her father's. Primo sat in his usual chair, at the head of the table, his eyes fixed on the doorway, his food completely untouched as he waited for her to appear.

"Sorry," she muttered, sliding into her seat two chairs down from her father, directly across from Dante. Relief shined from her brother's eyes as he regarded her. "I fell asleep, and well, you know... here I am."

"Here you are," her father agreed as he extended his hands toward Dante and her. They took them, bowing their heads as he quietly said Grace. Afterward, the guys eagerly dove into their food, while Genna just shifted hers around on her plate.

She still felt too queasy to eat.

They chatted about sports, her brother bringing up the Yankees, as Genna's mind wandered. She thought about Jackson, wondered how he had fared after their arrest. Had he been released, too? Did he even have anybody to call to get him out? Her father told her not to see him anymore, but well, she was never very good at listening.

And even sober, she still thought the guy was pretty damn cute.

"Genevieve?"

Her eyes shot to her father's when he called her name. "Yes?"

"Where's your mind?" he asked. "I've been trying to talk to you for the past few minutes."

"I, uh... nowhere. Sorry, I'm listening."

"I was asking about Umberto Ricci."

Her brow furrowed. *Why's he asking me about Dante's friend?* "What about him?"

"You and him ought to get together. You know, go out sometime."

She grimaced. "Really, Dad?"

"Yeah, what's wrong with him? He's a nice Italian boy. The two of you would make a good family together."

"He's Umberto! He's like, four feet tall." Not to mention the fact that he could never carry a conversation. Talking to him was painful. "Besides, didn't he just get out of jail? For the *second* time?"

"Yeah, so?"

"Jackson steals one car and he's the spawn of Satan. Umberto makes a living breaking the law and you practically try to marry me off to him! What gives?"

Primo scoffed and looked away, turning right back to his dinner. He wouldn't answer, but he didn't really need to. Genna knew why.

Umberto Ricci worked for him.

"Whatever," she muttered, shifting more food around on her plate. "I'm not interested in *making a family* with Umberto, but thanks, anyway."

Before her father could scold her for her curt tone, a ringing cell phone shattered the silence. Dinner was interruption-free time, all of their phones turned off and put away, except for one. It was one her father carried with him everywhere—one everyone knew was reserved solely for emergencies. Genna had never dialed that number before and hoped to never have to.

They tensed, watching as Primo grabbed the phone

and answered swiftly with a simple command: "Talk."

The call lasted less than thirty seconds. Her father hung up without saying another word. Sighing, Primo shoved his chair back, tossing his napkin down, as he looked between Genna and her brother. "Barsanti."

No elaboration. No explanation. It was unnecessary, anyway. Dinner was over twenty minutes early. Primo marched from the room, a man on a mission, while the word lingered around them in his wake, like a heavy, ominous cloud of noxious fumes, hell bent on poisoning whoever breathed it in.

Barsanti.

Fuck. Shit. Goddamn. Cunt. Cocksucker. None of those words held a fraction of the offense of uttering the curse *Barsanti* around the Galante household. If Genna's mother had been there, the mere sound of it would have driven her to prayers as she madly made the sign of the cross, outraged to have the blasphemous word spoken at her dinner table.

At that thought, Genna carefully set her fork down, giving up the façade of being interested in eating *ever again*, as her gaze drifted to the empty chair right beside her. It had been vacant for a little over four years, but every single night, without fail, a plate and silverware were set at it like someone might actually sit there again someday.

The chair across from it, too, remained uninhabited, also set for dinner, never again to be used. That one had been unoccupied for as long as Genna could remember. She had only been two at the time, much too young to recall what happened.

Dante had been five, though. It was his first memory... one she knew he would never forget. He carried the scars with him, mentally and physically, the skin on his chest thickened and distorted from extensive third-degree burns, his perception forever tainted.

"I should go," Dante said quietly, standing up. "Dad might need me."

Genna nodded but otherwise ignored him as he walked out. She always wondered what he thought at these moments, if he was reliving that day—their fatal run-in with the Barsantis.

To nobody's surprise, New York was a hot spot for organized crime. Five families shared stake in the illicit underground world, although two held the most power around Manhattan: the Galantes and the Barsantis. They worked amicably for a lot of years, sharing control equally, until one day the peace shattered, exploding into a fiery blaze.

Literally.

Since then, the vicious rivalry festered, a war between the families waging, the hostility so great that the mere mention of their existence made Genna sick with anxiety, and she was as far removed from the lifestyle as a Galante could possibly get. But as far as she was concerned, those people were monsters. Her father had taught her that since she was just a little girl, warning her, protecting her, so she would know to stay away.

"The only good Barsanti is a dead Barsanti," he'd said. "You see one, you run the other way."

Once her father and brother were gone, Genna went upstairs to fix her hair and put on make-up before heading out for the night. There was no way she was hanging around that house by herself with nothing to do but worry about what her family was up to. She drove straight to Harlem, parking in front of the townhouse where Jackson stayed. After locking up her black BMW, she knocked on the front door, expecting his sister to answer, or maybe one of his parents, but was stunned when none other than Jackson himself opened the door for her.

"Hey!" She rushed right at him, wrapping her arms around him in a tight hug that seemed to startle him more than anything.

He tensed, lightly patting her back. "Oh, hey, Genna."

"You're out! I thought you'd call me when someone sprung you."

"Yeah, well..." He nervously rubbed his neck, frowning. "I didn't think that was such a good idea."

"Why?" It hadn't been entirely *her* fault they got arrested. Sure, she started the car, technically, but it had been *his* idea to take it for a spin. "What's wrong?"

"Your dad doesn't think we should see each other anymore."

Her expression fell when he said that. *No.* "No."

"Look, I just think maybe he's right."

"Did he threaten you?" she asked. That would be *so* like her father. Wouldn't be the first guy he scared away from dating her. In fact, he seemed to scare everyone away. She couldn't even keep friends because of him monitoring her life and constantly intervening, sending his minions to wherever she was to keep an eye on them.

"No, he didn't threaten me. It's nothing like that."

"Then how do you know he doesn't want us together?"

"He told me," he said sheepishly, "when he bailed me out this afternoon."

"So *that's* it." Angry tears burned Genna's eyes, but she felt little in the way of sadness. No, this felt like betrayal. "He paid you off."

"I'm sorry, Genna," he said. "Really, I am. I didn't want to hurt you."

"You didn't," she said, backing away from him as she tried to ignore the pain nagging her chest that suggested otherwise. Man, it *did* hurt. It hurt like a son of a bitch. "I'm just disappointed, Jackson."

He tried to apologize some more, calling her name, but she was already off the steps and heading toward her car. She thought he didn't care who her father was, that he wouldn't be intimidated by the name... by the reputation.

Turned out, she had been wrong about him.

TWO

What had started out as a bad hair day, thanks to a malfunctioning alarm clock and dreary late spring weather, quickly spiraled out of control to arguably one of the worst mornings of Genna's life. By the time she reached the criminal court building in Chinatown for her hearing, she was drenched from a sudden rainstorm and running ten minutes late.

She sprinted down the hallway, her new black Jimmy Choos rubbing blisters on her feet, and crammed into the first elevator she came upon, skidding through just in time before the doors closed.

Her back was to an older man in coveralls, the scent of stale cigarette smoke and sweat surrounding him. She held her breath so not to inhale the stench, but she could feel every breath of his against the back of her neck as he wheezed. She tried to inch away, tried to get some space between them, but every time she shifted he seemed to move with her, pressing himself into her, brushing against the curve of her ass and driving her short skirt up further.

Worst elevator ride ever.

The man got off on the tenth floor, glancing back and giving her a playful wink. She shuddered as the doors closed again. *Ugh, gross.*

The elevator seemed to stop on every single floor on the way up, so by the time she made it to the twenty-third, she was actually *fifteen* minutes late for her hearing. She sprinted into the courtroom, shoving the door open so hard it disrupted the judge in the middle of proceedings. All eyes turned to her as awkward silence permeated the room. *Oops.*

"Sorry," she muttered to no one in particular as the judge turned his focus back on the case at hand. Her eyes scanned the courtroom, seeking out the lawyer her father had hired, and found him standing up front... with Jackson. *Wonderful.*

Jackson looked uncomfortable, dressed in a too-big black suit that did no justice to his physique; his hair was cut neatly, not the shaggy mop it used to be. She was so fixated on how he looked that she nearly missed the judge's words.

"This case is adjourned in contemplation of dismissal. I'm setting a court date for six months from now. If you can stay out of trouble until then, all charges will be dropped."

The judge banged his gavel, a small wave of murmurs flowing through the courtroom as Jackson smiled, his shoulders sagging with relief. He turned to leave, striding right by Genna, so close their arms brushed together, but he didn't so much as even look her way.

The entire thing reeked of Primo.

"Next on the docket is *The People versus Genevieve Galante.*"

Sighing, Genna tore her gaze away from the door where Jackson had disappeared out of and approached the lawyer still lingering at the front of the courtroom. He smiled politely at her as he shifted through his stacks of paperwork, putting Jackson's on the bottom as he moved hers to the top. "This should be quick. The judge just needs to sign off on the plea agreement we made."

"Why does Jackson get to walk free and I have to plead guilty?"

"That's just the way it worked out," he replied, his voice casual, but Genna caught the hidden meaning in the words. *That's the way Primo Galante arranged it.* Regardless of if her father wanted to admit it to her or not, she knew half of the people in the courtroom were in his pocket in one way or another, whether they owed him favors or he paid them handsomely. How else did the man, career criminal, manage to stay out of jail all these years?

"Miss Galante," the judge started, peering at her through a pair of thick wire-rimmed glasses. "The agreement made between your council and the district attorney for the lesser charge of unauthorized use of a motor vehicle in the third degree, a misdemeanor, is approved. The court hereby sentences you to 120 hours of community service and a $1000 fine. Your driver's license is also suspended until at which time you can complete your sentence."

The bang of the gavel echoed through the room before they quickly called for the next case. Genna's lawyer motioned for her to step out, but she just stood there, gaping at the judge.

"Is there an issue, Miss Galante?" the judge asked, eyeing her peculiarly when she refused to budge.

She opened her mouth to argue, to point out how harsh that sentence was, but the lawyer cut her off and spoke up instead. "No problem, your honor. My client's grateful for the court's leniency today."

Stepping in front of her, he physically led her away from the defendant's table and through the courtroom before she could really protest. She stepped away from him once they reached the hallway, throwing up her hands in disbelief. "You call that *leniency?*"

"It could've been worse," the lawyer said. "You could've gone to jail for the felony."

She glared at him as he casually strode away. "Could've been *better*. I could've gotten away with it like Jackson did!"

Frustrated, she sulked down the hall, in no rush now that everything was over. It was in and out within a matter of minutes. She approached the elevators, groaning when she saw a small crowd stuffing into one of them. She paused there, deciding to wait, and pressed the down button as soon as that one was gone.

In a matter of seconds, a second elevator dinged behind her. Genna spun around to look at it just as the doors opened, relieved to see wide-open space, the bright lights illuminating the shiny floor. She started toward it, her footsteps briefly faltering when she caught sight of a lone guy waiting in the corner.

Holy shit.

They stood eye-to-eye with her in six-inch heels, but he wasn't looking at her at all. His attention was fixed solely on a Blackberry as he typed away at the tiny keyboard. He casually relaxed back against the railing, legs crossed at the ankles, his sneakers so new even the bottoms were pristine white. His serious expression looked to be etched from the smoothest stone, his sharp jawline covered in a dusting of hair, but his skin appeared so, so soft, like the slickest satin. A warm tan glow swaddled him beneath the lights. He wore a pair of designer jeans and a long sleeved white button down, a cream-colored cable knit sweater overtop of it. His dark hair was perfectly styled or else effortlessly untouched, and just long enough to give the locks a slight messy wave. The tips of her fingers tingled with the urge to caress.

This guy... *no, this God...* had been zapped straight off the pages of GQ and transplanted right here in her elevator.

Thank you, Jesus, Joseph, and motherfucking Mary.

The elevator starting to close right in front of her face finally spurred her to action. Genna darted forward so quickly it captured his notice. Without breaking his stance, his eyes shifted from the phone to her, catching her gaze when she stopped in front of him. A trance fell over her as she stared into his eyes, golden splotches around the iris that faded like flames into the brightest blue, like an abstract Picasso painting come to life. A shadowy ring surrounded them, framing the vibrant color in darkness.

Never in her life had she ever seen eyes like his.

The elevator closed behind her as she stared at him, utterly speechless. *It's rude to stare.* Even a kindergartner knew that. But she couldn't look away.

He stared back boldly, arching a single eyebrow at her, a slight hint of amusement cracking his stony expression. The sight of it, the subtle curl of his lips into a smirk, made her stomach furiously flutter.

This day just got so much better.

They started moving as Genna swallowed thickly, trying to get her wits about her, trying to think of something to say to break the ice. Her lips parted, a shaky breath leaving in the form of half a word, when the elevator violently shuddered, alarming her back into silence. The lights

39

flickered, before abruptly, they started plummeting. Her heart was in her throat, hammering hard, the movement nearly knocking her off her feet. She stumbled in her heels, but a strong hand grasped her, stabilizing her enough so she could grab the railing.

Floors flew by in the blink of an eye before an ear-splitting screech echoed around them. They ground to a sudden stop, jolting her again, the motion making her vision blur as she gasped. "What the fuck was *that*?"

"Emergency brakes." His smooth voice held not a hint of anxiety. His accent was restrained, hardly enough for her to notice. New York, yes, like her own, but it held a slight hint of something else in it. New Jersey?

"Did we just...?" She shook her head, frazzled. "Are we...?"

"Stuck?" He stepped past her, the smell of his cologne—subtlety sweet and entirely sensual—infiltrating her senses. "Yeah, I'd say so."

He pressed the call button on the panel. When nothing happened, he repeatedly pushed the red alarm button. Genna could hear the alarm going off, the siren echoing through the elevator shaft. After a moment, he stopped, running his hands along the doors and gripping them in the center, prying them open just a crack to look out, but there was nothing to be seen.

They were trapped between floors.

"Just great," she muttered, reaching into her purse for her phone. She pulled it out, holding it up, the signal flickering between one measly bar and no service.

Hello again, bad day. Should've known you weren't done fucking me yet.

She continually struggled to get service, holding the

40

phone up as high as she could reach, as the guy retook his spot in the corner and pulled out his Blackberry. She watched him incredulously as he started typing on it, just as casual as he had been before. He cut his eyes at her as he finished, slipping the phone back into his pants pocket. "You're wasting your time. You'll never get a strong enough signal to make a call from in here."

"So, what, I shouldn't even *try*?"

He shrugged a shoulder. "I wouldn't."

"We're trapped in an elevator," she said, stressing the fact that they were *trapped*. "Maybe you're cool with that, I don't know. But this has the makings of a bad R. Kelly song, if you ask me."

Before the guy could respond, his phone chimed. He pulled it out just far enough to glance at the screen. "Like I said—not enough signal to make a call, but just enough to send out a message."

"You got ahold of someone?"

"Yeah."

She stared at him, shocked, when he planted himself on the grimy floor, his back pressed into the corner. How could he remain so calm?

"You might want to get comfortable," he said. "Knowing this city, it'll probably be a while before they get to us."

Genna stubbornly stood there for a few minutes, her feet starting to ache in the high heels, aggravating her blisters every time she shifted position. Sighing, resigned, she finally kicked them off, discarding them in the middle of the elevator. She sat down against the wall diagonal from him, tugging on her skirt and crossing her legs to keep herself covered, but she was pretty sure she flashed him the goods on accident. *Damn short skirt.*

"Great," she muttered. "I just can't catch a break."

"Bad day?"

"The worst."

"Ah, I doubt that," he said. "It can always be worse than it is."

Rolling her eyes, she gazed down at her hands and picked at her nail polish to distract herself. It was only two of them, but there was very little ventilation in the elevator. She could already feel the air warming up. "You sound like my lawyer."

"Your lawyer, huh? Were you here for a case?"

"Yes."

"What did you do?"

She hesitated, considering lying, but thought better of it. Why did she care what *he* thought? She didn't know the guy. "Stole a car."

"You?" he asked incredulously. "A car thief?"

She cut her eyes at him. "Technically, my boyfriend did it… or my *ex*-boyfriend, anyway. He walked away with barely a slap on the wrist, while I got enough community service to last a lifetime."

"That doesn't seem very fair."

"It's not," she said. "But whatever, that's just my luck today. Late for court, get fucked over by the Justice Department, and then the elevator tries to kill me. I'm pretty this day ends with someone shoving me in front of a train, which I'll probably have to take now, since the judge revoked my license for good measure."

"Wow." He seemed taken aback. "You weren't exaggerating."

"Told you. Worst day ever."

"I'd offer you moral support, but well…" He laughed to himself. "My morals are questionable at best, so how about I buy you a drink when we get out of here instead?"

His words made her smile. "That's nice, but I'm not old enough to drink."

He hesitated. "How old are you?"

"Eighteen."

"Ah, that's not bad. You're an adult. Besides, I said I had questionable morals, didn't I?"

"True." She felt the flush on her cheeks as she gazed at him, seeing the sincerity in his expression. "How old are you?"

"Old enough to buy you that drink, if you're up for it."

"Okay, uh…" She paused. "I don't even know your name."

"It's Matt."

"Matt, like short for Matthew?"

"Short for something, yes."

"Well, nice to meet you. You can call me Genna… Genna with a *G* and not a *J*. It's short for something, too, you could say."

"Genna."

The sound of her name from his lips sent a chill down her spine. She should've been upset, trapped in such a confined space with a virtual stranger, one whose eyes seemed to pierce through her with a scary intensity, but she oddly felt at ease. She liked the way he looked at her, the way he looked through her, like he really saw her.

People didn't look at her that way.

People always looked at her and saw her last name.

"So, Matt…"

"Call me Matty," he said. "It's what my friends call me."

"Matty," she repeated. "What brings you to criminal court?"

Dear God, don't let this stunning creature be some kind of perverted creep. I can't go out with a creep. Okay, maybe I can. Depends on how creepy. Ugh, please don't be creepy.

"Kidnapping," he said. "They found a girl tied up in my trunk."

Her eyes widened. Okay, that wasn't creepy. That was fucking *insane*.

His expression shifted before she could respond. He let out a laugh. "I'm kidding. My brother's on trial."

"Your *brother* kidnapped a girl?"

"No." He paused. "Well..."

She gasped, eliciting another laugh from him.

"I'm messing with you. He just got into a little fight. Nothing big, just a run-of-the-mill neighborhood scuffle."

If she had something within reach to throw, she would've hurled it right at his head. "That's not funny!"

"Yeah, you're right, it's not," he agreed. "For the record, though, I only tie girls up when they ask me to."

His voice ventured into playful but there was a serious note to his words that made her flushed skin glow brighter. Not creepy, but maybe a little freaky.

Now freaky I can date.

Looking away from him, she bit down on her bottom lip, trying to get herself together. Warm was putting it mildly. She could feel the sweat start forming along her brow. It was getting hot.

Sighing, Matty pulled his sweater off, tossing it on the elevator floor near her discarded shoes. Genna glanced over at him again as he shoved the sleeves of his white button-down up to his elbows. Vibrant color shined from his skin like a stained glass window woven into black etchings on his thick forearms. Tattoos. His arms were covered in *tattoos*. Genna let out an involuntary shaky breath, staring at them, captivated by the intricate designs.

Huh, so the God has a little bit of Devil in him...

"So tell me about yourself, Genna."

She grudgingly tore her gaze from his arms, meeting his eyes again. "Uh, there's not much to say. I've already spilled my guts to you."

"You told me about your bad day. Tell me about your good days."

"My good days?"

"Yes."

"Well... I guess I steal cars on my good days."

He laughed, slouching as he stretched his legs out. "Have you stolen a lot of cars?"

"Just the one. Guess I don't really have many good days. They're not all bad, they're just... *days*. That probably sounds stupid."

"No, I get it. Sometimes you just do what you gotta do to get through them."

"Exactly." Gorgeous *and* understanding? *Impossible.* "And my family, well... let's just say my father doesn't make it easy sometimes. He has all these rules and expects life to be lived to his standards, and I'm just not very good at following directions."

She was rambling. *Ugh, why am I rambling?* She hardly knew this guy, yet she was baring her soul like a dying hooker in confessional.

"My family's the same way," he said. "I like to think

45

there's always a positive side to everything, though."

"Not always."

"Yes, always," he countered. "Even on the worst days, you get something out of it. Like today. You got something out of today."

"What?"

"I don't know. A criminal record?"

She narrowed her eyes at him. "Funny."

"It happens to the best of us," he said playfully. "I'm just saying, sometimes good things come from bad things. I'm stuck in an elevator, but I've got a beautiful girl here with me, so I'm focusing on the girl and not the fact that I'm crammed in a tiny box. Because rest assured, if you weren't here, I would've been climbing through the trap door in the ceiling by now."

Genna's eyes darted up to the ceiling. Trap door? "Can we do that?"

"With the day you're having? No."

She peered at him across the elevator, seeing the amusement in his expression. He was enjoying teasing her. "Okay, your turn, then. Tell me about Matty."

"Not much to me." He shrugged. "I recently graduated college with a degree in communications."

"And what does one do with a communications degree?"

"Communicate? I don't know." He laughed to himself, a bitter edge to the sound. "Doesn't really matter. I minored in business analytics, though. I moved back home last month to help out my family, so that part's been a little more helpful on the job front."

"Yeah?"

"Yeah. It's just temporary, though. My mom's been

sick for a while. I didn't want to miss... well, you know. I wanted to be around for her."

"I get it," she said quietly. That was something Genna understood well. She felt the sting of the memory of her own mother constricting her chest. "So you're close to your family?"

"I'm Italian," he said. "That's kind of the name of the game."

She gazed at him, a small smile creeping up on her lips. A handsome Italian boy who understood family loyalty? This guy was the genetics jackpot. Her father was going to *love* him.

An hour passed trapped in the stifling elevator before they finally heard any attempts to reach them. By then, they were both laying on the floor, diagonally across the elevator, her flat on her back while he lay beside her, his elbow propped up as he gazed at her. It was uncomfortable, but comforting. Unnerving, but not at all alarming. She could feel his eyes on her, surveying her intently, seeing right through her just as he had done the first time their eyes connected. She babbled on and on, distracting herself, talking about everything but nothing at all.

It took a few more minutes for their help to find a way in. At that point, Genna was drenched with sweat, her clothes rolled up to indecent levels, dangerously close to saying to hell with it and just stripping right then, right there, and prancing around in her underwear.

Matty climbed to his feet once the fire department unbolted the trap door in the ceiling, but she just lay there, staring up at the lights above her. The air was hazy, each breath burning her lungs. She would've killed for some water... *maybe literally.*

"Come on," Matty said, extending his hand to her when a fireman started feeding a ladder in through from above. She took his hand, feeling his warm skin against hers as he helped her to her feet. She tried to quickly pull herself together, tugging at her clothes and fixing her hair before grabbing her shoes. Matty grabbed his sweater, using it to wipe the sweat dripping from his brow. His face gleamed under the lights.

How the hell did he make sweating so sexy?

They had them climb into the elevator shaft and across a ladder onto another elevator. They dropped down into that one, which took them straight down to the first floor. Genna breathed a heavy sigh of relief when those doors opened, a swell of fresh air reaching her. She stepped out, avoiding the curious gathering crowd of spectators as she hit up the nearest water fountain, before bolting straight for the front door. No sooner she stepped outside to the dreary afternoon, Matty joined her.

"So, how about that drink? What do you say?"

She looked down at herself, grimacing. If she thought she was having a bad hair day that morning, she couldn't even imagine what it looked like *now*. She wanted to go home, strip out of her mucky clothes, and fall straight into her comfy bed, never to resurface again. But there was another part of her, captivated and curious about this guy, that couldn't bear the thought of walking away from him already. If she did, chances were she'd never see him again.

He stared at her, awaiting her answer.

Fuck it. "Let's go."

Smirking, he pulled a set of keys from his pocket as he started walking away. After slipping on her shoes, Genna followed him, ignoring the burning pain as they rubbed against her blisters. He turned the corner, heading to a nearby parking lot as he pressed a button on his keys. Across the lot, lights flashed on a sleek blood red Lotus Evora seconds before he pressed another button and it roared straight to life. Her footsteps faltered, eyes darting to him with shock. "*That's* yours? The Lotus?"

"Why, you gonna steal it?"

Genna approached the foreign sports car, running her hand along the glossy paint, hearing the engine as it practically purred. She'd never seen one in person. They were rare, barely street legal. He opened the passenger door for her and she paused there, trying to contain her grin. "I guess you'll see, won't you?"

The leather stuck to the back of her sweaty thighs when she slid into the seat. Laughing, Matty shut the door and climbed in the driver's side. "Yeah, I guess I will."

Air conditioning blasted her in the face, cooling her instantly and soothing the burn of her cheeks. Thumping bass of hip-hop spilled from the speakers, vibrating her seat and sending goose bumps dancing across her skin when Matty threw the car in gear. They sped away from the criminal court building, effortlessly weaving through the afternoon Manhattan traffic, every turn smooth and agile, as they seemed to just glide along the street. Genna wanted to talk to him, wanted to ask him questions, wanted to know more, but she couldn't get any words to form. For the first time in her life, she felt utterly small. Not in the belittling way... no, she felt anything but depreciated. She was valued, and vulnerable, but oh so fragile, like she'd left her armor behind, completely powerless compared to the commanding creature beside her.

If she were a delicate ice sculpture, this stunning man

was a strong marble statue.

He drove northwest through Soho, one of the few neighborhoods Genna was entirely unfamiliar with. Her family ran the other side of the city so she tended to stay in those areas whenever she came to Manhattan, rarely crossing the invisible boundaries, never venturing too far west. Before she could dwell on that, he slowed the car near a brick building on the corner of a block, making a sharp turn into an underground parking garage, engine raring as Matty pulled into the first spot labeled *'reserved'*.

Carefully, Genna climbed out, eyeing him peculiarly as he locked up the car. She ran her hand along the smooth red paint again. "I can't believe you drive a freaking Lotus Evora."

"I'm surprised you've heard of it."

"I'm surprised you *own* one," she said. "There are only a few hundred in America, if even that. They're rare."

"I've never personally seen another."

Genna glanced at him. "I never thought I'd see *one*. That was… wow." She ran her hand along the sleek paint again. Cars were her first love, arguably her *only* true love. Guys flaked on her left and right, but she'd never had a car disappoint her before. "That was totally better than sex."

Matty laughed, stepping toward her, his gaze intense as he leaned close. "Something tells me you've been having sex with the wrong people, then."

Before she could respond, Matty motioned for her to follow him as he turned and strolled out of the parking garage. She stayed in step with him, looking around when they approached the building. The grimy brick was crumbling, the sign on the front barely legible. *The Place*.

She snorted. "The Place?"

"Genius, huh?" he asked, pausing in front of the thick red door.

"Either that, or it's the dumbest name ever. It doesn't even tell you what it is. Like, when someone says 'meet me at The Place', you don't know if you're going to a diner or some sort of underground cock fighting ring."

He grabbed the door handle, laughing, and pulled it open for her to go in. A sport's bar, it turned out, surprisingly bright and airy. Tables and booths were scattered around the space while a long bar spanned the side, wooden stools lining it. The lighting felt natural, a soft white glow, while everything else was shades of tan. A few guys sat at the bar, drinking beer from mugs and studiously watching ESPN, only a couple of the tables occupied at this hour.

Matty stepped in behind her, drawing the bartender's attention. The man, middle-aged with a sculpted goatee, grinned. "Matty-B! What's up?"

"Not much," Matty said, loosely draping his arm over Genna's shoulder to pull her to the bar with him. "Just came for a drink."

"What can I get you?" the bartender asked.

Matty glanced at her inquisitively, but she just shrugged.

"My usual, then," he ordered. "Two of them."

The bartender's gaze shifted from Matty to Genna. "She looks a little young to be drinking."

"And you're a little old to be checking her out," Matty responded casually. "So get our drinks, before I have to do something crazy to defend her honor."

Instead of being offended, the bartender laughed. "Whatever you say. Two Roman Coke's coming right up."

"We'll be at my table," Matty said, pulling her away

from the bar. "Send some water, too."

He led her to a booth in the far back corner of a separate room, where she slipped in across from him. It didn't take long for a waitress to bring their drinks. Genna gulped the water, parched, as Matty picked up his alcohol and swirled it around.

"A Roman Coke," Genna mused. "What's that?"

"It's rum and Coke. We just call it a Roman Coke around here."

"Because you're Italian?"

"And because when you get drunk enough, it all just slurs together anyway."

"Ah." Genna picked hers up, motioning toward him with it. "So what are we drinking to?"

"Today."

"Today?"

He nodded. "Right now, this moment. Let's drink to it."

Smiling, she clinked her glass with his. "Today, then."

They threw them back at the same time. The liquor hit Genna's taste buds and she grimaced, the vicious burn seeping down her throat and settling deep in her chest. "Ugh, is there even any Coke in this damn thing?"

He laughed, setting his empty glass down. "Just a splash."

"I couldn't tell."

"That's because I prefer it that way," he responded. "Strong and rough, enough to leave a lingering ache. I like it to hurt just a bit."

Oh good God. Those words sent a chill down Genna's spine, one she couldn't hide, as Matty waved for the waitress. Eyes never leaving Genna, he ordered another round of drinks.

"Another?" she asked, picking up the water to take another sip, this one to soothe the sting in her chest. "You said *one* drink."

A sly smile curved his lips. "I like to keep them coming."

"Is that right?"

"Absolutely." He stood, leaning across the table, his lips near her ear. "Maybe you'll let me show you later."

She coughed on her water, her face turning bright red as the double meaning of his words struck her. Spinning around in her seat, she watched as he strode through the bar, straight toward a group of guys that had just walked in. They all greeted him warmly as he spoke quietly, mouth moving furiously as he shook his head. Reaching into his pocket, he pulled out his Blackberry, typing something into it.

Genna turned away from them, nervously keeping her head down, when the waitress returned with their second drinks, just as strong as the first had been, barely any caramel color in the glass. Matty returned after a moment, slipping back into the booth across from her and wordlessly grabbing his glass.

"Friends of yours?" she asked curiously, watching as the guys headed back outside, not even staying long enough to have a drink.

"Something like that," he replied, relaxing back in his seat. "Friends of the family, anyway."

The burn in Genna's chest sparked a tingle after she finished her second drink, a tingle that spread throughout her body, extending down her limbs as the liquor kept flowing to their table. She scarcely kept track after a while as Matty joked around, entertaining her with random stories of the people who wandered into the bar.

The man who owned the butcher shop that Matty and his younger brother had stolen steaks from when they were just little kids, only to be forced to pay for them by their mother... after watching their father single-handedly eat every single one right in front of them as punishment.

The grocer who used to give the kids quarters when they came in so they could get something from the little prize machines by the door.

The guy who ran the ice cream truck for decades and used to slip them free popsicles when he came through their neighborhood.

He spoke fondly of everyone as if they were as close as family, but it didn't escape Genna's notice that hardly anyone even acknowledged him. They looked around him but never *at* him. He seemed to fade into the background, as if they couldn't see him, which baffled her, because she couldn't keep her eyes off the guy. The more she drank, the more she was set on fire from the inside out, the tingle engulfing into flames.

"Do you play?" he asked eventually, motioning toward some billiard tables in another separate nearby room.

Pool.

"Uh, no."

He threw back his drink, downing the rest of it in one gulp. "Come on, I'll show you."

She finished her drink hesitantly before joining him, the two heading straight to the only unoccupied table. She stood there, watching silently as he racked the balls for a game. After it was ready, he grabbed a cue stick and held it out to her. As soon as she took it, his hands gripped her hips, pulling her closer to him as his cologne washed over her. He turned her around, her back to his chest as his arms encircled her, grasping the cue stick.

She couldn't help it.

She shivered.

Holy fuck. He was intoxicating.

"Like this," he whispered, breath fanning against her cheek as he positioned her body, his hands overtop of hers. He aimed at the cue ball, striking it, sending it barreling down the table toward the others. The rest of the balls scattered, bouncing off the sides, a single red ball sliding right into a corner pocket.

He was pretty good.

"So now you aim for just the solid balls," he said, not letting go of her. He tugged her with him, positioning her once more, aiming for the cue ball again. He struck it, going for a solid blue ball, but it narrowly missed its mark, ricocheting back at them.

Matty did it again and again, pulling her around with him, body flush against hers, until he successfully sunk over half of her balls that way.

"You think you got it?" he asked. *No,* her head screamed, knowing if she said yes he would loosen his hold. And those tattooed arms? Christ, she *never* wanted them to let go of her. Her silent indecision made him chuckle. "Yeah, you got it."

She did.

Unfortunately.

The moment he stepped back, her body mourned the loss of his warmth. He grabbed a cue stick for himself as he took his first turn, sinking two balls right away and only narrowly missing a third.

Once it was Genna's turn, she aimed for the cue ball but barely grazed it at all. Her heart wasn't into playing a game, didn't really find it that interesting, but watching him? *That* she was into.

He didn't take it easy on her. He didn't let her win. Despite her massive head start, he demolished her quickly, the black eight ball smoothly disappearing into a side pocket.

Before he could say a word, Genna kicked off her heels and pointed her cue stick at him. "Set them up again."

Games flew by, as did more drinks, the flirting and laughter growing as time wore on. Matty got worse, the games taking longer as Genna hardly even paid attention to where her balls were positioned.

"I'll tell you what," he said as he set up their fifth game, a full glass of straight rum sitting on the edge of the table in front of him. Somehow, at some point, he had dropped the pretense of drinking Coke at all. "You manage to beat me at a game, and I'll give you anything you want."

"Anything?"

"*Anything.*"

"A hundred bucks?"

"Sure."

"Your watch?"

He glanced at his wrist—a silver-colored Rolex, probably white gold. Genna had noticed it earlier. Considering he drove what he did, she had a sneaking suspicion it might actually be real. "Of course."

"Your car?"

"Genna, if you can beat me, I'll give you a hundred bucks, my watch, *and* the Lotus."

Matty made a mistake... a big mistake. He had asked her if she played, and she didn't. Not often, anyway. It wasn't her thing. But that didn't mean she didn't know *how* to play. She had a brother, after all—a brother who regularly hustled around town for extra money.

A brother who taught her everything he knew.

"And if *you* win?" she asked. "Then what?"

He smirked. "Then I get whatever I want."

"Which is...?"

"You'll have to wait and see."

"Okay," she said. "Deal."

He leaned his cue stick against the wall and grabbed his drink. "You can go first."

Smirking, she lined up at the cue ball, striking it hard. A striped orange ball flew straight into the side pocket.

"Lucky break."

She cut her eyes at him. "That was skill, not luck."

"Is that right?"

"Yep."

"Then go on," he said, his voice tinged with humor. "Show me more of your skill."

He didn't have to tell her twice.

Genna sunk three more balls back-to-back, catching his gaze when she struck a fourth. It hit the corner pocket at a slight angle, bouncing off instead.

Matty gaped at her. Over half of her balls were gone. Had she not been tipsy, the game might have been over already.

"Your turn," she said, stepping back.

He set his drink down and grabbed his stick, eliminating four of his balls before narrowly missing the next. Genna knocked out another two, which he matched on his next turn, leaving them both with only one ball left.

Genna sunk hers right off, casting Matty a look as she aimed for the eight ball. He appeared to be sweating.

Panicked. "You hustled me."

She shrugged a shoulder, hesitating, before shifting position slightly and hitting the cue ball. It breezed right past the black eight ball, striking his last solid ball instead. It slammed against the side, flying back toward her, right into the corner pocket.

It ended her turn.

Genna strolled over to the other side of the room, toward Matty, and put her cue stick away. Matty silently motioned toward a side pocket before hitting the eight ball into it.

Game over.

He turned to her, discarding his cue stick against the wall, his expression somber. "The little car thief almost stole my car, after all."

"I did."

"So why didn't you go through with it?"

"Because there's something I wanted more than it."

He stepped closer, the tips of his shoes flush against her painted toes as he gazed down at her. "And what's that?"

"To know what you want from me."

Wordlessly, his hands grasped her head, his large palms covering her warm cheeks, flushed from the alcohol. His touch was firm but gentle as he tilted her face up, cradling her like she was something precious, something he would never dare drop. He stared at her again, staring *through* her, like he could tell all of her secrets just by looking at her.

Could he?

Licking his lips, he leaned down and slowly, carefully kissed her. It was soft and sweet, but it held so much power, unlike any kiss Genna had ever experienced before. He kept her locked in place, in total control, and she easily, willfully, succumbed to his touch, surrendering in his hands.

He pulled back much, much too quickly. Genna opened her eyes just as he did, meeting his intense gaze. After a moment, he took her hand, barely giving her enough time to grab her things before leading her away. He pulled her out the front door of the sport's bar as the sun started to set in the distance.

Where the hell had the day gone?

Before Genna could dwell on that, he opened a door right next to The Place and pulled her inside, toward a dark staircase.

"Where are we going?" she asked, brow furrowing as they started up the shabby steps. Ugh, had they *ever* been swept?

"My place."

"Your place?"

"Yeah."

"Your place is above The Place?"

He laughed. "Yes."

She blinked a few times. "You drive a Lotus yet you live above a bar?"

That made no sense.

None at all.

The moment he unlocked the door and pulled her inside the apartment, her eyes widened in surprise. It definitely looked better than she had expected. This place was clean, with plush furniture and glass tables. A black pool table stretched along the back wall, the bright blue felt matching a rug covering part of the living room floor.

Genna turned to face him when he shut the door, but she had no time to say anything at all. With no hesitation, he was upon her, lips feverishly meeting hers as he pulled her further into the apartment. This kiss was hard, frantic and passionate; it was nothing like the sweetness he'd shown her downstairs. She tried to keep up, but Matty was a force to be reckoned with.

A haze of alcohol and lust surrounded them, spurring them on. Genna wrapped her arms around him, pulling him tighter to her, desperate to feel more of him. His hands roamed her body, caressing skin, shoving her skirt up around her waist. Her breath hitched as a hand slid beneath her panties, fingers grazing her sensitive clit. Knees wobbled and vision blurred just from a simple touch of his hand, but she didn't have a chance to savor it.

Zero to sixty in the blink of an eye.

Her clothes were hastily discarded, a trail of unwanted material through the apartment as he dragged her over to the pool table. Grasping her bare thighs, he picked her up, setting her on the edge of it. She clung to him, drawing him closer as he fumbled with his belt. He got his pants unbuckled as she worked on his white button down, popping buttons as she tore it open. He yanked it off, throwing it to the floor, leaving him with just a white undershirt.

Genna didn't bother with it, not wanting to break the kiss, her hands stroking his strong biceps and running down his forearms, feeling his inked skin. He tore a condom open that he fished out of his wallet, discarding the gold wrapper on the floor so he could quickly roll it on. Genna wrapped her slim legs around his waist, desperate for friction, as he grasped a hold of himself and pushed inside of her.

The first thrust, hard and deep, elicited a gasp from her throat.

Oh shit.

She never got a chance to catch her breath.

Gripping her hips, firmly holding her there, he pounded into her over and over again, as she cried out from the sensation, her voice strangled. She lay back on the table, her body tingling, throbbing starting between her thighs as he hitched her legs over his shoulders to drive even deeper. There was never any let up, never any wavering with his brutal thrusts.

Matty was a fucking *machine.*

She could do nothing but take what he gave her, accepting all of him eagerly, her nails scratching his skin as she held on for dear life. He drove her to the edge, violently shoving her off of it as his name resounded from her lips, a barely contained scream that fractured as it escaped her throat. *Matty.*

The sound only seemed to drive him on, encouraging him to give her even more. Again and again he took her to the brink.

I like to keep them coming.

Christ, he hadn't been kidding.

His hand encircled her throat, gripping gently to pin her in place, the light pressure at the base of her neck sending a thrill through Genna's body. She had never had someone take total control over her, had never submitted so willingly to a touch. It was dangerous—so, so dangerous—but she'd never felt such a rush of adrenaline.

Fuck cars.

This… this was *everything.*

Eventually it got to be too much—too much pressure building and building, too much pleasure, too much everything. Overwhelming tears stung her eyes when she felt another orgasm bubbling up inside of her. He seemed to sense it. Was it something in her voice, the way she whimpered, crying out his name in a choked breath? Or could he feel it, attuned to her body like it was an extension of his? She wasn't sure. Either way, he backed off, dropping her shaky legs as he carefully slowed his movements and let go of her throat.

Leaning down, his lips found hers again, kissing her softly as he continued to push inside of her. His mouth slowly moved, exploring her skin before nuzzling into her neck, teeth lightly nipping at her flesh. Her hands slid beneath his undershirt, nails scraping the skin of his back as he thrust a few more times before grunting as he came.

Still deeply inside of her, he pulled his face back to look in her eyes. She panted heavily, trying to find her breath. The spot between her thighs, the place they were connected, terribly ached.

He hadn't been kidding about that, either.

His thumb grazed her lips, slightly swollen from his hard kisses, as a smile softened his expression. "I didn't think you could be more beautiful," he said, "but then you went and screamed my name."

Blush radiated down her body, originating in her cheeks and coating every centimeter of exposed skin, as he finally pulled out. Genna felt the loss instantly when he backed away, clenching her thighs together to stifle the void. He grabbed her hands, pulling her off the pool table and setting her back on her feet, but instead of letting go he drew her to him, wrapping his strong arms around her.

He was *holding her*.

The sensation startled her, as he stroked her hair, petting her lovingly as she snuggled up against his chest, smelling his cologne and feeling his warmth.

She'd never had someone hold her before.

She remained silent when he finally let go, grabbing her clothes and quickly slipping them on as he situated himself. He disappeared into another room—his bedroom, she assumed—and returned after a moment looking just as put together as he had been when she first saw him.

Her? Well... she was scared to encounter her reflection.

"You want something to drink?" he offered, casual and polite, as if he hadn't just fucked her brains out, leaving her a quivering mess. She watched him as he strolled to the small open kitchen, her gaze settling on a clock on the wall.

A quarter after nine at night.

She blinked rapidly. *Shit.*

She'd missed dinner.

"I should really be going," she said, trying to smooth her hair. "It's getting late."

Matty grabbed two bottles of water from his refrigerator before approaching her, holding one out. "You're not just trying to get away from me, are you?"

"No, of course not," she said quickly, grabbing the water. "It's just that, well, I should've been home hours ago. My father—"

"I get it," he said, cutting her off. "The *'send out a search party'* type."

She smiled, grateful he seemed to understand, as she opened the water and took a sip, the coldness soothing her gritty throat. She screwed the cap back on and grabbed her purse and shoes as she headed for the door. He walked her out, right on her heels as she descended the dark staircase, trying to pull herself together. *Deep breaths*, she thought. *Don't go spastic now.* But she couldn't help it. Her legs were like jelly, her heart still racing, her fingers trembling as she clutched tightly to her things.

The guy had knocked her world off its axis, and she was pretty fucking sure there was no fixing *that*.

Barefoot, she stepped out onto the sidewalk and glanced around cautiously. For the first time all night, the fact that she was in Soho seemed to really nag at her. *Enemy territory.* After dark, at that. The neighborhood was foreign, and all she'd encountered were friendly faces, but she knew deception often hid behind the kindest smiles. Psychopaths ran these streets, and maybe she wouldn't know any of them, but they'd certainly recognize her.

Her father had warned her of that over the years, one of the many things he'd pounded into her brain, something that seemed to just now sink in as she came down from her high of such an outrageous day. Music and belligerent shouting spilled out from The Place, the bar much rowdier than it had been just a bit ago. Any one of those voices could lead to her demise.

"I shouldn't try to drive," Matty said. "But I can get my brother to take you home. He should be hanging out around here by now."

"It's okay," she said, turning to him. "I can take a cab."

"Are you sure?"

"I'm positive. Besides, I mean, it's kind of early to be meeting the family, isn't it? Not that, well, we're ever going to get to that point, or that you want that, or anything..." She was rambling again. *Ugh.* "I'm just saying, you know..."

Did he know? She scarcely knew what the hell she was saying. She'd had plenty of boyfriends, none of which she had ever brought home to meet her father, but he always seemed to find out about them and scare them off, anyway.

But this one?

Genna wasn't sure anything could intimidate him.

Matty stepped toward her, his hands once again cradling her head, a serious expression on his face that silenced her blubbering, that calmed her fears. Slowly, he leaned toward her, pressing a soft, chaste kiss against her lips.

"That's what I want," he said quietly. "What I get for winning."

"What?"

"You."

"You had me," she whispered, cheeks flushing at the reminder.

"I did," he agreed. "But the past isn't what matters. I live in the present, Genna. I live in the *now*. I had you, yeah, but what I want is to *have* you."

The way he spoke intensely, so assuredly, left her frazzled. "We hardly know each other."

"So? We spent an hour together this morning trapped in a box with no way out. And you know what I realized that hour?"

"What?"

"I kind of liked a world where it was just you and me." He kissed her again before letting go and stepping to the curb to hail a cab. The yellow car swiftly pulled up, screeching to a stop right in front of them. Matty opened the back door for her as he held out his hand. "Let me see your phone."

She dug it out of her purse and handed it over to him. He quickly typed something into it before handing it back as she got into the back of the cab.

"I put my number in it," he said, leaning in the door.

"If you decide you want me, too, you let me know."

He shut the door before she could find the words to respond. The cab pulled away from the curb, infusing right into the evening Soho traffic. "Where to, miss?"

"Westchester County," she replied, rattling off her address north of the city as she settled back into the seat.

Sighing, she opened her contacts on her phone and found his right away.

Matty B

Pressing the phone to her chest, she bit down on her lip to contain her smile, unable to compress the emotions whirling inside of her that the sight his name alone elicited. Was it possible to fall for someone in just one day? Possible to have your heart stolen after only a mere few hours of knowing them? She certainly never thought so. But yet she felt it then, the stirring in her gut and the tightening of her chest that hinted at something more already, something much bigger than her. It was undeniable, irresistible. She was head over heels, unabashedly swept off her feet by Matty-B.

She groaned. *Insta-love. How fucking cliché.*

Genna made it home just after ten o'clock, pushing open the front door and cautiously glancing around. The house was quiet and dark, except for a dim light spilling out from the dining room. She crept that way, pausing in the doorway as she frowned.

The table had long ago been cleared from dinner, the staff gone for the night, food all put away, yet her father still sat in his chair, a single glass with a swallow of wine in front of him.

"Genevieve," he said, voice quiet—he knew she was there without even looking. His gaze slowly shifted from the empty table to her. "You missed dinner."

Sighing, she stepped into the dining room and approached him. "Sorry, I had a crap day."

His eyes surveyed her. "You look it."

She glanced down—dirty bare feet, wrinkled clothes, sweat-coated skin—and snickered. "Yeah, I'm kind of a mess."

"Yet you're laughing," he pointed out.

"It's been one of those days where that's really all you can do... *laugh*."

His expression shifted, eyes narrowing suspiciously as he continued to survey her. "Who is he?"

"Who?"

"The boy you were with," he said. "Who is he?"

Genna gaped at him. "How did you...?"

"I know that look, Genna. There's only one thing that makes a girl look *that* way."

"He's, uh..." It unnerved her when her father did that, reading her with just a look. "He's just a boy I met this morning."

"Does he have a name?"

"Matty."

"Matty," he echoed. "How very... American."

She laughed again. "Actually, for your information, he's *Italian*-American."

Primo looked pleasantly surprised. "How'd you meet?"

"We shared an elevator," she replied, stepping toward him to lightly kiss his cheek. "Now, if you're done interrogating me, I'd like to take a shower and get some sleep. I'm exhausted."

He waved his hand, wordlessly dismissing her.

"Oh, by the way," she said as she walked away.

"You're going to have to have someone pick up my car tomorrow."

"Where is it?"

"At the courthouse. The judge suspended my license."

"And you didn't drive your car home?"

"No." She looked at him incredulously. Didn't he hear? "I couldn't."

He eyed her peculiarly. "Curious."

"What?"

"Well, you've never really let that stop you before. You were driving cars years before you even *had* a license. This new boy of yours must be special."

"Yeah," she admitted, before adding in a whisper, "he just might be."

She hit the doorway when he spoke again, his voice so quiet she could barely hear. "You look like her. When you smile, you look *so* much like her."

Genna glanced back at her father, watching as he picked up his glass, his eyes focused on the blood red wine. He wasn't watching her, his words meant more for himself than anyone, but she gave her father a small smile anyway. "Goodnight, Daddy."

Matty stood along the curb and watched the taillights of the cab disappear into the darkness before he turned around to head into The Place. As soon as he opened the door and stepped into the busy bar, dozens of sets of eyes zeroed in on him like the scope on an assault rifle, eagerly waiting for his acknowledgment. They hadn't dared approach him earlier when he had company.

They knew better.

Sighing, he strode over to the bar, squeezing in along the side and tapping his hand against the hard, glossy wood. The bartender glanced over at him with a subtle nod, setting straight to work making him a drink. "Your friend leave?"

"Yeah, she needed to get home."

"Ah," he said. "She a *close* friend?"

Matty cocked an eyebrow at him. "Is that any of your business?"

"No, of course not," he said, sliding the Roman Coke down the bar to him before shifting the subject. "So, you working tonight?"

"Yeah, I'll be at my table," he replied, taking a step back. "One at a time, or I'll shut them all down."

The bartender saluted him. "You're the boss."

No, Matty thought. *My father is.*

Matty strode to the back of the bar, finding his younger brother, Enzo, already sitting in their usual booth, his arm around a young blonde girl clad in a tight red dress and deathly high heels, her hair teased and frozen solid, like she'd used an entire can of hairspray to hold it in place. Matty paused in front of them, glancing at the seat Genna had sat in just a few hours earlier, currently occupied by another girl. A friend of Enzo's friend, he supposed. He cast her a look, taken aback by the amount of make-up caking her young face—bright red lips, blue eye shadow, pink blush.

His brother seemed to appreciate women from all walks of life, but he had a particular type he always went back to, the one's Matty referred to as eighties music video girls. If they looked like they'd been spread out on top of a Thunderbird to a White Snake song, Enzo was hooked.

"Matty!" he said, holding his fist out for him to

bump it. "This is—"

"They have to go," Matty said, motioning toward the girls. He didn't much care to hear their names. There was only one girl on his mind tonight, and if AquaNet and Crayola lingered, he had a sneaking suspicion it would ruin his high. "We have some business to take care of."

Enzo sighed before waving his hand, dismissing the girls with the promise of reconnecting later. Once they were gone, Matty slid into the booth and pulled the Blackberry from his pocket, setting it down on the table in front of him.

"So what corner did you pick them up from?" he asked nonchalantly.

"I resent that, bro."

Looking over at him, Matty cocked an eyebrow.

"I found them walking down 10th Avenue," Enzo replied, grinning when Matty rolled his eyes. "What? Not good looking enough for you?"

"She looked like she got gangbanged by crayons, En."

Laughing, Enzo snatched a piece of ice from his glass and hurled it at him. Matty ducked in just enough time that it flew over his shoulder, skidding across the table behind him. "Just thought my brother might want a little pussy to loosen him up."

"I'm doing fine on my own," Matty said, turning on the Blackberry as he pulled out a small notebook, flipping it open to the last marked page. He could hardly read his own jumbled scribble. "I don't need you to hire hookers."

Enzo laughed loudly, but his amusement tapered off as he sat up straight, staring across the table with wide eyes. Reaching over, he snatched ahold of Matty's shirt collar, yanking it aside. "Holy shit, you're not joking!"

Matty grimaced, knowing exactly what his brother

saw. The back of his neck stung, the burning sensation running down his spine from where Genna had brutally dug her fingernails into his flesh. He smacked his brother's arm, pulling away as he tried to focus on the work.

"Don't hold out on me," Enzo said. "I want details."

"I'm not talking to you about my sex life."

"Come on," he pressed. "At least tell me who it was."

"It's no one you know. I just met her."

"You just met her, and she's already putting out like *that*?" Enzo laughed, shoving him. "You sure she's not a hooker, too?"

Matty cut his eyes at his brother, the look on his face silencing Enzo before he could even say, "Shut the fuck up."

Enzo held his hands up defensively. "You must really like her."

"More than I like you. In fact, right now, I'm really starting to *not* like you."

His laughter resurfaced. "You love me, bro."

"Doesn't mean I have to like you."

Rolling his eyes, Enzo swallowed down the rest of his drink before motioning toward the notebook. "So, how are the Yankees looking this week?"

Matty started plugging numbers into the calculator on the Blackberry, trying to make sense of the week's calculations. He was entrusted with the job of keeping up with the betting games, to note the odds coming out of Vegas and coordinate with the rest of the local bookies, but he also directly ran the books at The Place.

Being a bookie was far from glamorous, and certainly not what he had in mind when he enrolled in Princeton all those years ago, but a job was a job. "They're favored to win every day."

71

"Who are they playing?"

"Home against the Indians at the start," he said, "then away against the Mariners by the weekend."

"Put me down for a grand on Friday's game," Enzo said as he stood up.

"It's a twenty cent line this week," Matty said, shrugging off his brother's offended look. It was usually only a dime. "Either pay up or put your money on the Mariners."

"That's foul."

"I didn't set it," Matty said. "Gavin did."

For every dollar they wanted to bet, they had to fork over another twenty cents on top of it. For a thousand dollar bet, Enzo would have to shell out an extra two hundred. It had to be balanced out somehow so *they* weren't the ones losing money, and New Yorkers didn't like to bet against the home team without some incentive.

And for gambling addicts, scrounging up a few bucks to play the game, sometimes an extra dime was enough to push them over to the other side of the fence.

Sports betting—it was a tedious business, but taking all of those statistics classes had certainly paid off. It had taken him a while to get used to the system, learning firsthand from the best bookie in the city: Gavin Amaro.

A steady flow of betters stopped by their table; some trusted to wager large sums with their word alone, while others were forced to pay in advance. Matty plugged in the numbers, making sure the bets didn't get too uneven, so he'd come out on top no matter who won the games, while he jotted down names in the notepad. The Blackberry started ringing after awhile, trusted guys with a direct line to him, so they wouldn't have to personally come down to The Place.

Two hours a night, a few days a week, depending on

how he felt. Some weeks he only showed up twice, other weeks he immersed himself there every single night. They were at his mercy, much to their chagrin. He didn't do it for the money.

He did just enough to keep the peace with his family.

At exactly midnight, Matty turned the phone off and slipped it away, tearing the notes out of the notepad and sliding them over to his brother so Enzo would know who to hunt down if they didn't willingly pay up. He didn't care who was still there, who hadn't gotten a chance to get their bet in.

He was off the clock.

"So this girl of yours," Enzo said, nursing a beer across from Matty. He'd been staring at him the entire time, hardly able to restrain himself from interrogating him.

Nosey bastard.

"What about her?" Matty asked, motioning for the waitress to bring him another drink.

"How'd you meet her?"

"She was stuck in the elevator with me this morning."

"No shit?" Enzo looked notably impressed. "So the two of you took advantage of the privacy?"

"Hardly," Matty said, tipping the waitress when she delivered his drink. "I brought her back here for a drink afterward."

"And then you took advantage of the situation?"

"More like she took advantage of me," he muttered, sipping from his glass. "She hustled my ass in a game of pool. I nearly lost my car to her."

Enzo's eyes widened. "*You?* But betting is your thing, man. I don't think I've *ever* seen you lose a bet."

"It didn't happen today, but only because she let me

win. And thank God for that. I don't know what the hell I would've done otherwise. I put my car, my watch, *and* money on the game."

"Why the hell would you do that?"

"It's what she wanted."

"What did she put up?"

"Whatever I wanted."

Enzo stared at him, blinking rapidly. "And that was, what... pussy? Because you know, bro, that kind of makes her like a—"

"Shut the fuck up," Matty warned him again. As much as he loved his brother, he wasn't above beating his ass if he called her that one more time. "It's more than that. After the way she played me? I wanted *her* more than anything."

"She must be some girl."

He sighed, taking a gulp of his drink. "She is."

chapter THREE

Little Italy, a neighborhood in lower Manhattan, was a melting pot of their kind. Unlike the rest of the city, Little Italy wasn't clearly defined by boundary lines, segregating the different families. Here they ran the same streets, frequented the same businesses, and rubbed shoulders with one another in a sort of restrained civility.

Ground zero, her brother called it. *The point where all the explosions originate.* So much brewing hostility, so much distrust, only escalated by the constant run-ins on ground they each considered part of their territory, tensions running high day in and day out. It only spanned about four blocks, but they were the last unclaimed blocks in an overrun city, the last piece of the pie up for grabs.

Primo hated Genna going to Manhattan as it was, forbidding her from venturing into Little Italy, but she couldn't resist its appeal—she loved the deep-rooted culture, the locally owned shops and restaurants, the tight-knit feeling of the small neighborhood. So whenever she went—whenever they *knew* about it, anyway—Dante was always forced to tag along with her.

"So let me get this straight," Dante said, leaning back in the creaky wooden chair, pushing it up on its hind legs as he eyed Genna peculiarly. They were at *Casato*, a small café owned by the Amaros, another of the five New York families. The place was brightly lit from its vast windows, with a comfortable breeze blowing in from the propped-open doors. "You were stuck in an elevator yesterday and you didn't raise hell about it?"

"Nope," she said, lightly blowing into her cup of espresso. "There was no point."

"So who's the guy?"

"Excuse me?"

"Come on, for you not to flip out about something like that? There *has* to be a guy involved somehow."

Rolling her eyes, Genna took a sip of her hot drink. *Am I that fucking predictable?* "You know, you sound just like Dad."

"So I'm right."

"No," she said defensively, eyes narrowed at his smug expression. He stared at her, disbelieving. After a moment, she sighed. "Well… okay. There *was* a guy."

"Ha!" His chair dropped back down on all four legs, the ear-splitting screech drawing the attention of people around them. "Knew it."

"It's different this time," she said defensively, setting her drink down. "This one is different."

"How so?"

"I, uh… I don't know." How could she explain something she hardly understood herself yet? Dante was always picking on her about the guys she went for, but this was nothing like before. "From the moment I saw him, I couldn't seem to look away."

"So, what, he's attractive? Whoop-de-fucking-do."

"No. Well, I mean, he is, but it's not just that. There's something about him. It's unexplainable. He looked at me, and it felt like he was *consuming* me... like my insides were too big for my body and I was going to combust, like my heart was going to explode."

Dante stared at her, eyebrows raised. "That's, uh... that's the stupidest shit I've ever heard."

His laughter, brash and amused, rang out. Annoyed, Genna flung a balled up napkin across the table at him. "I'm being serious, Dante."

"That's what makes it even worse," he replied. "Are you sure it wasn't acid reflux you felt? Heartburn can be a bitch."

She sneered at him, picking her drink back up. "You just don't understand."

"I don't," he agreed. "I fall in love every time I fall into a new pussy, but I've never felt *that*... and if I did, I'd get to a doctor, STAT. That's just not normal."

She ignored him, instead shifting her attention to the plate in front of her, and picked apart the rest of her lunch in silence. The day before still felt so surreal, and absolutely incredible, and her brother wasn't helping. At all. She felt ludicrous, swept up in something so outrageous, so all consuming. She hardly knew Matty, yet she felt like she *knew* him intimately, like she had somehow always known him. Maybe that wasn't normal, but there was no denying it.

He had been on her mind all night long as sleep evaded her. She'd stared at her phone, typing out messages to him, but promptly deleting them before hitting send. What could she say? Nothing felt right.

He stole all words from her, leaving her speechless.

One thing was for certain, though: she was dying to see him again.

She finished her espresso before standing up and gathering her things. Dante was on his feet right away, tossing some cash down on the table for a tip, even though he hadn't ordered anything for himself. They strolled out of the café, into the cool afternoon. Italian flags flapped in the breeze, affixed to businesses, as red, white, and green decorations adorned the massive six-story buildings, canopies casting shade along the cracked pavement of the old sidewalks. People hung out on fire escapes, calling out to each other.

A few greeted Dante warmly, shouting his name from above. His gaze would flicker that way, a smile on his face as he waved politely.

It was strange to Genna, how loved her brother seemed to be by almost everyone they encountered. Not to say she didn't love him, because she did. She would be hard pressed to name someone closer to her. He wasn't just her brother—he was her best friend, too. He was her confidante. He was the one person she could count on, her constant in this world. But this was Dante, passive and playful... yet the people of New York revered him, treating him like he was so much more. No matter what she knew about his involvement with their father's business, regardless of the fact that she knew he carried a gun at all times, he was still just her harmless, overprotective big brother in her eyes.

"Where to now?" he asked, cutting his eyes at her as they walked south, casually swinging his keys around on his fingers.

"I wanna stop by the music store on Mulberry," she replied. "Then you can take me home. I'm sure you have other things to do."

It had to annoy him sometimes, she thought, being ordered to shadow her around like a bodyguard. He never complained about it… he never complained about *anything*, really. But she still felt guilty, him being treated like an employee within the family on account of her.

She never wanted Dante to resent her for anything.

They headed down the block and turned the corner onto Mulberry. Her gaze wandered the street as they walked, taking in the scenery, her footsteps faltering when a flash of bright red caught her eye, gleaming in the afternoon sunshine. A familiar car whipped in along the curb down the block, the loud bass of music coming from it echoing through the neighborhood.

No fucking way.

A Lotus Evora.

There was no way he was here—no way she'd run into him in the middle of Manhattan, a city of well over a million people. But what were the odds of someone else driving *that* car? One in a fucking billion.

She stared at it, watching with awe as the driver's side door opened and Matty stepped out. Her breath hitched, her heart thumping erratically, lodging in her throat. The very sight of him brought back all of those feelings her brother had laughingly dismissed just moments ago. Matty was even more handsome than she remembered, dressed impeccably in a light blue button down, sleeves rolled up to his elbows, showing off his tattoos.

Snatching a hold of her brother's arm, Genna yanked him to a stop, unable to drag her eyes away from Matty as he laughed radiantly, shouting to a group of guys stepping out of the music store in front of him… the same music store they were heading to.

"That's, uh…" *Holy shit.* "That's—"

"Barsanti."

That name, ground out in a harsh voice, drove her attention straight to her brother. *Whoa, Barsanti?* She turned to Dante, suddenly on edge, knowing he sensed serious trouble to speak that name out loud. Coldness rushed through her, bitter and unwelcome, sending a tremor down her spine. Dante's narrowed eyes shot daggers down the block, right to where the Lotus was parked.

Her gaze frantically followed his as Matty approached three others, greeting them. Immediately, she recognized Enzo Barsanti along with two others, vaguely familiar guys… ones who had come into The Place the night before.

'Friends of the family,' Matty had called them.

No. No. God, please, no.

He couldn't be, could he?

She would know, wouldn't she?

"Dante," she said, tugging on her brother's arm, trying to get his attention. He tore his gaze away from the group, his expression stone cold serious as he regarded her. "You know all of those guys?"

"Enzo Barsanti," he responded, focus going right back down the street. Enzo was a beast of a guy at only twenty, with the mass of a bodybuilder and enough hair coating him to make him damn near part-werewolf. "You know him."

"And the others?" she asked, desperate for this to be some kind of mistake.

"Two of his lackeys." Dante motioned toward the guys in similar red shirts, flanking Enzo. "Carl and Roy. Tweedledum and Tweedledee. Barsanti street soldiers."

"And the other?" she pressed, holding her breath as she waited for his answer. *Dear God, let him be a neighbor. He can move. Let him be an old friend. Friendships die.* Anything except what she feared her brother was about to say.

"Matteo," he said, voice as cold as ice. "Matteo Barsanti."

Her chest burned at the confirmation. She felt like she was going to puke. Matteo Barsanti. *Matty-B.* Adverse emotions flooded her system, her mind frantically racing, trying to make sense of it all as she recounted everything he had said to her the night before.

How could it be that he was one of *them*?

Had he known, she wondered? Watching him, seeing how at ease he seemed, how *cheerful* he was, she couldn't stop the sensation of betrayal that seeped into her bloodstream like poison. Devastation made her knees shake. The way he had looked at her, seeing through her, like he was reading her... had this boy, this seemingly perfect creature she stumbled upon, been playing her the entire time?

"Oh God," she gasped. What had she said? What had she told him about her family? She had spilled her soul to him so easily, and the whole time he was one of them.

Had he really hustled *her*?

"Guess the long lost son has returned," Dante said. "I was starting to wonder if he was even still alive. It's been a while since he showed his face around here."

"How do you know it's him?" Genna's voice was barely a strained whisper. It could still be a mistake, right? A big misunderstanding?

Please let it be a misunderstanding.

"Oh, I know," Dante said, not an ounce of wavering. "Trust me... I know the enemy when I see it."

81

Enzo turned then, his elated expression deteriorating when he caught sight of Dante and her. The guys at his side, attuned to their surroundings, quickly took notice of their presence. Matty's expression twisted with confusion at the sudden shift as he followed their gaze straight to them down the block.

Genna inhaled sharply the instant his eyes connected with hers, her chest constricting, treacherous sensations twisting her gut. He was a Barsanti. He was one of them. She should have been disgusted. She should've been consumed by hate. But looking at him, all she could feel were those butterflies.

Fucking tummy-fluttering butterflies that raised hell the moment his face lit up with a genuine smile at the sight of her. The breath left her lungs in a whoosh, strangling her. She watched, everything in painful slow motion, as Enzo leaned toward him and whispered something. She could see his lips moving, could practically make out the bitter word that made Matty's expression plummet.

'Galante.'

As much as Genna's family hated theirs, she knew they hated hers, too. They hated the Galantes just as much. And taking in his appearance, the way he blinked rapidly, shoulders tensing, eyes widening with disbelief, she knew... this was the face of a man who had just been knocked on his ass as hard as she had been a moment ago.

"Come on," Dante said, grabbing her arm and pulling on it, forcing her to take a few steps backward. "We're getting out of here. I'm not risking it."

"Not risking it?" she asked, grudgingly pulling her gaze away from Matty to turn around as her brother continued to drag her away. "You *never* retreat."

"If you weren't here, no problem, but I'm not putting you in harm's way."

She scoffed. "I'm not afraid."

"You should be," he said, his voice low as he cut his eyes at her. "Do you know what they'd do to you, Genna? Those people... those Barsantis? They're fucking savages. How many times has Dad told you that?"

Practically every day of her young life. "What are they going to do, kill me? Right here, in the middle of a busy neighborhood, in broad daylight?"

Dante's footsteps stopped abruptly, his grasp on her tightening. "No, Genna, they won't kill you. They won't *just* kill you, anyway. They'll stalk you, and they'll take you, because you're an easy target, and then they'll do things to you... things that'll make you *wish* they would just kill you."

His harsh words left her momentarily speechless.

"And that's when they'll kill you," he continued. "Only after you ask them, only after you beg them to end your misery. And they'll enjoy it. Believe me. They'll make sure when we find you... *if* we find you... that we won't even recognize you."

"How do you know?"

"How do I know?" He raised his eyebrows. "I know because Mom and Dad couldn't recognize Joey."

She flinched at his words, as if she'd been punched in the gut. "That's different."

"Is it?" he asked. "They killed him, Genna, and there wasn't even enough left for an identification."

"I know that," she said, tears stinging her eyes. "I know what happened."

"Yeah, well, I *remember* it, and I'm not going through that again."

Dante turned the corner, striding toward his car, while she lingered for a moment, casting a look over her shoulder, once more meeting Matty's eyes. He stared at her as if nothing else existed.

She wished, more than anything, that she could trust that look.

"Badass, huh?"

Matty tore his eyes from down the block when Genna jetted around the corner, obediently following her brother... her brother, the one and only Dante Galante. Who would've guessed? *Not me. Not in a million years.* His gaze fell on Enzo as he stood there, staring at him, grinning like a fool. "What?"

"The Ice Princess," he replied, motioning toward the corner where Genna had been just moments before. "Genevieve Galante. She's a looker, ain't she?"

Images flashed through Matty's mind: Genna beneath him, crying out his name, violently convulsing with pleasure so intense he saw tears in her eyes. When she came, over and over... Jesus, he'd never seen anything so beautiful before. "She's something, alright."

Enzo slapped him on the back jokingly. "Too bad she's one of them."

"Yeah," Matty muttered. "Too bad."

His day went from sky fucking high to in the shitter, and all it took was that one word: *Galante.* Ironic, he thought. The name meant gallant, brave, amorous, when as far as he was concerned, those people were anything but. The Galante family bred spineless, callous cowards, led by the biggest heartless brute of them all. *Primo.*

How could that girl, that glowing angel dropped from Heaven straight into his defunct elevator, be that barbarian's spawn?

Matty had been disconnected from the lifestyle for years—most of his life, it seemed—but he knew the stories as well as anyone. His father never failed to fill him in whenever he came to visit.

"Those cockroaches are at it again," he'd say. "Might have to take it to the mattresses soon."

Every visit, same thing for years… another war was brewing, much like the one that had ignited the deadly rivalry sixteen years ago.

He mulled over that as he drove to his parent's house, a vast townhouse near Central Park West. Enzo sat in the passenger seat, yammering away like a little yippee-ass pup. Usually he didn't mind his brother's need for constant chatter, but today he was making it difficult for Matty to think.

"They'll know you're here now," Enzo said as Matty pulled the Lotus up to the front of the house and cut the engine.

He glanced at his brother. "Who?"

"The Galante clan. They saw you're back."

Saying he was *back* was misleading, as if he were ever really involved in the first place. His little brother was the one knee-deep in the life. Enzo lived it. Breathed it. Loved it. As far as Matty went? He just tried to survive it. He'd been trying to survive it since he was a kid, too young to have to deal with having a bounty on his head.

The son pays for the father's sins.

Enzo burst in the front door of the house, leaping up

and slapping the top of the doorframes as he went, creating a ruckus as usual. Sighing, Matty walked in behind him, hearing the soft, feminine voice call out from the nearby den. "Boys? That you?"

"Of course it is, Ma," Enzo hollered, striding right through the downstairs as he headed straight for the kitchen. "Who else would it be?"

Stepping into the den, Matty paused momentarily and gazed at her sitting on the corner of the plush burgundy couch, huddled up with a thick fleece blanket like it was the middle of winter and not eighty-eight fucking degrees. Even sick and growing frail, she still had a softness to her face, her round cheeks slightly flushed, her hair naturally curly, her eyes vivid as they zeroed in on him.

"Hey, Sugar Cube," she said, lightly patting the couch beside her in a silent invitation.

He strolled over and sat down on the edge of the cushion. "Mom."

"You doing okay?" she asked, smoothing the hair on the back of his head. "You look a little down."

"I'm fine," he said. "Just having one of those days."

He could feel her eyes on him, assessing and judging. She didn't believe him for a second. His mother was an intuitive woman. Had to be, to be married to his father. And as much as he hated lying to her, he couldn't tell her this. No, he couldn't tell her the Galante girl had him wound tight, wrapped around her finger stronger than her legs had wrapped around his waist when he plowed into her on the pool table he'd gotten from his parents for his birthday.

Christ, he needed to stop thinking about that.

"You sure about that?" she asked hesitantly.

"Yes," he lied, turning to look at her. "More

importantly, how are you?"

"I'm hanging in there." She smiled, a knowing twinkle in her eyes. "It's good to have you around, you know. I've missed you."

"Missed you, too, Mom." Those words nearly caught in his throat. He'd missed *a lot*, but especially her. Despite the circumstances, being cut off from his family for years, he and his mother had remained close.

"So what are you up to?" she asked. "Any exciting plans tonight?"

"You could say that."

"Really? What?"

"I intend to spend it making dinner for the most stunning woman on earth."

Her expression lit up. "Is that right?"

"Absolutely," he said. "Then we'll probably watch movies."

"Really?"

His lips twitched as he fought back a smile at the barely restrained eagerness in her voice. "Yep."

"Anyone I know?"

"Oh, definitely."

Her eyes widened. "Who?"

"You."

All at once, her excitement turned to exasperation. She hit him lightly as she shook her head. "You can't do that to me!"

"What?" He laughed as he blocked her weak punches. "It's true."

"I thought you meant a girl," she said. "I thought you finally *met* a girl."

"A girl more beautiful than you? Impossible."

"As charming as you are, Matty, you'd think you'd have found someone to settle down with by now. You're pushing twenty-five for crying out loud!"

"I have time," he said, immediately regretting those words when he saw the reality in her eyes. He might, but she didn't. They all knew it, even if none of them wanted to admit that truth out loud.

"I just want you to be happy," she said softly. "I want *all* of you to be happy."

"I know."

Before they could get into it anymore, Enzo strolled in, clutching a peanut butter and jelly sandwich. He took a big bite out of it, obnoxiously chewing as he plopped down in a chair and threw his feet up on the corner of the coffee table. Their mother glared at him silently until he dropped his feet flat to the floor, tossing her a sheepish smile. "Sorry, Ma."

Upstairs, a door opened, heavy footsteps ambling down the hallway like steel against the hard wood. They approached the stairs, slowly descending them, each footfall sucking a little more of the warmth from the room.

Roberto Barsanti, short and stocky with a cleft chin and dark hair that faded to gray along the sides, oozed bitter coldness. He was severe—all business, all the time. Matty could never relate to his father, not like Enzo did, but he worshiped their mother and that was enough, for the moment, for him to maintain Matty's respect.

Roberto's beady blue eyes scanned the room when he stepped into the doorway, eyeing Enzo with approval and their mother with love, before shooting stern daggers straight at Matty. "Matteo."

He cringed. His father was the only one who insisted

on always calling him by that name. "Father."

"It's good to see you."

Unlike when his mother said it, Matty felt nothing genuine in those words. "You, too."

"Speaking of *seeing* people," Enzo said, words muffled from a mouth full of food. "Guess who we ran into today, Pops."

"Who?"

"The Galante kids."

Matty's chest constricted at the reminder, while his father sneered, his lip curling angrily. "Where?"

"Little Italy, of course," Enzo said. "Matty was picking me up when they were coming down the street."

"Did they say anything to you?"

"Nah, of course not," Enzo said, taking another bite of his sandwich. "Dante tucked tail and ran like a little bitch."

"En," their mother chided. "Language."

"Sorry, Ma," Enzo said, hardly missing a beat before continuing. "His sister followed him, but not before they both saw Matty standing there."

Roberto's eyes widened as that dawned on him. "Did they recognize Matteo?"

"Dante, most definitely. The girl, nah. It's doubtful she's ever even heard of him."

The few times Matty ventured to the city over the years, he had been around during run-ins with some of the Galante crew. Dante and him had come face to face for the last time when he was eighteen, but Genna?

Never saw her before yesterday.

"Yeah," their father agreed. "You're right. Medusa wouldn't know him."

Matty grimaced at that nickname as their mother gasped. "Bobby! Don't call her that! She's just a girl!"

"My apologies, Savina," his father said. "I forgot."

More like he forgot she was listening to their conversation. They had called her that for years, so much so it was the only damn name Matty remembered.

Medusa. The Ice Princess.

Despite himself, he snickered bitterly under his breath when it dawned on him—as many times as his father had warned him away from her in passing, cautioning him about the dangerous Galante girl, he'd unknowingly fallen right into her trap.

"Something funny?" Roberto asked, staring at him.

"No," Matty said, shaking his head. It wasn't really funny at all, but the whole thing was still starting to feel like a big goddamn joke.

Roberto studied him for a moment before striding over, leaning down and kissing Savina softly on the corner of her mouth. "Call me if you need anything, honey."

"I'll be fine," she said, smiling as she reached over and wrapped herself around Matty's arm. "I have my handsome boy to keep me company tonight."

Roberto's eyes shifted from her to Matty, and he saw the hesitance in his father's expression. It wasn't exactly distrust, but it was some apprehension, as if he hadn't yet decided what to make of Matty's ongoing presence.

Enzo jumped up, stuffing the last bit of sandwich into his mouth, noisily chewing as he held his fist out. Matty bumped his to his brother's before he jogged away, following their father out of the room.

Saturday night. They would be gone until the wee hours of the morning, robbing people blind and drinking themselves into a stupor, gambling and smoking, chasing skirts and doing whatever the hell else they did out on the streets.

"So, what are you hungry for?" Matty asked once they were alone, turning to his mother as he stood up.

She smiled softly. "We can just have some sandwiches."

"Nonsense," he said. "Tell me what you want to eat."

She pondered that for a moment. "Surprise me."

Surprise me. It would be no surprise. She knew exactly what he would make—it was the first thing she had ever taught him to cook, the one thing they always made together. It was her favorite meal: spaghetti with homemade meatballs.

Leaning down, he kissed her soft cheek before strolling to the kitchen. The staff had weekends off, so it was quiet and dark, the air chilly. Flicking on the light, he set to work right away, pulling out everything he needed for dinner. He tossed the meat in the microwave to defrost and pulled out pre-packaged pasta, knowing it broke every rule of an Italian kitchen, but he was in a bit of a time crunch. Besides, he knew she wouldn't complain... *much.*

He pulled out jars of her pre-made sauce and put it in a pot to simmer as he chopped up some onions and peppers, just enough for a little bit of a kick. He shoved up his sleeves and took off his watch before mixing together all the ingredients by hand, shaping the mixture into gooey round balls and slapping them on a baking sheet. He had just finished and was washing the gunk off his hands when he heard shuffling behind him.

"Need help?" his mother asked.

"No," he said. "I got it."

She ignored him, of course, and grabbed the pan of meatballs, placing it in the oven just as it preheated. She set the timer for twenty minutes before turning to the fridge and grabbing a bottle of red wine.

"Let me get that for you," he said quickly, reaching for the bottle, but she smacked his hand away and pushed past him, heading straight for the wine opener. Sighing, he leaned against the counter and put his watch back on, gazing at her as she struggled to uncork it. He kept his patience for as long as possible before sighing exasperatedly. *Stubborn woman.* "Give up yet?"

"Never."

He smiled at her determination. It took another few minutes, but she managed to finally pop the cork. She shot him a satisfied look as she grabbed a wine glass and poured a bit into it, taking a sip and closing her eyes, a look of sheer ecstasy crossing her weary face.

"Now that's good," she said, grabbing another glass and pouring a bit into it before holding it out to him. He took it and sipped, gagging at the bitter tang. She laughed. "Oh, quit whining and just drink it."

"I'm not whining," he said, taking another drink and grimacing. "Ugh, it's disgusting."

"*Now* you're whining," she pointed out as she motioned across the room toward the oven beside him. "And get your meatballs out before they're overdone."

He glanced at the stove just as the timer went off. *How the hell did she do that?* He pulled them out and plopped them in the sauce, letting them simmer while he boiled the pasta. Despite his protests, his mother insisted on setting the table for the two of them, dismissing his reservations with a sarcastic, "I'm not dead *yet*, you know."

He flinched at her words, trying to keep it from showing on his face, but she noticed, based on the apologetic look she cast him. Wordlessly, he dished them both out some food before joining her in the dining room and sitting down across from her. She immediately dove in, taking small savory bites as she hummed thoughtfully. "Pretty good."

"Thanks."

"You could've made your own pasta, though."

"I could've."

"And it could've been a bit spicier."

"It could've."

"But still… pretty good."

Like he said, she wouldn't complain *much*.

He picked at his food, his stomach protesting every bite he forced down, as his mind wandered back to thoughts of Genna. He replayed their night together, still trying to make sense of everything. The girl had clawed her way under his skin. What the hell was he supposed to do about it?

His dilemma must have played out on his face because his mother eventually stopped eating and pointed at him with her fork. "Okay, buddy. Spill it. *Now.*"

He raised his eyebrows. "What?"

"Don't *'what'* me, Matteo." *Ah, shit.* She used his real name. She meant business. "I can tell something's bothering you tonight, and I want to know what it is."

Sighing, he stared down at his plate, smashing a meatball with his fork. "You were right, I guess. There was a girl."

From the corner of his eye, he saw her tense—not what she had expected to hear from him. "A girl?"

"Yeah, but don't go getting worked up about it, Mom. I said there *was* a girl, not that there is one. It turned out she was everything I shouldn't want."

"But you still wanted her."

It was a statement, not a question, but he answered anyway.

"Yeah, I did." Man, he *really* fucking did. He hadn't wanted something—or someone—so much in his life.

"So what happened?"

"*We* happened."

"Oh." She was quiet for a moment as she started eating again. "So I'm guessing this girl figured out you're one of the notorious Barsanti boys?"

"You could say that."

"And that bothers her?"

"It should," he muttered. "If she's smart, and I think she is…" *Smarter than I might've given her credit for.* "…she'll never even look at me again."

"But you still want her."

Another statement. She knew him well.

"Yeah, I do," he muttered. "I shouldn't, but I do."

"I raised you to be independent, Matty. I know your father has expectations, things he wants you to do with your life, but I've always been proud of the fact that you made your own path. You've been that way for as long as I can remember. I'll never forget all those years ago, my strong-willed eight-year-old son, putting his foot down and standing up to his father for the first time. Do you remember that? That day?"

Matty sat quietly for a moment, surprised where the topic was diverting. "Of course I do. He wouldn't budge, though. I told him I hated him for it, hated him for making me stay away, and it didn't faze him a bit."

She laughed dryly. "You and I remember it a bit

differently. It certainly bothered him."

"He locked me in my room," he said. "When he finally let me out, he sent me and Enzo to live with Aunt Lena and Uncle Johnny. And when he came back for me—when I *thought* he came back for me—it was just to ship me off to boarding school."

"True," she said quietly. She couldn't deny those facts. "But you don't know how torn up he was about it. He asked me so many times, 'do you think he really hates me?' I always said no, hoping I wasn't lying to him, hoping you understood why he did what he did."

"I get he wanted to keep us safe…"

"But? I know there's a but."

"But he brought Enzo home. It was safe enough for Enzo to come back years ago, but not me. He's *never* welcomed me back."

"Now you're being ridiculous."

"Am I, Mom?" he asked, glancing across the table at her. "You know what the first thing he said to me when I came back to New York was? The first thing out of his mouth when he saw my face?"

"What?"

"Why are you here?"

"He just worries," she said. "He was concerned about why you came. He thought something was wrong."

"There *is* something wrong."

Her expression softened as she gazed at him. "Look, Matty, my point is you were such a little man back then, and you've grown into even more of a man now. It doesn't matter what people tell you... you do what you want. You always have. That's *why* he locked you in your room. If he hadn't, you would've defied him and gone anyway, despite the fact that he said you couldn't."

"What does that have to do with this?"

"Well, I don't expect any less from you now," she replied. "Life's short. Too short. Trust me. You'll *never* have enough time. So it doesn't matter if you think this girl might be all wrong for you. You want her? Then go for her."

"It's not that easy."

"Yes, it is. If she doesn't want you anymore? Her loss. Otherwise, there's no reason not to pursue what you want."

Matteo Barsanti.

Genna scarcely remembered there even *being* a Matteo Barsanti. He had become more of a phantom than a person, a ghost story, whisperings of a vague memory of the oldest Barsanti kid that nobody could quite recall in detail. His existence was sort of an urban legend, the Mafia Boss's son who seemed to vanish from society. Everybody had questions, but nobody ever dared ask for any answers.

Genna had been fifteen the first time she recalled hearing of him... her fifteenth birthday. Against her father's wishes, she'd stowed away into the attic of their house and rummaged through her mother's packed-up belongings, digging through all of her fancy clothes, admiring her jewelry, trying on her wedding dress. The things had been up there for less than a year then but a layer of dust already coated everything, like a lifetime had passed since she had been around to use any of it.

In one of the boxes, in a small wooden chest with a rusty metal clasp, Genna found a thick stack of photographs. She had sat right there in the middle of the dim attic, wearing her mother's pearls and one of her favorite sundresses, and sorted through the faded pictures. She had never seen any of them before, most of her brothers and her. On the bottom of the stack, the last few photos were of Joey and another little boy.

Flipping one over, Genna glanced at the back, seeing her mother's elegant cursive.

Joseph Galante & Matteo Barsanti
Seven years old

She stared at it, surprised. She knew the Barsanti family by that point, had their names and faces memorized as her father routinely quizzed Dante and her, ensuring they could recognize them out on the street. But never, in all of it, had anyone mentioned a Matteo to her.

After cleaning up the attic, she went downstairs, clutching one of the pictures. Her father sat in his office with the door wide-open. Curious, Genna paused in the doorway. "Dad, who's Matteo Barsanti?"

Her father's eyes darted to her. "What did you say?"

Stepping into the room, she held up the picture. "I found this, and on the back it says—"

"I know what it says." Her father was on his feet, tearing the photo out of her hands before she had even realized he moved. "Go to your room."

She gaped at him. "But—"

"Don't argue, Genevieve," he yelled, angrier than she had ever seen him before, his eyes glowing with rage, his hand shaking as he fisted the photograph. "And stay out of the goddamn attic. I'm not going to tell you again!"

She had later asked Dante, who brushed off her question with a half-assed answer. "He's not around anymore."

That was it. No explanation.

A year later, during one of her reckless rebellion moments, Genna was scrounging through her father's bedroom and found that photo in the drawer in his nightstand... half of it, anyway.

Joey's half.

Matteo had been carelessly ripped out of it.

She eventually got more out of Dante but nothing significant. Matteo was the eldest son, Joey's age... he would have been in his early twenties now. She assumed the boy had died, just like her brother had, but clearly he was alive and well.

And somehow managing to fuck with my life.

As soon as Dante and Genna made it home from Little Italy that afternoon, he strode right to their father's office. Voices carried out from in there, the various cars aligning their property telling her they were conducting business. In his haste, Dante had left the door open a crack behind him. Curiously, Genna tiptoed that way, standing against the wall beside the door, straining her ears to listen.

"I saw him today," Dante said. "Matteo Barsanti."

That silenced the other men right away.

"You're sure it was him? Matteo?" Primo asked. "No chance it was a mistake?"

"No chance."

Genna's stomach dropped.

"The Barsantis must think it's safe to bring him home and involve him in things," Primo said. "Why else would he be around now?"

His mother's sick, she thought. *He came home so not to miss this chance.*

"I don't know," Dante said. "But I'll find out."

Sighing, Genna pushed away from the wall before getting caught eavesdropping and headed up to her room, throwing herself down in bed and staring up at the ceiling. She laid there for what felt like forever, until there was a light knock at her door.

"Come in," she mumbled, not loud enough for anyone to hear.

The door opened anyway, her brother sauntering in, looking much more relaxed than he had been when they got home. Turning her head, she watched him as he sat down on the bed nearby.

"I'm sorry about earlier," he said right away. "I shouldn't have thrown Joey in your face like that to scare you."

She sighed. "You meant well."

"I did," he agreed, "but it still wasn't right. I shouldn't do that."

"Well, I forgive you."

"Thanks." Dante reached over, playfully nudging her. "So tell me more about this guy of yours that has you trying to spontaneously combust."

She shook her head slowly. "There's no point."

"Why?"

"I think you might've been right about it all."

"Yeah?"

"I realized I don't even know him," she said. "I was just fooling myself, being an idiot as usual, thinking he could be different when they're all just the same."

"Ah, I don't believe that."

"I'm a shit judge of character," she muttered. "I'm just gonna lay here and waste away, no point in even bothering anymore. I officially quit life."

Dante stood up, grabbing her hand to pull her up. She resisted, in no mood to even move, but he was undeterred, physically dragging her out of the bed. She grunted when her back slammed into the hard floor, but Dante still didn't let go, clutching onto her wrists and pulling her thorough the room.

"Stop," she whined as he dragged her across the carpet. "You're gonna give me rug burn!"

"No," he said. "My sister's not a quitter."

She fought him off, digging in her heels, but he just pulled harder, practically tackling her on the floor. By the time he got her to the bedroom door, she was engulfed in a fit of laughter and unable to fight him anymore.

"Okay, okay, I quit!" He narrowed his eyes, and she laughed harder. "I mean I *don't* quit. You win, okay?"

"Good," he said, yanking her to her feet finally. "Because those stairs would've hurt if I had to drag you down them, too."

A few minutes past eight. They were both late for dinner. Genna followed Dante downstairs, slipping into her seat. Their father said nothing about their tardiness, simply reaching across the table and taking their hands to pray. They all ate quietly, the atmosphere strained. A torturous hour passed before she finally had a chance to escape, slipping back upstairs as her brother followed their father into his office.

As soon as she reached her bedroom, she grabbed her cell phone out of her purse and flopped down on the bed.

Lying back, she gazed at the screen, opening her contacts to see his name.

Matty B.

Matteo Barsanti, just the touch of a button away.

Their families didn't just carry animosity—they were

100

mortal enemies, hell-bent on destroying each other. The two of them were a disaster waiting to happen, and they had just been fooling themselves if they thought anything good could come out of this thing.

Hesitating, her finger hovered over the screen for a moment before she hit the delete button, erasing him from her life just as quickly as he had been dropped into it.

chapter FOUR

120 hours of community service—three hours a day, five days a week, for the next two months. That was practically Genna's entire summer wrapped up in punishment. The court set up grueling graffiti cleanup duty in the Greenwich Village section of Manhattan, but her father quickly intervened and shut that down.

Greenwich Village was Barsanti territory.

Instead, she was scheduled to work in a soup kitchen in East Harlem, in a section of the neighborhood considered one of the sketchiest, but her father figured it would be the safest for her. None of *their* kind would ever dare venture that far east, he'd said.

She started the first Monday of June—dinner shift, from four to seven in the evening. Instead of bothering her brother for a ride, knowing he had better things to do than haul her around everywhere she needed to go, she called for a cab to take her. She showed up fifteen minutes late that first evening, wearing a nice black dress and high heels, her hair down and curled. She figured just because she had to do it didn't mean she couldn't do it in style.

Mistake.

The coordinator—a scrawny, tall man with gray hair and withered skin named Adam—met her at the door, took one look at her, and shook his head. "You know what you're getting into here?"

"Sure," she said, shrugging. They were feeding people. How hard could *that* be?

"All right, then," he said, tossing a grungy white apron at her. "Let's get started then."

As it turned out, she had absolutely no idea what she was getting into. She expected to slap dinner on a tray and mindlessly shove it along to the next person in an assembly line, never giving thought to the fact that someone had to *cook* the food.

And that someone, it seemed, was the same someone who served it.

By five o'clock, she was dripping sweat, her arms aching from hurriedly stirring a huge pot of chili, the front of her splattered by sauce, and her head itching from the hairnet she'd been forced to wear. In her eighteen years of life, she'd never cooked before—she never had to. Her mother was the farthest from domestic as a person could possibly get and Genna seemed to have inherited her kitchen skills. Her inadequacy earned her amused looks from the coordinator as he watched her scramble to be ready in time.

Lugging the heavy pot out of the kitchen, she stumbled in her heels and nearly dropped the chili. Grunting, she shoved it up on the serving counter, barely having time to catch her breath when the doors opened and people started filtering in to eat. From that moment on, it was nonstop as she ladled the chili into small Styrofoam cups, barely a few bites for each person, before plopping it on a tray and sending it down the line for sandwiches and cartons of milk.

When seven o'clock finally neared, her shift coming to a close, she was utterly exhausted, her feet aching, her muscles twitching. She almost longed for graffiti duty. On the way out, the coordinator met her at the door, where he stood most of the evening, greeting everyone who came along.

"I'm surprised you survived all night, Miss Galante," he said, glancing at his watch. She knew it was a few minutes early, but she was hoping he would let it slide. It was only about a half hour trip home, but she didn't want to be late for dinner. "Well, nearly all night. Will we be seeing you again tomorrow?"

"Of course," she replied. "And the next day. And the one after that, too."

And almost every fucking day for the next eight weeks.

"Good," he said. "And I assume in better shoes?"

"Absolutely."

She wouldn't make *that* mistake again.

The next evening, she took the train into the city, getting off right across the street from the community center that housed the soup kitchen, and made it there fifteen minutes early, dressed in jeans and a tank top, sneakers on her feet, one of her brother's Yankee ball caps backward on her head, her hair loosely braided. The coordinator smiled, greeting her much more assuredly.

"You ever made beef stew?" he asked, raising his eyebrows curiously.

"Nope," she said. "I've never made anything... except for chili now, of course."

That seemed to amuse him. "Well, no better time than the present to learn, huh?"

Every day was something new, something just as unappetizing as the day before—beef stew, corn chowder, potato soup—but Genna dutifully followed the recipes given to her, making sure she was ready by the time five o'clock rolled around. Friday was special, a full tray of food: some mystery meat contraption billed as meatloaf with instant potatoes, brown gravy, mixed vegetables and a dinner roll. Twice as many people came through then, keeping them constantly moving as she slapped slab of meat after slab of meat on the old plastic trays before shoving them down the line.

"Weekends are busiest," the coordinator explained, pitching in on the line to keep it steadily going. "More families come in, with more kids, so we try to make sure we have enough to sustain them all."

She stayed until seven that day, not stepping away from the line until the last person had come through. Pulling off the filthy apron, she tossed it in a nearby hamper and scanned the packed room. The tables were old, the cracked multicolored seats filled with bodies, not a single one vacant tonight. "Do you ever run out of food before you run out of people?"

"Occasionally," he replied. "Usually we have enough that some of them come back for seconds, though."

Her brow furrowed. "I've never seen anyone come back for seconds."

"That's because you're gone by the time that happens," he said. "Dinner shift ends at seven, officially, but we don't make anyone leave. Some of these people are still here come ten o'clock, eating until the food runs out. We let nothing go to waste, and for most of them, this is the only meal they'll get today."

That stunned her. She glanced around, taking in their faces. Most of them smiled as a wave of chatter rolled through the room. They didn't have a fraction of what she had in life, yet they looked more satisfied than she ever was.

She didn't think of herself as a self-centered person, but she felt extremely greedy then.

"You can go now," the coordinator said. "It's seven."

"No, I'd like to stay," she said, glancing at him. "If that's okay."

He smiled. "Absolutely. You're welcome to stay as long as you want."

There wasn't a lot of leftover food tonight, but enough that a few dozen were able to come back for second helpings— mostly parents, getting it for their children. It was civil and polite, no one fighting over who got extra or walking away angry. They seemed to be just grateful for whatever they were given.

It was after ten o'clock when she finally left the community center, where she promptly discovered her brother standing out front, leaning back against his car parked along the curb, his arms crossed over his chest. Her brow furrowed as she approached him. "Dante? Everything okay?"

"Dad sent me to check on you. You didn't come home for dinner so he got worried."

"How long have you been here?"

"An hour or so."

"Why didn't you come in?"

"I did," he replied. "I walked in, was gonna ask when you left, but I saw you were still working. Figured I'd let you do your thing and wait here for you."

"You didn't have to wait," she said. Dante just stared

at her. Yes, he did have to wait. Their father sent him for her, and there was no way he could have gone back home alone.

"Come on," he said, opening the passenger side door, and motioning inside. "Let's go home. I'm starving."

The thirty-floor luxury building stood on a street corner on Sixth Avenue in the Chelsea neighborhood, housing sixty vast condominiums, each one still vacant. Construction was just wrapping up, tenants expected to start moving in within a matter of weeks. Lights shined on the outside of the building, reflecting off of the expansive windows and illuminating the small trailer still parked on the lot.

A dim light shined within the trailer as electricity hummed from a generator connected to it. Matty pulled his Lotus straight up to the front of the new building, parking in the space designed for valet drop off. He locked his car doors and set off straight for the trailer, tapping lightly on the door when he approached it.

It only took a moment before it was pulled open a crack, suspicious eyes peering out at him. Confusion played on the guy's face momentarily before a smile split his hard exterior. He yanked the door open the rest of the way and stood there, grinning.

Gavin Amaro.

"Well, well, well," Gavin said, "if it isn't the one and only Matty-B."

The Amaros, along with the Genevas and the Calabreses, rounded out the five crime families that controlled New York's underworld. While they tried to maintain neutrality, the Amaro family was widely considered the

Barsantis greatest ally due to the fact that they were practically family.

Practically being key. Roberto Barsanti and Johnny Amaro shared no blood, but their children did. The men had married sisters, Savina and Lena Brazzi from the family that controlled most of New Jersey. While that wasn't enough to officially unify the families, it did give Matty someone on the outside that he could turn to. Gavin wasn't only his cousin, but he was also a mentor, and even someone he would call a close friend. And to people in the lifestyle, even those as far-removed as Matty, *friend* wasn't a term used lightly.

"Gavin." He nodded in greeting. "Good to see you."

"You, too," Gavin said, stepping aside and waving Matty past. "Come in."

Gavin closed the trailer door behind him before plopping down in an office chair along the back. A notebook lay open in front of him, papers strewn out all over the top of a desk.

The Amaro family books, Matty knew.

"How's it looking for you this week?" Matty asked, carefully sitting down on a padded bench off to the side. "We're still running a twenty-cent line."

"Same here," Gavin said, snatching up his pencil and getting right back to work. "Been a rough few weeks. Too many skipping out without paying."

"We haven't really had that problem."

"Of course not," Gavin said. "You have the Beast to go after them. Enzo runs the cheapskates straight out of your territory and into mine."

Matty smiled. "Yeah, he's useful for that."

"Useful for a lot, from what I've heard. He's earning a name for himself these days as your father's successor.

Everyone was worried for a while with you staying gone. They all wondered…"

Wondered what would come of the Barsanti family.

Gavin didn't need to say it. Matty knew. "Well, Enzo can have it. I'm happy where I am."

Gavin laughed dryly. "Nobody's *happy* running the books. We do it because someone has to, and half these jackasses can't even add or subtract."

Matty had no response for that. It was true.

"Speaking of jackasses," Matty said, "I was with Enzo in Little Italy the other day, and we ran into the Galantes."

"No shit?" Gavin said. "Primo?"

"No, it was just Dante," he said, hesitating before adding, "and his sister."

"Ah, the Ice Princess."

Matty hesitated. "Does *everyone* call her that?"

Gavin shrugged. "If the shoe fits…"

"So she's what? Cold?"

"Yeah," he said. "Cold *and* coddled. She's unapproachable, mostly because Primo goes after anyone who dares to even get close to his princess. He's overprotective, but you know, rightfully so, I'd say. He definitely has reason to keep her on lockdown."

"Does he ever let her out of his sight?"

"Rarely." Gavin continued to work in silence for a moment before swinging his chair around to face him, eyebrows raised questioningly. "Why are you asking me about Genevieve Galante?"

"No reason."

Gavin shook his head. "There's *always* a reason, so don't give me that bullshit."

"I'm just curious."

"About the Galante princess?"

"Yes."

Gavin stared at him peculiarly as if deciding whether or not to accept that answer. "Look, Matty, I'll tell you what someone told me once, a few years ago, when I got *curious* about a girl... don't plant your seeds in someone else's garden or you're liable to get buried six-feet under with fertilizer."

"Someone told you that?"

"I'm paraphrasing, but yeah, a friend out of the Chicago organization did."

"Chicago? You tried *planting your seed* in the DeMarco family?"

"Sort of. It's a long story, but I thought about it, when sometimes we just have no business even thinking it. Sometimes it just isn't a good idea. You don't go petting a poisonous snake, you know? No matter how pretty it might be."

"I'm not trying to pet anything. I'm just..."

"Curious. Got it." Gavin stared at him for another moment before turning back to his work. "I heard she's been working at a soup kitchen over in East Harlem, the one at the community center. Doing a stint of community service for some trouble she got into."

Community service. "I bet they have the place guarded."

"You'd think, but no, she's pretty safe there on her own. Her brother lurks around sometimes when he's not otherwise occupied. You know, like when the family's busy in other boroughs, like in Brooklyn, like tonight..."

"Tonight?"

"Yeah." Gavin glanced at his watch. "Right about now, actually."

Matty stood up and started for the door. "Thanks."

"You're welcome. But Matty? You get caught petting something you shouldn't be, and you didn't hear any of this from me."

FIVE

Monday night. Chili. *Again.*

"Do you serve the same thing every week?" Genna asked, lugging the big pot to the serving counter without nearly falling this time. Her apron, covering her dark skinny jeans and black fitted t-shirt, remained mostly white today, only a few specks of tomato sauce staining it.

"Usually," the coordinator said. "We serve what we can get, and well, the way the economy is, that's not much. People aren't banging down our doors with donations, nor is there a line of volunteers anxious to help."

She had noticed, her first week, that it was the same few people working every day. The others kept to themselves, not nearly as friendly as the coordinator. She had a sneaking suspicion they also weren't there from the kindness of their heart.

The night passed quickly as she ladled out the chili, filling the small Styrofoam cups nearly to the brim this time before plopping it on a tray and passing it down the line. People strode past to collect their dinner, some she recognized from the week before, a few even striking up friendly conversation as they went.

Her shift was winding down at a quarter till seven. She stared into the pot of chili, stirring the watery mixture, watching the beans and chunks of tomato swirling around. Sighing, she started scooping out the rest of it into cups when someone slowly approached, a throat clearing in front of her.

"Coming back for seconds?" she asked, glancing up with a smile on her face. The moment her eyes connected with his, the chili from the ladle in her hand turned over, completely missing the cup and splattering right down the front of her apron. Gasping, she jumped back, realizing what she had done, while dozens of eyes in the room turned toward her at the sound of the commotion.

She scarcely noticed, though, her gaze going back to meet *his*.

Matty.

"Seconds," he said as he stared straight at her. "Because the first time around was so good, huh?"

Genna's blood ran cold. She had no idea what to say, not expecting to ever see him again. Her mind was a flurry of questions. What did he want? Why was he there? She just gaped at him, unable to find the words, as she stared into his bright eyes.

Ugh, why does he have to be so goddamn attractive?

"Miss Galante?" the coordinator called from across the room. "Everything okay?"

"Uh, yes, fine," she shouted, tearing her gaze from Matty. It didn't escape her notice that he visibly cringed at the sound of her last name. "Just had a little accident, but I've got it handled."

She quickly untied the apron and pulled it off,

tossing it in the hamper off to the side. She did her best to ignore Matty's presence as she went to work cleaning up the mess, but she could feel his attention on her the entire time. It unnerved her on more than one level, her stomach fluttering while another sensation tried to drown it out.

Fear.

A Barsanti was there, standing right in front of her, breathing her same air, and there was nothing she could do about it.

When she turned back around, the coordinator was approaching them.

"Are you going to help our guest?" he asked, raising his eyebrows as he motioned toward Matty. "He's been waiting patiently."

"No," she said. "He's just leaving now."

She said it matter-of-fact, like if she believed it enough, maybe it would make it so, but Matty seemed to dig his heels in and push back. "Actually, I'm not going anywhere."

"But you have no business here," she said quickly. "This is a soup kitchen. People come here to eat."

"Maybe I'm hungry."

"Then go somewhere else."

Before he could bite back, the coordinator interjected. "That's no way to talk to one of our guests. We turn *nobody* away here."

"He can afford to buy his own food," she ground out. "Jesus, just look at him! He's wearing a Rolex."

"We don't judge people. Nor do we question their circumstances. He said he's hungry. Feed him. *Period.*" The coordinator started to walk away but hesitated. "And Miss Galante? I expect you to apologize to him, too."

Once the coordinator was gone, she turned her focus to Matty again. Slowly, she dumped a small ladle of chili into a cup and slammed it down, breaking open the flimsy bottom, watery tomato sauce seeping out onto the tray. She shoved the tray down the line, her eyes not leaving his. "I apologize, Mr. Barsanti. I guess I forgot your kind likes to take advantage whenever possible. I assure you—I won't make that same mistake again."

He stared at her in silence for a moment, not seeming at all offended by her words. "Sounds like a Galante apology if I've ever heard one."

She glared at him as he moved away. A Galante apology? What was *that* supposed to mean?

Matty politely greeted the other servers, charming them, before snatching up his tray at the end of the line. He confidently strolled through the community center, making something as ordinary as walking look like an art form, and slipped into a chair at the end of a table, away from others.

Unbelievable.

Seven o'clock. Genna strode away from the serving counter, her shift officially over, but instead of heading for the exit her feet instinctively veered straight toward him. She paused at the table in front of him, her hands on her hips, her expression stern. "What the hell do you want?"

He poked in his broken cup with the plastic spoon, not looking up as he answered. "I want some more meat in this chili. Geez, you kind of skimped on it, didn't you?" Instead of looking at her, he glanced down the table at some others eating. "Hey, is your chili kind of, uh… pitiful?"

"Yeah," a man agreed.

"Always is," someone grumbled.

"They should do something about that," Matty said.

"Yeah, well, beggars can't be choosers, so either eat it or get out," Genna growled. As soon as those words came out of her mouth, she realized how unsympathetic she sounded. Her gaze darted around at the others nearby, seeing a few scowling at her. "I, uh... I'm sorry. It's just that..."

"She didn't mean to sound like an insensitive bitch," Matty said casually, picking up a spoonful of chili and eyeing it with distaste. "It's just a family trait."

She leaned forward, her palms flat against the table as she glared at him. "You have a lot of fucking nerve coming here. How did you even know how to find me?"

His gaze slowly shifted from the food to her, a mere few inches of space between their faces. She stared at him, watching as his lips twitched. The urge to kiss him overwhelmed her, memories of the way his mouth felt sending chills down her spine, but she fought it back.

That could never happen again.

Never.

"I have my ways," he said quietly. "You're not a hard person to track down. It was just a matter of finding the right moment. You know, when *they* were busy."

He didn't elaborate, or specify, but she knew he meant her family. She was in no hurry to get home tonight because her father was out of town and her brother was taking advantage of the old man's absence to hustle a bit down in Brooklyn, so there would be no family dinner. Nobody expecting her.

Her expression quickly melted from anger to dread as her stomach lurched. How could *he* know that?

"Like I said—I have my ways," he said, answering her unspoken question. "I knew they wouldn't come looking for you tonight, so it was my chance."

"You don't have the balls to hurt me," she said, her voice hard as she forced confidence in her words... although she scarcely believed them herself. This guy was the damn definition of dangerous, especially with the emotions he stirred up inside of her. She wanted to simultaneously punch him in the face and rip off his clothes, and she wasn't sure which part of her would ultimately win that battle.

"Oh, I have the balls," he replied, cocking an eyebrow at her. "Or have you forgotten? Because I haven't."

"You're so full of yourself." She felt the red-hot blood rush to her cheeks at the reminder. Um, yeah, she had been full of him, too... filled to the hilt, so much so she still felt the achy void from when he'd pulled out. "You weren't *that* great, you know."

"Judging by the way you screamed my name, I have to say you're lying."

His words were loud enough to draw attention to them. Groaning, Genna shot daggers at a few of the meddlesome eavesdroppers, embarrassed, as she yanked out the chair across from Matty to sit down. She leaned across the table, her voice low again so nobody else could hear. "This is *my* father's territory. You're supposed to stay on the other side of Central Park. You're not allowed to come over here."

Without responding, Matty reached across the table toward her. The moment his hand shot out, she scooted back, the chair legs screeching against the floor as she moved out of his reach, her heart thumping erratically. She swallowed thickly, trying to shove down the fear that movement elicited. His hand froze mid-air, lingering there for a moment, before he slowly dropped it back to the table. "You're afraid of me."

"You're one of them."

"I was one of them the day we met, but you weren't afraid then."

"You didn't know who I was," she replied. "You had no reason to hurt me then."

"I have no reason to hurt you now."

She scoffed. "Liar."

"How do you know I'm lying?"

"Your lips are moving."

"Look, this has nothing to do with my father's business," he said. "Whatever issues our fathers have... it has nothing to do with me."

"It has something to do with all of us," she argued.

"Why?"

She gaped at him. Why? How could he ask that question? "It's always been that way. Your family... your family is vicious!"

"Don't act like you Galantes are all roses," he replied. "You've got more thorns than you do petals, princess."

Princess. The way he said it made her hair bristle. She stared at him as he turned back to his food, picking up the flimsy sandwich and tearing it apart to inspect it: two pieces of white bread, a slab of chopped ham and a slice of cheese, hard around the edges from exposure.

"If this isn't about business," she started, folding her arms across her chest, "then why are you here?"

"I wanted to see you," he said quietly.

"Well, here I am," I said. "See me? Good. Now what do you really want?"

His eyes drifted right back to her as he let go of the sandwich. Reaching across the table again, this time he moved slowly, deliberately. Genna sat still, her back as stiff as a board, her eyes fluttering as the back of his hand grazed against her flushed cheek, sending tingles dancing across her skin. He brushed aside some wayward hair that fell from the Yankee's cap and tucked it behind her ear. "Is it so hard to believe I *just* wanted to see you?"

"Yes," she admitted.

"Well, it's true," he said, dropping his hand again. He turned back to his tray once more, grabbing his spoon and scooping up some of the chili. This time, instead of just staring at it, he shoved the spoonful in his mouth and started chewing. Genna cringed, watching as his face contorted with disgust, but he choked it down and took another bite. "Who made this crap?"

"Me," she said, watching him with surprise. "I can't believe you're actually eating it."

"That's what it's for, isn't it? It would be a dick move to take food and not eat it."

"Well... nobody would blame you," she said, watching as he took yet another bite. "Family trait and all."

He cut his eyes at her, smirking when she threw his insult right back at him. Genna sat there, watching in awe as he ate every bite of food on his tray, forcing it down without gagging, as if he were trying to prove some point to her. He opened the milk and chugged it before crushing the empty carton with one hand. "I need a drink."

"They'll give you another milk."

"Not milk."

"There's a water fountain on the other side of the room."

He pushed his empty tray aside. "Not water, either. I want a drink... a real drink."

"Ah, a glass of rum."

"And Coke," he said.

"There was no Coke in that rum."

He laughed, relaxing back in his seat as he gazed at her. "There was."

"I don't care what you say."

"Come with me, then," he said. "Let me *show* you. I'll make you one myself."

Instinctively, she shook her head. Was he crazy? He expected her to go somewhere with him? "I can't."

"You can," he insisted. "Christ, you already let me take you into the heart of Barsanti territory."

"I didn't know you were—"

"It doesn't matter," he said, cutting her off. "You went there, knowing it wasn't safe, and you didn't even bat an eyelash. You trusted me to keep you safe, and I did, didn't I? You got home safely, didn't you?"

"Yes, but—"

"So what makes you think I won't keep you safe now?"

"Because you know who I am."

"And I'm telling you I don't care."

"But it changes things," she said. Even he couldn't deny that. Regardless of if *he* cared, so many others would.

"It does," he agreed, leaning closer, his eyes flickering from her eyes to her lips, almost if by some instinct. And somehow, she knew—he was fighting the same urge she had fought earlier. "We have to be so much more careful now."

Those words washed through Genna, dulling a bit of her resolve. She stared at him, examining his face, trying to find some hint of deception, something to give away the ulterior motives she was certain he must have, but he merely gazed at her, wide eyes full of sincerity. *Ugh, why did he have to look so damn genuine?* She wanted to believe he was a wolf in sheep's clothing, sent to lure her, to devour her, but at the moment he looked like a sheep that knew it was dangerously close to being skinned alive, but a sheep that was willing to walk into the slaughterhouse on its own anyway. "I can't go with you back to that place."

"What place?"

"The Place."

He cracked a smile at that. "We'll go somewhere neutral then."

"There is nowhere neutral."

"Little Italy?"

She scoffed. "Please, at least half of that neighborhood knows who we are."

Her, anyway. Sure, they knew the Barsantis, but she wasn't yet sure how many people would be able to identify *him*. She couldn't risk it, though. All it would take was one person recognizing them together for all hell to break loose.

He sat in silence for a moment. "Somewhere else, then."

"There is nowhere else." Her eyes narrowed as she regarded him, still trying to figure out if this was some kind of ruse. "How do I know this isn't a trick? That you won't walk me straight into an ambush?"

"You don't know. You just have to trust me."

"I need some kind of guarantee," she said. "Some kind of security."

"Then you pick the place. We'll go wherever you want."

"I don't know anywhere."

He sighed exasperatedly, running his hands through his hair. "We're getting nowhere here."

He was wrong. They were most definitely getting somewhere. Little by little, he was breaking down her walls despite the voice in the back of her mind, screaming, crying, and warning her away. She wasn't an idiot, and despite what she had told her brother, she knew she was a good judge of character. It was something her father had instilled in her, teaching her how to spot a schemer a mile away, teaching her how to con a conman in return. And this guy sitting across from her was either as genuine as they came, or he deserved a fucking Academy Award.

Wolf in sheep's clothing, maybe not, but he was undoubtedly Satan, tempting her to the dark side. *Forgive me, Father, for I want nothing more than to sin and sin and sin again...* "Can I ask you something?"

Matty's brow furrowed. "Sure."

"How do you fix your hair so your horns don't show?"

He let out a loud laugh as he shoved his chair back. "Funny."

"It was, wasn't it?"

"Yeah, it was a good one," he said, standing up. "I'm surprised it came from *your* mind, to be honest."

Genna smiled, amazed how easy the teasing came for them. *Must be in our DNA.*

"I can't linger here too long," he said, gazing down at her. "My car's parked outside, and well, someone's bound to take notice eventually."

She nodded. He was flirting with disaster coming here, even with her family preoccupied. Her father may not personally catch him, but someone else could. He had eyes and ears all over the city. "You were stupid to come here in the first place."

"You pronounced *fearless* wrong," he said, reaching over and lightly grasping her chin, tilting her face slightly more toward him as he gazed at her. "Thanks for the chili, Genna. Best soup kitchen meal I've ever had."

"You eat at soup kitchens often?" she asked as he started walking away.

His footsteps faltered briefly as he glanced back at her, his lips turning into that condescending—yet damn sexy—smirk. "No, but I might start."

Walking into the East Harlem soup kitchen was like stepping into the busy underground subway station. A continuous flow of people shuffled through, methodic yet still chaotic, and despite the fact that there seemed to be someone always cleaning, the place constantly remained filthy. An unpleasant odor hung in the air from an unknown source that Matty suspected might've been whatever concoctions they were brewing in the kitchen, strong enough to make him cringe when he inhaled.

He strolled in toward the end of dinner service again, immediately seeing Genna behind the partition. Even wearing a filthy apron, dressed down in jeans and a t-shirt, she made him pause to take her in. A smile lit up her face, the kind of smile that could replace sunshine without you even noticing a drop in temperature. The girl was *radiant*. She laughed, and heads involuntarily turned toward her like a flower turning toward the light.

Ice princess? Hardly. She was the opposite of cold.

Christ, just the sight of her made Matty want to speak in fucking verse like he was Shakespeare incarnate.

Genna glanced up as he approached, her expression dimming a bit, worry evident in her eyes as they darted all around, doing everything not to look at *him*. He got it... he did. She didn't trust him. He couldn't say he blamed her.

After a moment, she skeptically met his gaze, her cheeks flushing. "What do you want now?"

There was an edge of antagonism to her voice that made it hard not to laugh. Matty's thinly veiled amusement made her eyes narrow further as she glared at him, awaiting an answer.

"Just stopping by," he said. "But don't worry, I'm not going to steal any of your food this time. I brought my own."

He held his bag of take-out up for her to see, to make his point, since she had given him grief for taking food from people who needed it. He expected maybe an eye roll at most, but the flare of anger caught him off guard. "You brought your own food? Are you stupid? You can't do that!"

"Why?"

"Why? It's *rude*! How dare you bring that in here and tease these people. What is it, anyway?" Before he could respond, she reached over the divider and snatched the bag straight out of his hand, opening it up to glance inside. She shifted the food around, surveying the contents. "French fries and what, a cheesesteak? Got onions and peppers on it?"

"Of course."

She snatched a fry, popping it in her mouth as she hastily closed the bag up tightly, her eyes darting beside him. "Hey, you. Yeah, you... guy with the green shirt. You like cheesesteaks?"

Matty turned, looking at the guy beside him as the man's eyes widened. "Uh, yeah, sure."

Genna thrust the bag over the divider, straight to

him. "Here you go. Eat it. Enjoy yourself. My treat."

The man grabbed the food, quickly saying his thanks, and darted away before anyone could take it from him. Matty turned back around, gaping at Genna as she grabbed a paper cup and dished out some kind of brown gunky stew into it.

"Enjoy your dinner, Mr. Barsanti," she said, slamming it down on the tray before shoving it down the line. Matty stood there for a moment, dumbfounded, but she said nothing more, brusquely dismissing him with a wave of the hand before continuing to dish out more stew into cups.

Not wanting to hold up the line or make a bigger scene, Matty walked away and grabbed a tray from the end. He headed across the room, straight to the same seat from last time. He stared down at the food, picking up the plastic spoon and shifting the stew around, the potatoes and carrots turning to mush at a simple touch. Beef stew, he assumed, although he barely found any beef at all.

Hesitantly, he took a small bite, cringing as he swallowed it down. It tasted like nothing but water and salt. He couldn't fathom eating this crap every day.

It took longer this time, but Genna eventually wandered over at a few minutes after seven, yanking the chair out across from him and plopping down. Crossing her arms over her chest, she stared at him pointedly. Unlike yesterday when she'd been on the defense, scrambling to comprehend his presence, this girl appeared entirely in control, an air of authority surrounding her. Confidence oozed from her pores, bordering on downright cocky.

Matty knew it was an act, but damn if it didn't turn him on.

"You owe me a dinner now," he said, matter-of-fact.

"I gave you a dinner," she said, motioning toward the food in front of him. "Even cooked it myself."

"Yeah, well, do me a favor?" he asked, taking another bite of the beef stew. "Never cook for me again, because this? This isn't your strong suit."

She dramatically gasped, grabbing her chest with feigned hurt. "You mean I don't live up to your expectations? How ever will I go on?"

Without responding, he made a point to choke down every damn bite of the god-awful stew before washing it down with the milk, desperate to get the salty taste from his mouth. Sighing, he tossed the carton down on the tray and gazed at her. "So how about a drink, Genna?"

Her self-assured expression wavered a bit, skepticism shining through. "Are we going to do this every day?"

"Do what?"

"Do *this*," she said, waving between the two of them. "This thing where you pretend like there could actually ever be something between you and me."

"There could be," he said. "There was."

"That's the past."

"And I told you I don't live in the past."

"Then why are you here?"

Christ, she was infuriatingly stubborn. Leaning forward, he shoved his tray aside. No words came from his mouth as he stared in her eyes, drinking in the pale blue hue, so unnaturally light they appeared almost gray, void of color. Like the iciest stone.

"Don't look her in the eyes," he said quietly. "She's dangerous."

She blanched. "What?"

"That's what they say about you. I'm sure your family

warned you about me, told you to stay away, but you're not the only one, Genna. I've heard it all, too. They have a lot of names for you... the Ice Princess... Medusa... they say you're the worst kind of monster, the kind that can bring a man to his knees, that can shatter his world with a simple stare."

She blinked rapidly, looking away for a moment, before curiosity got the best of her. She turned right back to him. "I've heard Ice Princess before, but they seriously call me *Medusa*?"

He cracked a smile at the incredulous tone to her voice. "They do."

She remained quiet for a moment, contemplatively chewing on her bottom lip, her gaze leaving his once more. This time it didn't return. "If they warned you about me, why don't you just... stay away? It would be so much easier."

"I don't do things just because they're easy. Despite what you might think, I don't have sinister intentions. I risk coming here, because one of us has to take that risk. One of us has to be willing to take the chance. But if you want me to stay away, if you want nothing to do with me, fine. Just tell me. I'll stay away. You'll never see me again." Pushing his chair back, he stood up and leaned across the table. She tensed, her eyes closing as he brought his face close to hers, his cheek brushing against hers as he whispered in her ear. "It's too late for me, though. I already looked the soul-stealer in the eyes."

Grabbing the tray, he started to walk away when the sound of her voice stalled his footsteps.

"Matty?"

Turning, he raised his eyebrows questioningly.

She stared at him for a moment, frowning, as she let

her hair loose from beneath her ball cap and ran her fingers through the wavy strands. "It's not, uh... it's not because my hair looks stringy like snakes, right? Because I promise it's usually better than this."

He burst into laughter, shaking his head. *This damn girl...* "You're beautiful, Genna. The prettiest little car thief I've ever seen."

Matty stepped out of the community center, keeping his head down and walking swiftly up the block and around the corner, to where he'd parked the Lotus in a dark alley. Pulling out his keys, he pressed the button to unlock the car doors and hit the remote start, the engine roaring to life down the block. His phone buzzed in his pocket—his personal line, not the Blackberry, which was locked in the car's glove box. It had been vibrating constantly for the past few minutes, but he hadn't wanted anything to interrupt his conversation with Genna. Opening his car door, he slipped inside, out of sight, as he pulled his phone out.

Enzo.

"Yeah?" he said, answering it as he shifted the car into gear, wanting to get out of East Harlem. Lingering could easily get him killed. He had come tonight without confirmation that the Galantes were busy. For all he knew, they could be watching him.

"Jesus, Matty," Enzo said, voice frantic. "Where the hell are you?"

"Near Central Park." Close enough, anyway. "Why? What's up?"

"It's Ma," he said. "She's been taken to the hospital."

Coldness washed through him as he gripped the gearshift tightly. "Which one?"

"NewYork-Presbyterian."

She'd had a seizure, he said. They found her unresponsive. Matty drove straight up north to Presbyterian, meeting his family in the waiting room twenty minutes later. They didn't question where he'd been or why it took him so long to answer his phone, and for that he was grateful.

He had no idea what he'd say if they did.

They ran some tests and decided to keep her for observation. Life didn't stop for Enzo and his father, who were in and out constantly, but Matty didn't leave her side for two days. He could do his part anywhere. When they kicked him out of her room, he took up residence in the hospital lobby, eating food from the cafeteria that rivaled the crap Genna made and fielding phone calls for bets out of The Place.

It was Thursday night, well past visiting hours, when he lounged in the small uncomfortable chair, the muted television giving him enough light to sort through the figures in his notebook. His mother was sleeping soundly, her soft snores filling the quiet air, the sound nearly lulling Matty to sleep along with her.

He felt like he hadn't slept in forever.

The door opened and he glanced across the room, expecting it to be a nurse coming to eject him, but was surprised to meet his father's gaze. He hadn't been around since earlier that morning.

Roberto quietly approached, smoothing Matty's mother's hair and gazing down at her as he spoke softly, although his words were clearly meant for Matty. "I'm surprised you're still here."

"I'm not leaving her if I can help it."

"I didn't mean at the hospital."

"I knew what you meant."

He was surprised Matty was still in New York.

Slowly, his gaze shifted to Matty, expression stern. "I take it you haven't changed your mind about my offer?"

Matty shook my head. "That other stuff's not for me."

He'd agreed to take on the books, but that was as far as he went in the family business. If he had to be involved, if he had to lend a hand, he'd stick with staying behind the scenes. He wanted nothing to do with the violence and hatred, nothing to do with the rivalry.

"You're wrong, Matteo. It's *all* for you. I built this entire empire for you, and it saddens me that you want very little to do with it."

"Saddens?" he asked. "Or maddens?"

"Both," his father admitted. "You're my oldest, and it upsets me to see you snub the family legacy."

Hell of a legacy, Matty thought, but he said nothing. It would only cause a fight—a fight they needn't have *there*, of all places. Roberto seemed to realize that also, his gaze turning from Matty back to the hospital bed.

"Go on home, Matteo. She's being released in the morning. There's nothing more you can do here."

He hadn't wanted to leave, but he knew his father wouldn't take a refusal lightly. Roberto was used to people following his every word, which was what caused the rift between them in the first place. Matty wasn't very good about being submissive.

Glancing at his watch, he saw it was nearing seven o'clock. "Yeah, you're right."

He started to leave, striding past his father, when the man reached out and grabbed his arm, stalling him. "I know you don't want to get involved, but certain things are unavoidable. You're a Barsanti, and unless you find a way to stop being one, there will forever be a target on your back after what's happened. So be careful, you know. Stay where we can protect you."

The message was loud and clear: stay out of Galante territory. Matty nodded, acknowledging those words, but he didn't heed them.

As soon as he was in his car, he drove straight to East Harlem.

It was a few minutes past seven when he made it to that side of town. He approached the community center and was about to swing the car into a parking spot along the curb when he caught sight of Dante lurking out front.

Cursing, he sped right past, hoping like hell the Galante boy hadn't noticed him.

Genna had a crappy day at home, followed by a crappy night at the community center, topped off with the crappiest of crappy: her babysitter-slash-bodyguard was waiting for her outside when her shift was over.

That never boded well.

Dante stood along the curb, hands shoved in his pockets, his brow furrowed as he stared down the street. Slowly, Genna approached, grabbing his arm and proceeding to startle the fuck out of him. He jumped, immediately glaring at her. "Dammit, Genna, you scared me!"

"Sorry," she said, glancing past him. "What are you looking at?"

"Nothing, I just thought I saw..." He paused as he eyed her peculiarly. "You haven't seen any Barsantis lurking around here, have you?"

Her eyes widened. *Oh, shit.* "Of course not."

"I must've been seeing things," he said. "It almost looked like that car from Little Italy, but even they're not that stupid, right?"

"Right." Too bad they *were*. Stupid, stupid boy. He hadn't shown up at all in days. She had shrugged it off, scoffing, telling herself it was for the best, that she shouldn't be surprised since he was one of them... they were flakey, and she shouldn't want him anywhere near her. But yet... she'd missed him. She'd found herself waiting for him, watching the door, disappointed when her shift was over and he was nowhere to be found. She'd even worried. *God, what the hell's wrong with me, stressing about one of them?* "Had to have been someone else. It wouldn't be them. Not here."

"Yeah," he agreed. "You'll tell me if you see any of them, right?"

"Of course," she said, frowning. She hated lying to Dante. He was her person, but he wouldn't understand this. How could he? She scarcely did. "We should go before we're late for dinner."

"Ah, yeah, that's why I'm here," he said. "Dad needed to leave town for a few days, so it's just you and me."

"Oh?"

"Yeah, I have plans this weekend, but I thought you and I could do something tonight."

"Aw, you get a bit of freedom and there's nobody else you'd rather spend it with?"

"Of course there is," he said, "but you'll do, anyway."

She rolled her eyes, nudging him as she strode to the passenger side of his car while he climbed behind the wheel.

"So where do you want to go?"

"Doesn't matter to me," she said.

He raised his eyebrows. "Genna, with no opinion? I'm starting to like the new you."

She laughed as he started up the car and swung out into traffic, speeding down the busy street. "I'm still the same me."

"No, you're not," he said. "Come on, the Genna I grew up with would've flounced community service by now and forced Dad's hand to pay off whoever he needed to pay off to get her out of the mess. You've been *way* too accepting of this all."

"It's not so bad," she said, shrugging. "I mean, it's not easy, but it's not like I'm doing manual labor. I'm just cooking."

"And how's that working out?"

"Terrible. Apparently, I'm a crappy cook."

"Doesn't surprise me a bit," Dante said, casting her a playful smile. "I always said you'd make a good *trophy* wife."

They went to dinner at a steakhouse in the Upper Eastside. Genna took off the ball cap and ran her fingers through her hair, trying to make herself half-assed presentable before joining her brother inside the restaurant. He was at ease, lounged back in the booth, sipping from a glass of complimentary wine. As soon as Genna slid in across from him, the waiter turned to her. "Wine, miss?"

She was about to say an emphatic "hell yeah!" when her brother cleared his throat, waving the waiter away. "She's only eighteen, man."

Genna glared at Dante as the waiter strode away, taking her alcohol along with him. "That's foul."

"You're my little sister," he said. "It's my job to look after you."

BY ANY OTHER NAME

Rolling her eyes, she drank the glass of ice water, waiting for the waiter to return. She ordered a steak and baked potato, and flirted her ass off, trying to convince the man to bring the wine back to no avail. Dante watched her with amusement, steadily drinking his own alcohol, rubbing it in.

"So tell me," he said eventually. "How's your guy?"

She tensed, fork mid-air, as her gaze darted across the table at her brother. "What guy?"

"Mr. Eyes on Fire," he said. "What happened with that?"

"I, uh... nothing," she muttered. "Nothing happened."

"Dad said his name was Matthew or something? Matt... he called him Matty."

She blinked a few times, avoiding his gaze. *Not good.* "Err, yeah. It was, uh... it wasn't what I thought it was."

"Pity," he said. "But you know, if you want me to hook you up with Umberto—"

"Oh my God," she said loudly, cutting him off. "If you even try, Dante, I swear, I will make your life a living hell."

"Come on, why not?"

"I'll go back to Jackson before I even entertain the idea of dating Umberto."

"What's wrong with Umberto?"

Before she could come back with a response and ask him what was *right* with Umberto, Dante's phone rang. Casually, he pulled it out and glanced at the screen, casting her a contemplative look before answering it. "What's up, Dad?"

Dante listened to their father quietly for a moment,

eyes squarely on her. Genna stuck her tongue out at him when the waiter returned, once again filling his wine glass. *Jerk.* He stifled a laugh, his expression straightening out as he focused back on the call. "We're planning to move in this weekend... I don't think we'll get much resistance, you know, since it's Little Italy... yeah, Umberto's in on it with me, no big. We got it under control."

Dante picked up his glass of wine, teasingly taking a sip and theatrically rolling his eyes back in his head like it was the greatest thing he'd ever tasted. Genna flung some of her potatoes at him, but Dante merely brushed them away, focusing back on the call.

"Speaking of them, I thought I saw the oldest today... he's driving that sports car, you know, the fancy red one? Flashy fucker. How stupid can he be? Even Enzo knows how to fly under the radar, and he's about as dumb as they get."

Genna tensed, staring at her brother.

"Well, word on the street is Savina's sick. Yeah, cancer or something. She's being treated up at Presbyterian in Washington Heights... probably where he was heading when he drove through East Harlem, but you'd think he'd know better and stay west."

Genna shifted food around her plate, her appetite long gone as she absorbed her brother's words.

"Yeah, drove right by the community center... I don't know if they know that Genna's working there, but we might want to think about having some people watch it. You know, just in case."

Her heart dropped into her stomach as her fork hit the plate, slipping from her fingers. Dante cast her a strange look.

"I should probably go. Yeah, I'll keep you updated."

He hung up, slipping the phone back away as he focused on his plate. "You'll be okay, you know. We'll keep you safe."

"I, uh... I'm not scared." Not scared of what she should haven been scared of, anyway. "You don't have to look after me."

Dante was quiet for a moment, cutting up his steak in silence, before merely dropping his silverware and giving up the pretense of eating. "You know, that day... *the* day..."

"*The* day?"

He nodded.

The day Joseph Galante lost his life in an explosion.

"What about it?" Genna asked. Dante rarely talked about it.

"I almost died that day, Genna."

"I know you did," she said quietly.

"You know why I didn't?"

Slowly, she shook her head.

"Because I was too busy trying to look after you. I wasn't in that car with Joey because I was waiting for you. So, in a way, you saved my life. Watching you saved my life. I've been doing it since I was a kid, and I'm not going to stop doing it now."

Sighing, Genna picked up her glass of water and sipped it, trying to drown out her feelings. Her stomach felt sour, a sense of bitter betrayal inside of her simmering. "You think Matteo Barsanti is trouble? That he's... *bad*?"

Dante shrugged a shoulder casually. "He's a Barsanti, isn't it?"

"Yeah, I guess he is," Genna muttered. "I saw a picture of him once, in our house."

"I know," Dante said. "Dad told me."

Genna eyed him peculiarly. "He did?"

"Yeah," he replied. "He said you were snooping around Mom's stuff and found it."

"Did he tell you he got pissed at me for it?"

"He said he might've overreacted a bit."

"I'd say! He grounded me on my birthday."

"Yeah, well, he was upset. He doesn't like to be reminded that we used to get along with those people."

"And Matteo and Joey... they were...?"

"Friends, yeah," Dante said. "Best friends."

"But then... that day happened."

"Yeah," Dante confirmed. "The day."

The day Roberto Barsanti killed his son's best friend.

chapter SIX

Dinner service had just started, the doors of the community center opening for the visitors to filter in. Genna stood at her place in the line, methodically and indifferently slapping precarved wedges of meat onto the plastic trays before pouring lumpy gravy overtop of it and sending it down the line. People ambled by, some speaking, most just silently moving along. Only a few minutes had passed when a vaguely familiar scent wafted around her, carrying across the barrier with a soft breeze.

Without even looking up, a smile lightly touched her lips, her heart swelling with unbridled emotion.

Fucking feelings.

"What the hell is that?"

Genna slowly glanced up, meeting Matty's gaze as he stopped right in front of her, deep in the middle of the line today. "Meatloaf."

"That," he said, waving toward the tray, "is *not* meatloaf. I put up with the chili, and I suffered through the beef stew, but that? That's *unnatural.*"

"You should've been here yesterday," Genna said. "I

made one hell of a pot of corn chowder."

He visibly grimaced. "People actually ate it?"

"Every last bite," Genna confirmed.

"And they survived?"

"Yep."

He shook his head as he took a step back out of the line. "I'm sorry, Genna, but this is where I draw the line."

Genna's brow furrowed. She slapped some meat on a tray, not wanting to hold up the line, and watched incredulously as Matty turned around and stormed right out the door, brushing past people waiting for dinner.

The bastard *left*.

The exhilaration she'd felt just a moment ago withered away. Sighing, she turned her focus back on the trays, continually dishing out the food and sending it on its way. *It's for the best*, she told herself. *He need not be there, anyway*. It wasn't safe.

Friday. The evening passed agonizingly slow. It was nearing seven o'clock, the food already all gone for the night. There would be no seconds for anyone. They'd hardly had enough for skimpy *firsts*. Genna started cleaning up when a throat cleared behind her. Turning around, her eyes widened when she came face-to-face with Matty again. "You're back."

He nodded, hands in his pockets. He looked at ease.

"Well, sorry for you, but the food's all gone," she said, motioning toward the empty pots and pans. "We ran out."

"I didn't come here to eat."

"Then why are you here?"

"You know why," he said, stepping closer to the divider between them. "Go somewhere with me."

She shook her head. "I don't know anywhere."

"I do," he said.

She eyed him warily. "I need some assurance."

"You know the number for 911, don't you? Use it if you feel the need."

"How do I know if I'll even have the chance?" she asked. "What if it's a trap?"

"Give me a break. Do you seriously think I'd do that?"

"I just--"

"Listen to me," he said, cutting her off as he glanced around to ensure nobody was listening. "I get it. You didn't expect this, you didn't expect me to be who I am, but I didn't either, Genna. I didn't expect you to be one of them. But you are, and I am. It is what it is. I've done everything I can think of to get you to put some trust in me, so tell me... what else can I possibly do? What do you *need* me to do? Because I'll do it, whatever it is."

"I don't know," she said quietly. "It's not *you*."

"You don't trust my family," he said.

"Yes."

"I'm not going to let you get hurt," he said. "If you're afraid I'll call them, that I'll tell them where you are, then take my phone. Take it so I can't call *anyone*."

He pulled a cell phone out of his pocket and slipped it beneath the divider between them. Genna stared down at the white iPhone, slowly reaching for it as her brow furrowed. "I thought you had a Blackberry."

"I do," he said. "It's my business phone. I'd give it to you, too, but it's in the glove box of the car."

She picked up the phone, eyeing it momentarily. "Why do you need two phones?"

"If you go with me, I'll tell you," he said. "Come on,

what do you have to lose?"

My life, she thought, but those words caught inside of her, blocked by the swell of her chest, refusing to come from her lips. No matter how much the well-trained voice of warning in the back of her head screamed it, she couldn't listen. She didn't believe it.

Before she could respond, there was a commotion at the door. She looked that way, straight past Matty, and blinked rapidly when a bunch of guys in red and white uniforms strolled in, carrying boxes and boxes of pizza. She watched, stunned as they started setting them on all the tables in front of people. Shocked, her eyes widened as she slowly turned back to Matty. He hadn't moved, his gaze still on her, a smug smile tugging his lips. "You…"

"Tell me something," he said. "Is it really *me* you're afraid of? Do you honestly think I'd ambush you? Because I assure you, there are much easier ways to get to you than this, if that's what I wanted."

Her attention shifted back to the room, watching as the meatloaf was shoved aside, forgotten for the moment, discarded, as they dove into the freshly delivered food. There had to have been at least a hundred boxes, some still coming in. "Did you do this just to impress me?"

"Does it impress you?" he countered. "Me buying dinner for everyone except for you?"

She turned to him, slowly shaking her head. She wouldn't admit it out loud, but yes, she was damn impressed, mostly because never in her life had she thought a Barsanti would be capable of being so generous. Although, a part of her was unsurprised, as she gazed at Matty. Hadn't he been that way since the very moment they met? He'd bought her an abundance of drinks and followed it up with even more orgasms.

The boy was a giver, for sure.

"The place you know of," she hedged. "It's safe?"

He nodded. "Completely neutral ground."

Carefully, she untied her apron and pulled it off, tossing it aside. She gave him no answer, but based on the way his expression brightened, his shoulders relaxing, she knew he knew... she was conceding. Every bit of denial inside of her, every bit of resolve, had disintegrated as she admitted the truth to herself. He didn't scare her, not in the least.

What scared her was the way she felt about him.

Wordlessly, she strode through the community center with him right on her heels. Her breath hitched as she neared the door, feeling the palm of his hand press into the small of her back. They ducked right past the coordinator, too overwhelmed with the sudden anonymous donation of dinner to even notice their retreat or bid Genna goodbye. Her heart thumped wildly as she wrapped her arms around her chest, grateful night had fallen, hoping maybe the darkness would conceal her sins.

"This way," Matty said, his breath tickling the back of her neck as he leaned down to whisper. She shivered when he shifted his body, blocking hers from sight as he led her up the block to a dark alley. As soon as she stepped around the corner, she spotted the front end of the Lotus, partially concealed. He pressed the button on his keys, unlocking it, the lights illuminating the space around them, before it roared to life.

"Remote starter," Genna said, shaking her head.

Matty walked around and opened the passenger door. "It's practical."

"It's *pretentious*." She paused there, eyes vigilantly inspecting the busy neighborhood, before slipping inside.

There was no second-guessing, no wavering, but Genna felt like she couldn't breathe as he sped from the neighborhood, tires squealing as the car weaved through traffic. He turned the radio down, the thumping bass barely a dull vibration, as he drove north through familiar terrain.

"This is Galante territory," she said, surprised, when he headed for Washington Heights. Somehow, for some reason, she had expected him to take her in middle ground, somewhere along the invisible boundaries where nobody was quite sure who controlled what.

He let out a laugh. "Your father doesn't own the GWB."

She watched out the windshield as he sped through the streets, going straight for the George Washington Bridge leading out of Manhattan, out of New York. "You're taking me to Jersey?"

"Yes."

She tensed slightly, shifting around in her seat as the car merged into traffic on the bridge, heading west into New Jersey. She had detected it the first time she heard his voice, the subtle Jersey accent to his words. Was that where he'd been all those years when he disappeared from society? She knew her father worked closely with the crime family in New Jersey, the Brazzis, as did the Barsantis, but neither one wielded any control over there. Their rivalry stayed within New York. *Neutral ground.*

Apparently he *did* know a place.

As soon as they crossed into New Jersey, Matty headed south. Nearly an hour had passed before they approached a small suburban neighborhood, the cookie-cutter houses modest and uniform, the lawns perfectly manicured, sprinklers watering the grass in the darkness as subtle porch lights lit up the surrounding areas. It was quiet and still, most of the houses dim at nearly nine o'clock at night. He pulled the car into a cul-de-sac, swinging into the driveway of a white house on the very end. He hit a button in the car, the headlights shining upon a garage door as it slowly lifted. Once it was up, he pulled the Lotus in, out of sight, and hit the button once more for the door to close.

Matty cut the engine but sat there, reaching over toward the glove box. He popped it open, pulling out the familiar Blackberry, and plopped it on her lap. Genna carefully picked it up, running her fingers along the scratched screen as he wordlessly got out of the car.

The house was quaint, only one story with a small kitchen and two stuffy bedrooms. Matty flicked on the living room lights while Genna explored the rest of the place on her own, not waiting for an invitation. A subtle odor seemed to cling to everything, the air stale as dust wafted around, stirred up from her movement. It was fully furnished with various shades of brown, homely yet sort of impersonal. Someone had lived in the house, certainly, but it wasn't what Genna would call anyone's 'home'.

"Did you live here?" she asked hesitantly, swiping her hand along the smooth wooden countertop separating the kitchen from the living room, a bit of grime collecting on her fingertips.

"Once upon a time," Matty said, lurking near the front door as he carefully watched her. "Figured it was easier to just relocate to New York for a while than to commute every day."

"To see your mother?"

"Yes," he confirmed, no wavering in his voice. "So I moved into the apartment above The Place with my brother."

Her expression fell, shoulders tensing as those words struck her. "Enzo lives there, too?"

"Yes."

She shook her head, staring down at the plush tan carpet. How close she had gotten to being caught, to being ensnared by them. She hadn't just wandered into enemy territory... she'd walked straight onto their base, making herself at home in their nest, like she actually belonged there. And the worst part? The worst part was she'd almost felt like she had. She had felt secure. Her guard had been down, one of the most vulnerable moments of her life.

She was lucky to have walked back out at all, much less completely unscathed.

Physically, anyway. Emotionally was an entirely different story, the aftermath still constricting her insides and scarring her very being.

Slowly, Matty strolled over toward her, coming up behind her. The back of his hand rubbed against the bare skin of her left forearm, caressing her, as his other hand swept her hair back over her shoulder, out of the way. Leaning down, he gently kissed her neck, sending chills through her body. "You don't have to be afraid."

"I'm not," she said. Horrified was more like it as her eyes fluttered closed, the warm sensations flooding her. She cocked her head to the side, instinctively giving him more of herself. "Your brother... he really could've hurt me."

His arm encircled her, pulling her back to him as his lips trailed down her neck toward her shoulder, leaving feather-light kisses. "He wouldn't."

"How can you say that?"

He kissed back up her neck, his lips finding her ear. "Because I wouldn't let him."

She wanted to believe him. God, how she wanted to believe this stunning creature could keep her safe instead of being the catalyst for her demise, but it was difficult. One night of passion couldn't wipe away a lifelong animosity. "I'm not so sure you could stop him."

Matty let out a bark of laughter as his mouth left her skin, but he didn't loosen his hold on her. "Genna, have you ever met Enzo?"

She scoffed. "I know who he is."

"Errnt!" He cut her off, the brusque noise making her flinch. "Not what I asked. I asked if you've *met* him."

"Of course I haven't."

"Then how can you say what he'd do? How can you judge him if you've never even spoken to him?"

"He's a Bar—"

"Barsanti. Got it." Matty loosened his hold, swinging her around to face him. "I am, too. Been a Barsanti since the day I was born."

She rolled her eyes. "I'm well aware."

"Yet you trust me."

"Don't get ahead of yourself," she muttered. "Just because I'm trusting you doesn't mean I trust you yet."

"Whatever. All I'm saying is maybe you ought to give him the benefit of the doubt. I know my brother, and he might not be the most chivalrous guy around when it comes to women, but I've never heard of him hurting one."

"No women tied up in his trunk?"

He laughed. "Nope."

"Huh." Her breath hitched as Matty gripped her hips,

his eyes flickering to her lips. "There's a first time for everything."

He leaned closer, his expression suddenly sober, all hint of joking gone. "Trust me, Genna."

"I'm trying," she whispered.

His lips met hers, softly, sweetly, as he kissed her. Genna wrapped her arms around his neck, trembling as she reciprocated, her lips parting and tongue darting out to mingle with his. She lost herself in his embrace, his arms tightly wrapping around her, holding her close as the scent of his cologne ignited her senses. He pulled back from the kiss after a moment, pressing his forehead to hers. Genna opened her eyes, seeing his still closed, a serene look softening his sun-kissed face. She tilted her head, pressing a soft, chaste kiss to his bottom lip, when a sudden loud ring disrupted the silence.

Every muscle in Genna's body grew taut at the foreign sound. "What's that?"

Matty stepped back. "My phone."

Her eyes widened instinctively from apprehension, but he just laughed at her expression and playfully nudged her chin.

"Don't look so terrified," he said. "You have it."

She'd nearly forgotten. Sliding out of his reach, she grabbed her purse from where she'd left it by the door and pulled out his ringing phone. She glanced at the lit-up screen, the short name prominently displayed. *En.*

"Enzo?" he asked nonchalantly. She hesitated before nodding slowly. En. Enzo. "Not surprised."

She eyed him cautiously. "Why?"

He motioned toward his watch. "It's almost ten o'clock."

"So?"

"So technically I'm supposed to be working," he explained. "He probably called the Blackberry and is wondering why it's shut off."

Genna's gaze shifted from the quiet iPhone in her hand to the Blackberry lying on the top of her purse. Before she could say anything, his phone started ringing again. En.

"You probably want to turn it off," he said. "He'll just keep calling."

Genna stared at it for a moment, her finger hovering on the button, but she hesitated. Carefully, she stepped toward him instead, holding the phone out. "Here."

Matty took it, eyeing her peculiarly as the phone stopped ringing. Within a matter of seconds, it started ringing once again.

"Go on," she insisted. "You can answer it."

Matty pressed something on the screen, the ringing instantly stopping, but instead of bringing it to his ear to talk he looked away. He declined the call. Genna watched him with surprise as he turned it off and set it on the nearby counter.

"I work for my father," he said quietly. "That's what the Blackberry is for. It's my direct line."

"And you're supposed to be working?"

"Yes."

"Right now?"

"Yes."

She hesitated. "You're not, right?"

"Not what?"

"Not working," she clarified. "Right now."

His expression softened as he stepped toward her, his hands lightly gripping her hips. "I don't mix business and pleasure, Genna. And you? Well, you're not business to me."

"Does that make me pleasure then?"

A smile touched his lips as he pulled her closer to him. "Hmm, well, that's certainly the way I remember it."

Genna's heart thudded hard in her chest when he leaned down to kiss her. Tingles shot down her spine as another sensation bubbled up inside of her: anxiety. It was wrong, so very wrong, so why did it feel so right?

His lips never left hers as he pulled her through the house, to a darkened back bedroom with nothing but a king sized bed. Her nerves skyrocketed, fizzling and fraying as she tried to ease her worries. She was admittedly far from inexperienced, but this felt different than anything she had ever done before.

He busily went to work on her clothes, carefully discarding them. She nervously followed his lead, shaky hands trying to unbutton his shirt. He pulled her hands away after a moment, tearing it off and tossing it to the floor. The white undershirt was pulled off right after, and Genna's breath hitched as her eyes came into contact with his bare chest for the first time. The ink up his arms extended to his shoulders, peeking out along his chest. She scanned it instinctively, her stomach in knots when she saw the fancy scrawl over his heart:

Barsanti

If only she had taken his shirt off last time. She would have known. She would have seen. How would she have reacted? She couldn't fathom it. Standing there, knowing what she knew, believing what she believed, the sight of it—a physical reminder spelled out on his flesh—made her weak in the knees.

Before she could dwell on it, Matty pulled off her bra

and tossed it to the floor. His mouth captured her nipple, a shiver running through her, her mind going blank, as he pulled her into the bed and hovered over her. He teased her flesh as they discarded the rest of their clothes, before he reached over and grabbed a condom from the bedside stand. Her heart thudded hard when he pulled away to put it on, her hands nervously reaching up to cover her breasts. Modest, she was not, but nervous? Hell fucking yeah.

"Relax," he whispered, his body covering hers as he pushed himself between her thighs, spreading her legs. His lips lightly found her jawline, peppering kisses along her face. "It's just me."

Was that supposed to comfort her? She wasn't sure, but it somehow did. She relaxed, wrapping her arms around him as she closed her eyes, anticipating.

The first thrust again took her breath away. This time she caught it, inhaling sharply, as he pulled back out. Her eyes opened, immediately meeting his in the dark room, seeing the cocky grin lifting his lips. His strokes were deep and hard, but he moved agonizingly slow, taking his time between thrusts and savoring the moment. His hands were planted on the bed beside her, propping himself up.

"Feels different, doesn't it?" he asked.

"It does," she agreed, suddenly queasy as she admitted it out loud. "I feel kind of like Julia Roberts."

"Pretty Woman?"

"Sleeping with the Enemy."

He let out a light laugh, gazing down at her. "Ah, it's not *that* bad."

"No?"

"If anything, I'd go with 'I Love Trouble'. Because you, princess, are undoubtedly *trouble*."

"And what? You love me?"

The moment she said it, her vision blurred, her stupid heart skipping a beat at the notion. She expected mocking laughter, but he merely smiled as he shifted position, pushing her knees further up to thrust even deeper, more of his weight pressing upon her. Gasping as he filled her, she wrapped her legs around his waist, her fingers trailing down his spine, caressing his back.

It went on for forever and a day, yet it ended much too soon. Genna and Matty lay in bed together, nothing but a flimsy sheet covering them. Neither said a word, their hands speaking volumes for them both as they lightly caressed sweaty skin. Genna ran her hand down his chest as she lay in his arms, her head near his heart, while his fingertips lightly drew patterns on her back, tickling her. She fought off a laugh, squirming slightly from his touch as tingles engulfed her entire body.

"You wanna watch a movie or something?" Matty asked, his voice soft but seeming magnified in the quiet room. "I don't have much here, but there are some DVDs in the living room. No Julia Roberts, though."

"Ah, no Notting Hill?"

He laughed. "No. Got Silent Hill, though."

She cringed. A horror movie? "I'll pass."

He continued to caress her back, making no move to get up, and said nothing more. Peacefulness settled over Genna as her eyes slowly drifted closed.

Sleep took her away.

Something jolted her awake much later. Darkness still shrouded the space around her, deep and all consuming. There was no light in the room, no clock, but she could tell it was the middle of the night, well past midnight, creeping near dawn, with the way the blackness seemed to cling to everything, unyielding and cold. Genna sat up in bed, wrapping the sheet around her as she looked around.

She was alone.

Standing up, she found her panties and pulled them on before grabbing Matty's white button down shirt and slipping it on, buttoning it up enough to cover her. The rest of his clothes were gone, she noticed.

Slowly, she walked to the doorway when she heard his voice off in the house, firm with a hard edge to it, although he spoke low, as if not wanting to be overheard. Peeking out, she saw him sitting at a table with a dim lamp lit up around him.

"No, no... I got it... I'm working on it as we speak."

Genna's chest constricted. Working on what?

"Yeah, I'm sure... don't worry, it's handled."

Genna took a step backward, back into the shadows of the bedroom, straining her ears to listen to him.

"Yeah, it'll be done tonight. I'll let you know when I'm finished."

Tonight? Finished with *what?*

Matty let out an annoyed groan. "Yeah, I'm with her now... don't even start, En. I told you—I'm not talking to you about what I do with my dick, so don't even ask for details."

Genna inhaled sharply. *Oh God.*

"Look, I gotta go. I'll be in touch."

Matty let out a deep sigh and quietly muttered to himself before he raised his voice once more. "You can come out now, princess. I know you're awake."

Taking a deep breath, trying to calm her frantic heart, Genna stepped out of the bedroom but didn't make any move to approach him. He didn't look at her, his attention on a small notebook in front of him as he tapped a pencil against the table.

When she didn't come any closer, he cut his eyes at her, raising an eyebrow. "Something wrong?"

"You're, uh…" Her voice shook, despite her attempts to steady it. "Are you working?"

"Yeah."

Her stomach lurched. "Yeah?"

"Yeah," he said again, tossing his pencil down so hard it bounced off the table and hit the floor. "Trying to, anyway. Just not into it tonight."

"What's *it*?"

He gazed at her for a moment, his expression softening. "How much did you hear, Genna?"

"Enough. You told your brother you'd have it handled tonight, then you mentioned me… that you were with *me*."

"That's what you think you heard?"

"No, that's exactly what I heard."

"Wrong," he said, reaching down to snatch up his pencil again, using it to point at her. "I never said your name. He knows I'm with a girl, *my* girl, but he doesn't have a clue who she is."

"He doesn't?"

"Nope," he said. "Kills him, too, not knowing who I'm dating."

"Dating?" Genna said. "Is that what we're doing?"

"You got another word for it?"

No, she didn't, although they hadn't really dated. They couldn't, really. Could they?

"Anyway, since I neglected work earlier, I had to get out of bed and try to handle it… *it*, being the books," he said, motioning toward his notebook.

Hesitantly, Genna approached him, seeing the elaborate math problems worked out in the margins of the pages, answers circled while others were scribbled out. She paused right beside his chair, gazing down at it. The books. He was a *bookie*? "This is what you do?"

"Yes." He sighed, gazing down at the notebook, scribbling a few more things down before tearing out a page filled with names and numbers. "I spend my days doing mathematical statistics."

"So, you're kinda like a geeky gangster, then."

He laughed, grabbing her around the waist. She yelped as he pulled her down onto his lap. Leaning toward her, he kissed the exposed skin of her chest near the peak of her breasts. "You could say that."

"Huh," she said. "Fascinating. Where does the communications degree come in?"

"Hmm, well... I have decent, uh, oral skills."

Genna blushed at that. "I wouldn't know."

"You wouldn't, would you?" he said. "I'll have to remember to show you next time."

"Next time?"

"Yeah. I'd show you now, but, well..." He held up the paper he had torn from the notebook. "My brother's waiting for this, and it's better I go to him than for him to try to find me."

"Understood," she said standing up from his lap, mourning the loss of his touch the moment she was away from him. Man, she had it bad. "I'll get dressed."

She pulled her clothes on quickly, meeting him back in the living room as she slipped on her shoes. Matty grabbed his keys, and the two of them set out for his car.

"I can drop you off at your house on my way," he said, looking in the rearview mirror as the garage door opened.

She looked at him incredulously. "Are you crazy?"

"Possibly," he said, smirking as he backed up, pausing to close the garage door again, before taking off down the street. "Crazy about you, anyway."

"Yeah, well, you have to be certifiable to even think about going to my house," she said. "My father would *kill* you."

"Your father's out of town," he said. "He's up in Connecticut. And your brother, well... word is he has a girl down in Little Italy he's going to be spending the weekend with."

She gaped at him. "How do you...?"

"Give me some credit here, Genna," he replied. "I know what I'm getting myself into."

Shaking her head, she looked away from him and glanced at the clock on the dash. It was almost three in the morning. "You're not as good as you think you are. My brother saw you."

"In East Harlem?"

"Yeah."

"I figured," Matty muttered. "I saw him standing there so I kept on going. I didn't even think to check where he was before I swung by. It was a rough day."

"Your mom was in the hospital," Genna said quietly, recalling the conversation Dante had with their father.

"How do you...?" he started, laughing dryly as he cut off, shaking his head. "I guess we're not the only ones who keep tabs on the other side."

"Of course not. You seem to baffle them, though."

"Why?"

She hesitated, silence enveloping the car. The radio was turned off, the air so quiet that Genna could hear every one of her shaky breaths. "They can't figure out why you're here."

"You didn't tell them why?"

She scoffed. "I'd never."

"Because you don't want them to know about us?"

She gazed at him in the darkness, surprised by his earnest tone. "I just don't want to give my father a reason to kill you."

He laughed dryly. "Your father doesn't need a *reason*. He'd try to kill me just for existing."

"He wouldn't."

"He *has*," Matty said, a hard edge to his voice. "He's already tried, princess. It's certainly nothing new."

His mocking tone made the hair on her nape bristle. "When?"

He shook his head, casting a glance at her. "Not now."

"Then when?"

"Just… some other time," he said. "I'd rather not get into it right now. But trust me when I say I'm not afraid of your father. There's nothing he could do to me that he hasn't already tried to do to me… tried, and failed. And always will fail."

Genna looked away from him, gazing out of the window, and said nothing else as they drove back through Manhattan. Matty drove straight to Westchester County, right to her house without her having to offer an address or any sort of directions. She wasn't surprised, not really, but it still unnerved her that *they* knew exactly where to find her at all times.

He pulled straight up to her front door and put the car in park, grabbing her arm to stop her when she tried to get out. He pulled her toward him and softly kissed her lips.

"Thank you," he said quietly.

"For?"

"For trusting me, even if you don't trust me."

She hesitated, glancing from him to her house then back to him again. "You got me home safe."

"Yeah."

"You said you would."

"I did."

"Guess that means I have no reason not to trust you now."

He smiled softly, letting go of her arm. "Does this mean you decided you want me? Because you still haven't called me like I told you to."

She rolled her eyes. "That's because I deleted your number."

"Seriously?"

She pulled out her phone, laughing to herself. "Yep."

Wordlessly, Matty reached over and grabbed the phone, once more plugging his number into it, before handing it back to her. "Don't delete it this time."

She smiled playfully, waving the phone toward him as she got out of the car. "I make no promises."

SEVEN

La Traviata. The drinking song.

The music echoed through the dining room, so soft the others didn't seem to notice it, but it was all Matty could hear. Over and over, again and again.

It was his father's favorite song.

His father's favorite opera.

It grated on Matty's every nerve.

He sat at the table, pushing the food around on his plate, not hungry in the least. He wasn't sure why he'd agreed to this charade of a family dinner.

Probably because it was Mom who asked me to come.

His mother, who sat across from him, smiling happily as she ate dinner, her gaze drifting between all of them. Matty smiled whenever she looked at him, grateful to see the adoration in her expression. She loved him. He knew that. He *believed* that.

He couldn't fathom a life without her, but he knew it would happen—sooner, rather than later. He could see how tired she already was.

Matty pushed his food around some more, taking a

few bites, when the song started up again. Sighing, he dropped his fork and sat back in his chair as ringing echoed through the room from his pocket. Pulling out his phone, he glanced at the screen to see a new text message from a foreign number... one he easily gathered belonged to Genna.

So, I've been thinking...

He quickly typed back, holding his phone near his lap. **About what?**

Before he could put his phone away, it dinged with another message. **About those oral skills you're supposedly certified in.**

He replied right away. **Certified? Princess, I practically have a PhD.**

"All this texting and technology," Roberto grumbled.

Matty ignored his father, texting Genna again before she could respond to his last message. **So I've been thinking too...**

"It's what's hurting families, you know," Roberto continued. "It's destroying society. Kids these days can't even make it through dinner without their telephones."

Sighing exasperatedly, knowing the man wouldn't drop it, Matty started to put his phone away when it rang again with yet another message. *Fuck it.* Dismissing his father's unrestrained groan of annoyance, Matty glanced at the message and smiled.

About my oral skills? ;)

No, he replied. **I was thinking about going on a date... although, now I'm thinking about THAT, too.**

"What's got you smiling, Sugar Cube?"

Matty put his phone away and glanced over at his mother, seeing her look of curiosity. Before he could respond, however, Enzo chimed in. "Must be his girl again."

"His girl?" his parents said at the same time.

"Yep," Enzo said. "She's had him lit up like the fourth of fucking July for weeks."

"En, language," their mother chided before turning her focus right back to Matty. "So this girl..."

"Mom," he warned. "Please."

"Oh, fine." She waved him off. "I was just being nosey."

"No, I'd like to hear about this girl," Roberto said. "Does she have a name?"

"Yes," Matty said. "Everyone does, last I checked."

Roberto's eyes narrowed at his sarcasm before he turned to Enzo. "Enzo?"

"Don't ask me," Enzo said, holding his hands up defensively. "He won't tell me shit."

"En!"

"Language, I know," he grumbled. "Sorry, Ma, but it's true. I figure he's gotta be ashamed of her, right?"

"Huh." Roberto glanced at Matty again, judgment clear in his eyes as he regarded him coldly. "Or else he's ashamed of *us*."

"Enough," his mother said, the happiness gone from her expression. "Not tonight, fellas."

"Apologies, Savina," Roberto said, pushing his chair back and standing up. "We have some work to attend to, anyway. Dinner was lovely, honey. Enzo?"

"Right behind you," Enzo said, already on his feet. The two of them made a speedy exit for Roberto's office, while Matty just sat there, staring at his plate. His gaze shifted to his mother's after a moment, seeing the curiosity back in her eyes.

"Between you and me," she said quietly. "Which one

are you ashamed of?"

"Neither."

"Then what is it?"

He sighed, answering silently. *I'm afraid you'll all be ashamed of me.*

She stared at him, her expression softening. "I'm not going to ask you any more. I won't do that to you. I just want you to be happy, Matty."

That was all she ever wanted—their happiness. But what about hers?

Before he could dwell on that his phone chimed again. He pulled it out, glancing at the screen.

Like a real, live date?

A few seconds later, another message came in. **With me?**

"Her name's Genna," he said quietly, shaking his head. *Only her.*

"Genna," she repeated. "Is this the same girl we talked about before? The one you thought you'd lose because you're a Barsanti?"

"Yes."

It took a moment, but a soft smile touched her lips as she said the name again. "Genna."

"Don't get ahead of yourself," he warned her, seeing that look on her face, the same daydreamy look she had last time, the one that said she was envisioning grandchildren.

"Genna Barsanti has a nice ring to it," she said, ignoring him. "I always complimented Cara about that name."

"Cara?"

"Yes, my old friend Cara Galante. Their daughter, Genevieve... they sometimes called her Genna."

Matty stared at his mother, seeing the knowing twinkle in her eyes. She wasn't stupid, not in the least.

"I, uh... I should go," he said, standing up and walking around to the other side of the table to kiss his mother's cheek. "Thanks for dinner."

"Anytime. Maybe you'll bring Genna along next time."

"I wouldn't count on it, Mom."

Not as long as my father's around.

"I'll pick you up."

"You can't," Genna whispered into the phone as she strode into her closet and snatched her favorite pair of black stilettos from their place on the shelf. "They're here."

"Ah, right."

"How about I just meet you somewhere?"

"Where?"

"I don't know. Where are you at?"

"The Place."

"Is it safe for me to come there?"

"Uh, sure."

She sighed, sitting down on the bed and holding the phone in the crook of her neck as she slid on her shoes. "You don't sound very sure."

"Well, it's Soho. How safe is it ever for you?"

True. "How about I—" A knock on her door cut her off mid-sentence. "—I'll call you back."

She hung up, tossing the phone down on the bed just as her door was pushed open. Standing up, she ran her fingers through her wavy hair, loosening some more of the curls, as Dante strode in.

"Hey," she said casually, glancing at him on her way to her bathroom. "Need something?"

"Nah," he said, following her, pausing in the doorway as she grabbed some hairspray and coated her hair. "Heard you were going out."

She cut her eyes at him. "So?"

"So I was just being nosey as hell," he admitted, eyeing her peculiarly. "You haven't been out since, you know..."

"Since I got arrested," she said. "Been awhile, huh?"

"It has. I was starting to worry you actually *did* give up on life."

"Of course not," she said, grabbing her lip-gloss and putting a layer over her lips before turning to face him. "Why?"

He shrugged a shoulder as he turned away and strolled through her bedroom, tinkering around with things as he nonchalantly busied himself.

"Oh God," she groaned, flicking off the bathroom light and stepping into the bedroom behind Dante. "No, Dante. Please tell me he didn't order you to follow me tonight."

He cast her a sideways glance, sighing, as he offhandedly flipped through a book on her desk. "You know how it goes."

"This is ridiculous!" she said, throwing up her hands in frustration. "I'm not twelve, you know. I'm an adult. I don't need to be babysat."

"I'll just drive you wherever you're going."

"And what, wait out in the parking lot?" she asked incredulously. "Hide out in the corner of the restaurant? Sit two rows back from me at the movie theater?"

"Is that what you're doing? Dinner and a movie?"

"Does it matter?"

He started to respond, but she cut him off before he could get anything out, because yes... it mattered. They both knew it. It mattered to their father.

"This isn't fair," she ground out, glaring at her brother, although she knew it wasn't his fault. "At all."

"It's the price you pay for being one of us."

She shook her head. *It's the price I pay for looking like my mother.*

"Look, just let me drive you," he said. "I have some things to do tonight. I promise I won't lurk. I'll just drop you off and be on my way."

She hesitated. "You promise?"

He held up his fingers. "Scouts honor."

"Fine," she said, grabbing her purse and spouting out the first thing that popped into her mind. "I'm meeting some friends in Harlem."

"What friends?"

She shot daggers at him. "I conceded to a ride, Dante, but not an interrogation."

He let out a laugh, pulling his keys from his pocket. "I was just being nosey. For real that time."

Genna headed downstairs, stopping by her father's office quickly to say goodbye. She strode in, right past one of his associates, the two men abruptly stopping talking as soon as she appeared. Sighing, Genna kissed her father's cheek and stepped away as he eyed her, clearly assessing her. "That dress is kind of short, isn't it, honey?"

She rolled her eyes, not humoring him with an answer. It was blood red and fell nearly to her fingertips, a layer of long-sleeved lace covering the skin-tight tube top dress. Short, maybe, but it was a hell of a lot more modest than most hanging in her closet.

"I'm heading out, Dad," Dante hollered from the doorway, where he waited for her. "I'll be back later."

"Give your sister a ride, will you?" Primo replied, his voice casual, although it made Genna glare at him. It was an act, she knew. That had been arranged hours ago, and there was no question about it. It was an order.

"Already on it," Dante said, waving goodbye as he motioned for Genna to go ahead of him. She headed outside, her brother right behind her. They both climbed into his car, and he raised his eyebrows as she clipped her seatbelt in place. "Where to?"

"I told you—Harlem."

"Where at in Harlem?"

"You know where Jackson lives?"

Dante's expression fell. "Genna..."

"There's a pizzeria across the street from it," she said, waving off his concerned look. "Drop me there."

There was also a train station less than a block away.

Dante was quiet most of the ride, driving her straight to where she requested, no questions asked. It wasn't until they arrived at the pizzeria and Dante pulled in along the curb that he spoke up. "Really, sis? You can do so much better than that loser."

"Who?"

"Jackson."

She shot him a smile. "Who said I was meeting Jackson?"

Dante's eyes drifted across the street, to where Jackson lived, before he shook his head. "Just be careful, okay? Don't steal any cars."

"I won't."

"And call me. If you need a ride… if you need *anything*… just call me. Okay? I'm supposed to keep an eye on you all night, but well… I don't want to do it any more than you want me to. So just keep your ass out of trouble, and it'll keep *me* out of trouble."

"I promise," she said, genuinely meaning it. "There won't be any trouble tonight."

"Good. Have fun."

Genna climbed out of the car and strolled into the pizzeria, immediately taking a seat at the first empty booth along the window. She sat there, watching outside as her brother's car pulled into traffic.

After slowly counting to a hundred in her head, she got up and walked back out, heading straight for the train stop less than a block away.

Thirty minutes later, Genna stepped out into Soho, two blocks down from her destination. Keeping her head down, she swiftly navigated the streets, heading for The Place, as she pulled out her phone and dialed Matty's number. It rang, and rang, and rang as she caught sight of the faded sign of the sport's bar. She slowed as she neared it, hesitating on the corner near the parking garage.

"Hello?" he answered, his voice guarded, just as she was about to hang up.

"Hey," she said, her eyes darting around neighborhood as she dodged past the bar and grabbed the other door, slipping into the stairwell leading to the upstairs apartment.

"Thought you bailed on me," he replied.

"Of course not," she said. "Just had a bit of a

problem getting away from my brother. Where are you?"

"The Place."

"Inside of it or above it?"

"Above it," he said. "Why? Where are you?"

"In your stairwell."

As soon as those words were from her lips, she heard footsteps upstairs, the door opening. Matty appeared in the doorway, phone to his ear, a smile lighting his face when he spotted her. Genna stood there, at the bottom of the steps, gazing up at him. He wore the same thing he wore the day she first laid eyes on him, except in striking shades of gray and black this time instead of the warm tan and bright white. He looked dark, and sleek, and downright dangerous.

He ended the call, slipping the phone in his pocket, as he shut the door quietly behind him and sauntered toward her. His gaze swept over her body, scanning the length of her form, as he paused right in front of her.

"Well, well," he said, reaching out and grasping her hips, his hands seeming to instinctively find the curve of her ass as he pulled her toward him. "You look good enough to eat."

Heat overcame Genna's cheeks as she wrapped her arms around his neck, standing eye-to-eye with him with her heels on. She couldn't stop the blush from rushing down her neck and engulfing her body in tingles. "Thanks."

"I'm serious," he said, his husky voice not at all betraying his words. "I want to drag you upstairs and take that dress off of you right now." Leaning down, he kissed her neck, nipping at the skin near her shoulder. "With my teeth."

She shivered, her eyes closing briefly at the sensation. "Why don't you, then?"

"Because I promised you a date," he said, pulling

back to look at her again, smiling softly as he nudged her chin. "Besides, my brother's home."

Her expression slowly fell, her eyes drifting past him toward the closed door.

"Don't worry," Matty said reassuringly when she dropped her arms from around him. "He's passed out, probably won't get up until the sun goes down."

He took her hand, linking their fingers together, and Genna's heart pitter-pattered in her chest at the sensation. Matty squeezed her hand as he pulled her toward the door, opening it and glancing around before leading her out. They strode past The Place, around the corner and to the parking garage. Genna kept her head down, gaze away, as Matty casually greeted the parking attendant near his car. Pulling out his keys, he pressed the buttons to unlock it and start the engine from afar.

She climbed inside the car, suddenly, strangely, nervous. Why? She wiped her sweaty palms along her thighs as she took a deep breath to steady herself when Matty got in behind the wheel.

"You okay?" he asked as he pulled out of the lot and weaved into traffic.

"Yeah, just, uh..." She shook her head. "I guess we're actually dating now, huh?"

He smiled softly. "Guess so."

There was no questioning where they were going, no surprise when he headed north. Genna relaxed a bit in the passenger seat, watching out of the side window as they sped along the GWB, and laughed when they passed into New Jersey.

"What's so funny?" Matty asked, casting her a quick glance.

"It's kind of fucked up that we have to cross state lines to *date*, isn't it?"

"Could be worse."

"How?" she asked, raising an eyebrow at him. "Seriously, I want to know."

"Well, we could have to leave the *country*."

"That might be better," she muttered. "In that case, we'd be far away... away from them."

"Which *them*?"

"All of them," she said. "The whole lot of them, the Barsantis and the Galantes."

"You'd leave your family?"

She wavered, pondering his question. The silence was so pervasive that all she could hear for a moment was her own heartbeat thrashing in her ears. "I'd miss my brother, but yeah... I would. Honestly, Dante would have it a lot easier without constantly having to watch over me."

"Huh."

"What?" She eyed him warily. "Would you?"

Unlike her, he didn't hesitate. "I can't leave my family, Genna... not when they already left *me* a long time ago."

She gazed at him for a moment before reaching over and grasping his hand on the gearshift, entwining her fingers with his. His eyes left the road momentarily, distracted, as they settled on where they were connected.

Although she wondered, although she wanted nothing more than to hear his story, to hear his side of everything, to know what he knew, to see what he saw when he stepped back and observed everything, she said not a word the rest of the drive, letting the silence once more submerge the car. Matty drove through Jersey, toward his old house, but swung into a more commercial area, driving to a busy steakhouse. He parked the car, and Genna started to pull her hand away, but he grasped it tightly and pulled it to him, pressing a soft kiss on the back of her hand before finally letting go.

The steakhouse was busy, dozens of people packed in around the door, patiently waiting for tables. Genna sighed, looking around for somewhere to sit, when the hostess glanced over, taking note of their presence. Something flickered in her eyes, something akin to recognition.

Genna's stomach sunk. *Oh no.*

"Mr. Brazzi!" the hostess said, smiling. "Just one?"

"Two," Matty said, returning her smile as he motioned toward Genna. "I have a guest."

"Wonderful," the lady said, snatching up two menus. "Follow me."

Genna cast apologetic looks at the waiting diners, who appeared none too happy that they jumped ahead of the line. The hostess led them to a table in the far back, and Genna slid into a chair across from Matty.

"Brazzi?" she asked incredulously when they were left alone. "What's up with that?"

He smirked, opening his menu, but he scarcely even look at it. "It's my mother's maiden name. Savina Brazzi."

"Ah."

"I just took on the last name out here. Helped keep, you know, *certain people* from finding me."

"Certain people, as in…?"

Matty didn't respond, but his expression was answer enough for her.

The Galantes.

"I still want to hear that story," she said, following his

lead and opening her menu.

"What story?"

"The story of whatever my father did to you."

"Not tonight," he muttered. "I have plans for you, so I ought to keep trash talking about your family to a minimum."

"Plans, huh?"

He nodded as the waiter approached with wine and wordlessly poured a bit in both of their glasses before setting the bottle right on the table for them. Matty smirked as the man strode away. "How's that saying go? Wine you, dine you, sixty-nine you?"

Genna flushed at the husky notes in his voice, the gritty sound seeming to glide along her skin and make her hair bristle as she let out a shaky breath, unable to contain the grin that glossed her lips. "Is that right?"

"Unless, of course, you're not planning on coming out of that dress later," he said, his gaze burning through her once again, like he was drinking in her soul.

"Well, uh," she said, glancing down at herself. "I like this dress. I might wanna keep it on."

"Huh." Matty looked away from her, his gaze going back to his menu. "In that case, order something cheap."

Gasping, Genna thrust her leg out under the table to kick him when he laughed. Before she could think of something witty to say, or something to say at all, the waiter approached their table again. "Are you ready to order, or do you need a few more minutes?"

"I'm ready," Matty said, closing his menu again and folding his hands on top of the table. "Genna?"

"I, uh..." She hadn't even looked at hers yet, and with the way Matty flustered her with just a simple stare, she wasn't sure she would *ever* get around to looking at it. And the way he breathed her name, emphasizing the 'a' at the end, the slight Jersey twinge in his voice accentuating it, nearly made her toes curl. "I'll just have the..." She peeked down at the menu, naming the first thing she saw. "...Classic sirloin. Well done."

"What size?" the waiter asked, jotting it down.

"Uh... ten," she said, closing her menu. "The ten-inch one."

Before it was even entirely from her lips, Matty let out a sharp bark of strangled laughter he'd clearly struggled to contain. The waiter stood motionless, his surprised gaze flickering to her briefly, before he shook his head and finally jotted something down.

"What?" Genna asked, glancing at Matty curiously. What the hell was so funny?

"Ten inches, huh?" Matty picked up his glass and motioned toward her with it. "Maybe we could've skipped the *wine-ing* portion of the plan. You might already be good to go."

That cracked the waiter's serious façade as he chuckled. Genna opened her mouth to ask him what the hell he was talking about but froze when it struck her: *the ten-inch one*. Mortified, she covered her face. *Oh, God.*

The waiter cleared his throat. "And for you, sir?"

"I'll have the same," Matty said, taking her menu from her and handing both back to the waiter. "The ten-*ounce* steak, though."

"I'll have it right out to you."

The waiter couldn't seem to scurry away fast enough. As soon as he was out of earshot, Genna groaned and dropped her head to the table, knowing her face was bright red. "I can't believe I said that."

"I can."

Lifting her head back up, she narrowed her eyes at him, seeing his lips twitching from amusement as he took a sip from the glass of wine. She watched his throat muscles when he swallowed, oddly aroused at the bob of his Adam's apple, and nearly missed the painful grimace that contorted his face when he set his glass back down.

"What's wrong?" she asked, picking up her own glass and taking a sip, savoring the bitter tang on her tongue. "You can drink rum straight, no problem, but a little wine is too much for you?"

"It's disgusting."

"Oh, quit bitching and drink it."

Matty raised an eyebrow at her when she spoke. "You sound just like my mother."

Genna balked at that. His mother? "You're comparing me to a Barsanti?"

"Technically, she's a Brazzi. And need I remind you, I'm—"

"You're a Barsanti," she said. "Well aware, thanks."

"Besides, my mother's not like the rest of them. Or I guess I should say the rest of *us*. She's different. She always has been. If it weren't for her, I wouldn't have ever gone back to the city."

"And afterward?" Genna asked hesitantly. "When she's, well… you know… what then? You'll leave again?"

Matty gazed at her for a moment. "Haven't thought about it."

"You haven't?" How could he have *not* thought about it?

He shook his head. "I don't like to think about things in terms of *after*, Genna."

"But that's all there is," she said. "The *after*. Every moment is just the aftermath of whatever came before it. I mean, hell, even time is measured by the after. *After*noon. A quarter *after*."

"Not always," he said. "Sometimes it's a quarter 'till."

She narrowed her eyes at him. *Smartass.* "Whatever, I'm just saying…"

"I know what you're saying," he said. "But still, when it comes to my mother? I don't like to think about the *after*."

Sighing, Genna sipped her wine and lounged back in the chair. "I know how you feel, you know. I mean, I don't know *exactly* how you feel, but I get it. My mom…"

"I know," he said quietly.

"You know?"

"Of course," he said. "That surprises you?"

"Well, considering your family had nothing to do with *that*… or, well, at least I don't think…" She shot him a playful look of suspicion that made him grin. "I didn't know if you'd know…"

"My mother told me about it when it happened," he explained. "Said she died in a car accident."

"Yeah," she muttered. "My dad hates me driving because of it. He watched her drive away one afternoon and she just never came back, and I guess he's afraid of the same thing happening to me. Took me forever to convince him to let me get a license, and even still, every chance he gets, he makes it so I *can't* drive. He's always forcing Dante to chauffer me around."

"He doesn't try to drive you himself?"

"No. He hasn't driven since… well…" *Since Joey died from the car bomb attached to his car.* "Let's just say I can't remember a time when he *did* drive."

Matty nodded, his gaze shifting from hers as he glanced to his glass of abandoned wine. He nudged it out of the way, away from him. She knew, watching his expression softening, that he knew what she was talking about. "Let's talk about something else. We're always talking about our families, and well, frankly, the last thing I want to think about tonight is what awaits us tomorrow. I'd rather think about tonight... and you... and making sure you get all ten-inches you asked for."

She snorted with laughter, taking another drink of her wine, the atmosphere instantly lightened again. As if on cue, the waiter appeared then with their food, sliding their plates on the table in front of them.

"Can I get some steak sauce?" Genna asked, glancing around the table, noticing there was none.

"Yeah," Matty said, grabbing his knife and pointing at her steak. "Nothing worse than taking in ten inches dry, huh? The wetter, the better, they say."

She glared at him when the waiter laughed and set off to grab some steak sauce. "Funny."

Matty shrugged. "I thought it was."

Playful innuendos slipped out left and right over dinner as they ate and laughed, the banter flowing freely between the two of them. The alcohol relaxed Genna as it simmered in her bloodstream, loosening her taut muscles. The air in the restaurant grew stifling after a while, warm and crowded with conversation from the tables surrounding them, the endless chatter occasionally intruding in their stolen moment of peace. Matty sighed eventually and stood up. "Let's get out of here."

She looked around for their waiter. She hadn't seen him in a while. "Did you pay the check already?"

She couldn't even recall the check even coming.

"They'll bill me," he said, holding his hand out to her. "Come on."

"Are you sure?"

"They've done it before."

Shrugging it off, Genna took his hand and stood up, putting up no argument as he led her from the restaurant, out into the warm, quiet night.

They drove through town, straight to the small white suburban house Matty had taken her to before. Genna strolled inside, pausing in the living room as Matty flicked on the light and tore off his sweater, tossing it on the couch. He shoved the sleeves of his gray button-down up to his elbows as he approached.

"You really do look beautiful tonight, Genna," he said quietly, pausing in front of her. Softly, he pushed some hair out of her face and tucked it behind her ear, the back of his hand brushing against her flushed cheek. "*Shall I compare thee to a...* uh... whatever the hell Shakespeare compares thee to."

Smiling, Genna draped her arms around his neck. "A summer's day, but I'm more like a winter storm."

"Ice princess," he joked, softly kissing her as he gripped her hips. "You feel warm to me."

"Maybe you're just cold, too."

"Might be," he said. "But I don't think you're made of ice. You're like a volcano, Genna. You've been dormant all this time, all that passion building up and brewing right under the surface, just waiting for the right tremor to cause the explosion." He kissed her again, his hand drifting down her leg and slipping beneath her dress. "And I think I got just the shockwave to set you off, princess."

Genna shivered when his hand slid between her thighs, her breath hitching when his fingertips grazed along the edges of her lacy thong. "I changed my mind."

"About?"

"I think I wanna take the dress off."

"Nope. The dress stays on... and the shoes, too, while we're at it."

She raised an eyebrow at him. "Oh?"

He smirked, pulling his hand away as he took a step back, his gaze slowly, methodically, raking down her body. When he reached her toes, his gaze trailed back up to her eyes. "Definitely."

Genna let out a surprised yelp when he grabbed her hand and tugged her toward the bedroom. She followed him, light-headed as she swayed a bit, whether from the wine simmering in her bloodstream or the looks he cast her, she wasn't sure. As soon as they were in the bedroom, Matty pulled her to him and kissed her deeply, his hands once more on her hips as he led her to the bed. Slowly, he laid her down and hovered over top of her, breaking from her mouth to kiss down her jawline, his lips finding her neck. He kissed and caressed her skin, licking and sucking, leaving small red splotches along the way.

Matty trailed kisses down her clothed chest, teasingly biting at the red lacy fabric as he slid her thong off, his hand lightly stroking her inner thigh. Genna arched her back, tingles coating her body and a rush of pleasure washing over her when she felt his teeth nipping the flesh shielded by her dress. Her hands found his hair, running through the dark locks as he moved down even further, along her stomach, until he settled between her parted thighs.

Gripping her hips, Matty locked her in place on the

bed and trailed wet kisses up her inner thighs before reaching her aching center. The moment Genna felt his mouth on her flesh, his tongue gently, teasingly grazing her clit, she sucked in a sharp breath that left her body as a shaky cry of pleasure. "Oh, fuck..."

She was a goner.

Matty took her to the brink quickly, easily, with nothing but a gentle touch and a wordless tongue. He played her body like an instrument, plucking her strings and stroking her keys, leaving her a quivering mess yet again.

Crying out, she gripped his hair tightly, fisting the locks, as her thighs clamped around his head. Her heels dug into his back, wrinkling his shirt, dirtying the fabric with the soles of her shoes.

Orgasm rocked her like an earthquake, curling her toes and sending her heart racing. When the pleasure faded, she loosened her hold on Matty, softly running her fingers through his hair when he shifted his body to look at her.

"So?" he said, arching an eyebrow in question as he hovered over her again.

"So," she whispered, "I think you might've graduated summa cum laude." She cracked a smile. "Get it? *Cum* laude?"

Matty laughed, shaking his head as he kissed her quickly. "That was a terrible joke."

She shrugged. She thought it was pretty funny. "Matty?"

"Yeah?"

"Can I take the dress off now?"

"Abso-fucking-lutely."

Hours later they lay together, sweaty and tangled in the rumpled sheets. Genna had no sense of time—could've been minutes or hours, but it felt as if the world had stopped as she lay in his arms.

Heavy darkness permeated the air. Midnight?

"We should probably go soon," she said.

"You're right," he said, although he made no move to get up or even let go of her.

A few minutes passed before she mumbled, "My family's probably expecting me."

"Yeah," he said, softly kissing the top of her head. "Mine, too."

A wild ruckus surrounded The Place, the racket only growing louder when Matty opened the outside door to head up to his apartment. He paused at the bottom of the stairs and sighed exasperatedly, the soles of his feet vibrating to the rhythm of guitar riffs.

Just great. Enzo was home… and obviously not alone.

Trudging upstairs, his feet heavy from exhaustion, Matty opened the door and stepped inside. Music blasted him, the classic rock so loud he cringed. Bodies packed the living room—three guys and three girls. Enzo sat on the couch with a girl on his lap. Beside them was another girl—a young girl—her face caked in make-up. AquaNet and Crayola from The Place, Matty recognized.

Carl and Roy Civello, two Barsanti street soldiers, brothers with a reputation for being all brawn and no brains, flanked Enzo, while the last girl sat on the floor, huddled over the coffee table, snorting lines of something. She tilted her head back, her eyes closed in euphoria, her skin damn near as ghostly white as the powder she inhaled.

Unbelievable.

Matty shut the door behind him, the movement drawing their attention. Enzo glanced over, his face lighting up with a grin. "Matty-B! What's up?"

"Nothing," Matty muttered, not loud enough for his brother to even hear as he tossed his sweater down on one of the stools surrounding the small bar near the kitchen and walked over to the stereo. He turned the music down, low enough that he could *think*, ignoring the protests from the girls. "I could hear that shit from the street. You're lucky nobody called the cops."

Enzo scoffed, holding his fist out for his brother to bump it. "Who's gonna call the cops on me?"

"Somebody who doesn't know any better," Carl said, laughing, as he draped his arm over Crayola's shoulder.

Matty didn't entertain that with a response, instead walking into the kitchen for a drink. He glanced around, spotting a nearly empty bottle of rum on the counter, and grabbed a shot glass to pour himself a shot. He tossed it back, grimacing at the hot, bitter liquid as it scorched his throat. He stood there against the counter, his eyes closed, as he let the burn settle into his chest.

After a moment, he opened his eyes and poured another shot when Enzo strolled it. "Looking good tonight, bro."

Matty cast him a quick look, seeing his brother sizing him up.

"Hot date?" Enzo asked, grabbing the bottle of rum and pouring himself a shot. He clinked his glass with Matty's before they both tossed them back. The second shot was smoother, numbing Matty's chest just enough to fill the sudden void he felt... the void from having to drop Genna off at home and drive away, unsure of when he would get the chance to see her again.

"You could say that," he replied.

"Same girl?"

"Yeah," he said. "Same one."

"You ever gonna bring her around?"

Matty shook his head. "Probably not."

"Why?" Enzo pressed. "Afraid I'll steal her? Because I won't. Well, you know... depends on how hot she is."

Matty laughed dryly at that. "You couldn't steal her from me if you tried."

"Wanna bet?"

"I'll pass." Matty set his shot glass down and stepped away from the counter. "I'm going to bed."

"But it's still early."

"It's three o'clock in the morning."

"Exactly," Enzo said. "The sun doesn't come up for another few hours."

Matty punched his brother lightly in the shoulder as he passed him, heading for his bedroom. "Goodnight, En."

"You'd think getting some pussy finally would loosen you up," Enzo hollered after him, "and not wind your ass up even tighter!"

Matty flashed him his middle finger before ducking into his bedroom and shutting the door behind him. Kicking off his shoes, he plopped down on his bed on his back and stared up at the dark ceiling, listening to the continual commotion in the living room.

"Your brother's kind of got a stick up his ass, doesn't he?" one of the girls asked, her voice a loud drunken slur. "Geez."

"Don't talk about my brother," Enzo said.

"But—"

"You heard me," Enzo said, a hard edge to his voice. "He deserves respect, and if you can't respect him, then you can get the hell out."

"Come on, En," Carl said. "Even *you* just said he was wound tight."

"Yeah, well, he's *my* brother," Enzo said. "It's my job to give him shit. But you? Fuck, especially *you*, Carl... you know better. You don't talk about a Barsanti."

"Yeah, you're right," Carl muttered. "Sorry."

"What did he do?" one of the girls asked.

"What do you mean?"

"You said he deserves respect," she responded. "What did he do to deserve it?"

"It doesn't matter what he did," Enzo replied. "He didn't have to do anything. It's who he is and what he's been through. It's about what he's had done to him."

"And what's that?"

"You know what?" Enzo raised his voice, a tinge of anger sparking the words that surprised Matty. "How about we call it a night?"

The girls protested, once more, but Enzo brushed them off, quickly clearing the apartment as he practically forced them out the front door. He slammed the door after they were gone, the vibration so intense it rattled the walls and echoed through the apartment. Matty considered getting up again, considered going to talk to his brother, but instead he just lay there, Enzo's words running through his mind.

It's about what he's had done to him.

Matty tried not to dwell on it, but this was twice in one night it had been brought up, thrust front and center in his mind, the evasive whispering of the day his perfect world had deteriorated around him. A long time had passed since then—over sixteen years—but he still remembered it clearly... remembered the confusion, and the terror... remembered the heartbreak, and the anger... remembered the misery.

The misery. He remembered it most, because it still lingered. He felt it often, weaseling its way into the corners of his being, infiltrating his life, and tainting his happiness with the memory. It left a dark stain on everything good in his universe, and he knew... he fucking *knew*... when he told Genna, that it would scar what he had with her, too.

Closing his eyes, Matty sighed.

It's about what he's had done to him.

Vibrant multi-colored balloons had covered nearly every inch of space, coating the floor as others hovered in clusters around the low ceiling, the curly strings hanging down nearly to the floor of the dining room. The table had been shoved against the far wall, presents piled high on it, the entire room rearranged to accommodate all of the godforsaken balloons.

There had been two hundred of them, to be exact: a hundred at his feet and a hundred above his head. Matty remembered, because his mother had told him earlier that morning. He strode around the room, weaving through the maze of strings, as his little brother Enzo snatched balloons off the floor and threw them around like balls, chasing them, landing right on top of them, the flimsy latex bursting.

Pop.

Pop.

Pop.

They were down by about twenty already.

Matty's gaze kept drifting to the vast window nearby, out into the front yard. Dozens of cars aligned the driveway—

family, and friends of the family, but there were very few kids, although the party was supposed to start long ago.

Matty's eighth birthday.

La Traviata played from the speakers as voices echoed through the house, the adults drinking and chatting, already knee-deep in festivities, seemingly oblivious to Matty's growing concern.

The Galantes weren't there.

They were supposed to be.

Why weren't they?

"Mom!" he called, his voice tinged with whining. "Why isn't Joey here yet?"

Savina stepped into the doorway, smiling sadly. "I'm not sure, sweetheart. I called and got no answer, so they're probably on their way. You know Joey wouldn't miss your party."

"Wait until he sees all of my balloons," Matty said excitedly just as Enzo ran by, clutching a blue one, and face planted right on the floor, the balloon bursting. *Pop.* "If there's any left, anyway."

Minutes passed... five, ten, fifteen... with no sign of Matty's best friend. Growing frustrated, Matty sought out his mother again. He strode through the dining room and stopped in the doorway, seeing his mother clutching the phone to her chest, a frown on her face, as Roberto stood in front of her, his expression severe.

"*None* of them are here," Roberto said sharply. "Not a single one, Savina."

"They'll come," she replied. "It's Matty's birthday."

"That means nothing."

"They're our friends," she said. "Primo is his godfather! They'll come."

"They're not coming," Roberto said, his voice dropping low. "They're sending a message with this."

"What message?"

Before Matty could hear his father's response, a flash of something outside caught his attention, the sound of an engine roaring. He turned toward the window, watching the car pulling up toward the house.

"There's a car here, Mom!" Matty hollered. "Maybe it's Joey!"

His parents both stepped into the dining room, but neither had a chance to speak before it happened.

Pop.

Pop.

Pop.

Matty thought it was the balloons. Instinctively, naively, his gaze darted around at them, confused. Within a matter of seconds, his mother grabbed him and threw him to the floor, snatching a hold of Enzo as he ran past, clutching a balloon. She threw herself on top of them, pinning them there with her trembling body, as the noise grew louder, blanketing the air around them.

Pop.

Pop.

Pop.

Incessant gunfire lit up the house, a hail of bullets raining in on them, shattering the windows, disturbing the curtains, and destroying everything all around. Enzo screamed, terrified, as he struggled beneath their mother, but Matty just lay there, too stunned to even move, tears streaming down his flushed cheeks as he violently shook.

It was over as fast as it started. It took less than a minute to knock his world off its axis, to annihilate his life and leave nothing but devastation.

Matty opened his eyes, again staring up at the ceiling in his dark bedroom. The living room was quiet now, Enzo having shuffled off to his own room for the night. The sudden silence was deafening.

He never saw his best friend again.

A week later, Joey was dead.

chapter

EIGHT

"So, uh, where are we going?"

Matty glanced at where Genna sat in the passenger seat of the Lotus. "I told you..."

"You said I'd see."

"Exactly. You'll see."

Genna cut her eyes at him, feigning irritation, but Matty could see nothing more than apprehension. She absently rubbed her palms on the thighs of her dark jeans as she surveyed the neighborhood outside the car windows. It was probably nowhere she had ever been before, yet she knew all about these streets.

They were streets she was *never* supposed to step foot on.

Her question didn't linger in the car for long. Within minutes Matty was pulling up in front of his parents' residence. Genna's anxiety skyrocketed, her fidgeting turning into damn near tremors. "Are we...? Is this...? Dear God, please tell me this isn't your family's place."

"It is."

She gaped at him. "Why are we here?"

"For dinner."

"Are you fucking kidding me? Hannibal Lecter took me *home*?"

"Hannibal?"

"Yeah, you twisted cannibalistic fuck."

Despite himself, Matty laughed at that. *Silly girl.* "I have no plans to eat you, Genna." He paused, raising his eyebrows playfully. "Well..."

"*Not* funny."

"Yeah, you're right. Come on."

He parked the car and climbed out, hearing the passenger side door thrust open right away. "Seriously, Matty? Matty... Matty... Goddammit, Matteo!"

He grimaced when she used his real name, casting her a sideways look. "Don't call me that."

"Fine then, Michael Myers... but slow the fuck down and tell me why we're at your childhood house of horrors."

"I told you... for dinner." Through her outward portrayal of anger, Matty still saw nothing but anxiety. She was starting to seriously sweat. He couldn't say he blamed her. But he hadn't told her in advance for this exact reason, knowing it didn't sound even the least bit rational. "You trust me, right? That's what you said. You trust me now."

"Yes, but—"

"Then *trust* me," he said, holding his hand out to her. "Please."

"Fine," she ground out, rubbing her palms on her jeans once more before slipping her hand into his. He took it, squeezing reassuringly, before leading her toward the house.

Matty didn't knock, opening the front door and stepping right inside, having to practically drag Genna across the threshold. He closed the door behind them as Genna clung to him, her eyes darting around the foyer like a feral cat backed into a corner, looking for a way out. Sighing, he pulled her to him, yanking his hand from hers to drape his arm over her shoulder, tucking her into his side.

She played like she was so unbreakable, so ferocious, so fearless, but moments like this reminded Matty that the ice princess was nothing more than a façade, disguising the fact that she was the most vulnerable of them all.

"Matty? Is that you, Sugar Cube?"

The soft voice wafted out from the den, comforting Matty, but the sound of it had an adverse effect on Genna. She cowered at his side, her hand gripping the back of his shirt.

"Yeah, Mom, it's me," he called out.

Seconds later she appeared, chatting as she approached. "I was wondering if you were going to stop by tonight. Your father and brother just..."

His mother froze there in the doorway, her words trailing off, the smile on her face fading quickly as her mouth dropped open with shock. Blinking a few times, she stared at Genna.

"Left?" Matty guessed, finishing her sentence. "I know. I waited until they were gone."

"I see," she said, drawing out the words, unable to drag her eyes away from Genna. She shook it off after a moment, the smile returning to her lips as she pulled herself together. "So, uh, come in. Have a seat."

She motioned toward the den. Matty started that way, dragging Genna along with him. She didn't put up a fight but ducked her head shyly as they passed his mother, her cheeks flushed. He sat down in the chair, pulling Genna down onto his lap, as his mother took her usual spot on the couch. She pulled the blanket over herself, curling up, with her eyes on the two of them.

"Genna, this is my mother, Savina," Matty said, motioning between the two of them. "Mom, meet Genna."

"Oh, we've met before," Savina said.

Genna eyed her warily. "We have?"

"Certainly," she said, smiling. "Although, you were just a wee little one the last time you were here, so I'm not surprised you don't remember. Feels like just yesterday to me, though."

"Here?" Genna asked. "I was *here* before?"

"Your mother brought you kids over plenty of times to play."

"We *played*?" she asked, disbelief in her voice. "Like, us and... them?"

Genna's skepticism only made Savina smile wider, a light laugh echoing from her. "Absolutely. Matty and Joey were the best of friends. They would try to run off and do their thing while Dante and Enzo trailed behind them, annoying the boys like little brothers often do."

"And me?"

"You were more interested in wreaking havoc than anything."

"Still is," Matty said playfully, earning an elbow to the chest from Genna when he laughed.

"Those were the good ol' days," Savina continued, letting out a deep sigh. "We didn't always go head-to-head. We used to exist peacefully."

"What happened?" Genna asked hesitantly. "What changed?"

"These fools Cara and I married chose power over friendship," Savina said bluntly. "They chose money, and notoriety... instead of choosing each other, like they should have. Don't get me wrong—they're great men. They're *both* great men." Before Matty could speak up, to argue, his mother pointed at him, her expression stern. "They are. They've just gone astray, and I hope they see the error of their ways before it's too late."

"It was already too late as soon as it started, Mom," Matty said. "It took them less than a week to destroy both families."

"I wouldn't say they *destroyed* us," she countered. "We're still here, aren't we? And look at us, sitting here together again. All we need is for Genevieve to stick pennies in my light sockets and it'll feel just like old times."

Instead of clamming up, Genna seemed to relax more, easing back into Matty's arms as a soft smile touched her lips. "I shorted out the electricity in my house a few years ago playing with a light socket."

"Told you," Matty said, wrapping his arms around her. "*Still* wreaking havoc."

They casually chatted some more before Matty excused himself, leaving Genna in the den with his mother as he headed for the kitchen. Flicking on the light, he set to work pulling out everything he would need to make dinner, this time starting with the basics to make it all from scratch. It would take a while, but he wasn't worried—he knew Genna would be fine. His father wouldn't be home until late, long after they were already gone, and he knew his mother wouldn't breathe a word about the visit.

Spaghetti and meatballs. Matty had his sleeves rolled up, his hands dirty as he worked on fresh pasta, the sauce already simmering on the stove. Every now and then he heard laughter filtering out from the den, but it had been quiet for a few minutes.

Almost *too* quiet.

He considered going back in there to check on them when quiet footsteps in the hallway drew his attention. Glancing up, he watched as Genna stepped into the doorway.

"Hey," he said. "You okay?"

"Yeah... your mom fell asleep."

"Not surprised," he replied. "She's been tired lately. I'll wake her when the food's done."

Genna smiled softly, walking into the kitchen, her gaze scanning over the mess he had made. "So you cook?"

"I do."

"Are you any good?"

"Well, I'm better than *you*."

She scoffed playfully, nudging him when she stopped beside him. "That's not saying much. Everyone's better than me."

Matty pulled the meatballs out of the oven before starting to boil the pasta. He stirred the sauce before holding a spoonful of it out toward Genna. She tasted it, slowly licking her lips afterward.

"So?" he asked.

"So, I guess you're pretty good."

Smirking, he put the meatballs in the sauce to simmer. "You *guess*?"

"Yep," she said, leaning back against the counter as she crossed her arms over her chest. "I reserve judgment until after I taste the whole thing."

"Fair enough."

Matty finished cooking, feeling Genna's intent gaze on him the entire time. Once the food was done, Genna offered to set the table as Matty went to get his mother. She was sleeping soundly, her head propped up on the arm of the couch. Her face was passive, her body at ease.

He considered letting her stay asleep, but he knew he would hear it from her later if he didn't wake her. Gently, he shook her, his voice soft. "Mom, dinner's ready."

Her eyes opened, confusion on her face that morphed into a sheepish smile. "Oh my, I must've dozed off."

Genna was already sitting at the table when they walked in. They took their seats, immediately starting to eat. Matty took a few bites, having no appetite, too focused on the women sitting at the table.

He never, in a million years, thought it was possible to have them both there with him. They talked quietly, an ease in their conversation as she openly welcomed Genna into their home.

"This is good, Sugar Cube," his mother said. "Much better than the last time you made it."

He was about to thank her when Genna spoke up. "Sugar Cube?"

Matty was rolling his eyes before his mother even started to explain.

"He's so, so sweet," she said, "but so, so *square.*"

Genna laughed, nearly choking on her drink.

"I'm not *that* bad," he said defensively.

"You're not," his mother said reassuringly, reaching over and covering his hand with hers. "You used to be so much worse. You've loosened up a lot these past few weeks. Wonder why that is..."

There as a knowing twinkle in her eye as her gaze drifted to Genna.

"Probably because I've got *two* beautiful women to spend my days with."

"I'm glad you do," his mother said. "I'm happy you have her, too."

It didn't escape his notice that Genna's cheeks flushed at the acknowledgement.

Dinner went by way too quickly, darkness falling outside. As much as Matty wished he could stay longer, as soon as he cleaned up the kitchen he knew they had to get out of there. Against his wishes, his mother walked them to the door, hugging Genna tightly. "It was so great to see you, Genevieve."

"You, too, Mrs. uh..."

She stumbled on the last name.

"Call me Savina."

"Savina."

Genna stepped off the porch, heading for the Lotus, as Matty eyed his mother warily. She looked even more exhausted now, her face pale, sweat beading along her forehead. Just dinner had sapped every ounce of energy out of her.

"I'll come back after I drop her off," he said. "I'll wait with you until Dad gets home."

"Nonsense, I don't need a babysitter," she said, waving him away dismissively. "You have a good night."

Sighing, he leaned over to kiss his mother's cheek as she hugged him. "Goodnight, Mom."

"Night." He started off the porch when she called his name. "Matty?"

"Yeah."

"Thank you."

He stood there, staring, as she headed back inside the house and shut the door. Sighing, Matty headed for the car and slipped into the driver's seat.

He raised his eyebrows at Genna. "So?"

"So you're a good cook," she conceded, reaching over to cup his cheek before softly pressing a kiss to his lips. "But more importantly, I'm beginning to think you're a wonderful person."

Matty stood along the side of the lot, leaning back against the construction trailer as he watched the traffic flow by along Sixth Avenue. It was the middle of the afternoon, the temperature steadily creeping up so sweat beaded along his back, making his dark button down stick to him uncomfortably.

"This place seems like it took forever to build," Matty said, motioning toward the structure. "I remember when you guys first broke ground. I was just starting college."

"Yeah, we milked it for every penny we could," Gavin said casually from where he sat on the trailer steps, sipping from a bottle of water. "Couldn't delay it any longer, though. The city was starting to get pissed it wasn't finished."

"Turned out nice," Matty said. "How much does one of these places go for?"

"Uh, around four thousand a month or so," he replied. "You in the market for a new place?"

"No."

"Then why you asking?"

"Just making conversation."

Gavin cut his eyes at him, a look of skepticism on his face. "Ah, come on, Matty-B. Cut the shit. You know I hate small talk. Just say what you came to say."

"Why do you think I came to *say* anything?"

"Because contrary to how you're acting right now, I know you hate small talk, too. You always have a point for everything, so get to it."

Matty stood there for a moment in silence, continuing to watch the cars whizz by, before he let out a deep sigh. "I'm in deep, and I don't know what to do about it."

Gavin shook his head. "You pet it, didn't you? I told your ass not to, and you did it anyway, didn't you?"

"I didn't *pet* anything," he said.

"You didn't?"

"No, I scooped it right up and took it home and called it my own."

"Jesus Christ." Gavin looked at him incredulously. "Some shit's not meant to be had. No matter how pretty it is, you can't try to tame a wild animal and expect to *survive*."

Matty shrugged. "I've done pretty good at surviving."

"You've either got a lot of guts or no brains, and based on the fact that your preppy ass went to Princeton, I'm wondering how the hell you walk around carrying such big balls." Gavin put the lid on his water as he stood up and faced Matty, eyeing him peculiarly. "The Prodigal Son and the Ice Princess, huh? Sounds like a terrible fairy tale. You know, the kind where the big bad wolf eats everybody in the end."

Despite himself, Matty laughed at that. "It does."

"So you're in deep and you don't know what to do about it," Gavin continued. "You want my advice? Is that what you want?"

"Yes."

"Get the hell out."

Matty's expression fell. "What?"

"I don't mean walk away from her. I mean get out of *this*... the life, everything you came back to but I know you don't want. Walk away from it. Your father will be pissed, but come on... let's be real... when isn't Uncle Bobby pissed at you?"

Matty couldn't seem to remember a time the man wasn't at least disappointed. He had never lived up to his standards, and even if he stuck around, he knew he never would. His heart wasn't into it. He couldn't follow in his father's footsteps.

Gavin lightly punched his shoulder. "Come on, let's go have a drink and commiserate. I'll even let you buy."

"Thanks." Matty laughed as he pulled out his keys. "Why are we commiserating?"

"Because of beautiful women and the hell they put us through."

"Speaking of which, whatever happened to your girl?" Matty asked curiously. "The one you were warned away from?"

"Ah." Gavin shrugged. "Guess she ended up wherever she was meant to be."

chapter
NINE

"How'd you learn how to play?" Matty asked, shifting the cue stick from hand-to-hand, his eyes on Genna and not the pool table. She shrugged, trying to keep her focus on the game, but he wasn't making it easy.

Fucking attractive man and his goddamn distracting eyes.

She lined up, gracefully striking the cue ball, the loud crack echoing through the otherwise quiet apartment as the vibrant red ball flew into the side pocket. Her eyes flickered to his, drinking in the genuine curiosity. "Dante taught me."

"He must be pretty good."

"The best," she confirmed, knocking the cue ball into the green one. It hit the corner, bouncing right back. *Damn.*

Matty scoffed. "I wouldn't go *that* far. I like to think I'm the best."

"That's not thinking," she said, clutching the cue stick with both hands in front of her as she eyed him. "That's dreaming. And dream on, buddy. My brother is definitely better than you."

"How do you figure?"

"I can't beat him, but I can beat you."

"You've never beat me."

"But I could."

"You wanna bet?"

Genna watched as he hit the black eight ball, knocking it in the corner pocket and ending that game. He was undoubtedly good. In another life, it would've been amazing to watch him and Dante in a match.

"Okay," she said. "What are we betting?"

"Whatever you want," he said, smirking. "Except for my car."

"Ah, man." She dramatically frowned. "What about the watch?"

He cast a glance at his Rolex. "Fine. But if I win, I want your panties."

Her eyes widened. "What?"

He stepped toward her, their toes touching, his nose brushing against hers before he softly pressed his lips to hers. "I want your panties." *Another kiss.* "In your mouth." *Another kiss.* "Gagging you." *Another kiss.* "As I fuck you from behind."

Oh. My. God. Genna shoved away from him, her cheeks burning at the mental images that flashed through her mind. Matty merely chuckled, studiously racking the balls for the next game.

"We have a deal?" he asked.

"Yep." She had no intention of losing, so it didn't matter what he wanted. That watch was about to be hers.

He motioned toward the table. "Ladies first."

"You sure?" she asked. "I don't want you crying foul when I win because you let me go first."

"I won't cry *nothing*. Go, princess." He winked. "I

always heard you were good at breaking balls."

She rolled her eyes as she took her first try, breaking hard but scoring nothing, the cue ball flying into a side pocket instead. Groaning, she brusquely waved for him to go. She was off to a bad start.

Smirking, Matty took a turn, sinking a striped ball. He always went for the stripes, she noticed. Back and forth they went, both intently focused on the game, scoring until all that was left was the black eight ball.

Matty's turn. *Ugh.*

"Eight ball, corner pocket," he declared, self-assured, bordering on cocky, as he motioned toward the pocket diagonal from him. He lined up, taking his time. He struck it, the ball soaring that way, angled slightly too far left. It hit the edge hard, ricocheting back, and rolled straight into the side pocket right in front of Genna.

His smug expression fell as her lips curved into a grin. Wrong pocket.

"I won," Genna declared.

Matty cursed under his breath, tossing his stick aside as he strolled toward her, carefully unfastening his watch. He pulled it off, holding it up by the band and dangling it in front of her. "I guess you did."

"Don't look so surprised," she said, snatching the Rolex with a laugh and quickly putting it on as she leaned back against the table. The watch was gaudy, heavy and overwhelming on her frail wrist, but she wore it with pride. "This is real, right? It's not, like, gonna turn my wrist green and make my hand fall off, is it?"

"Of course it's real. It was a graduation present."

"Well, it's mine now, since I *schooled* you." She grinned. "Told you I'd beat you."

"You didn't beat me. I lost. There's a difference."

She rolled her eyes. "Whatever."

"And I think, since you didn't *beat* me, I should get what I want, too."

"You think so?"

"Mmmm, I do," he declared, pausing right in front of her, pinning her there. His hands stroked her hips before drifting further down and shoving her skirt up toward her waist. He slowly caressed the bare skin as he hooked his fingers on the sides of her black thong. Smirking, he crouched down in front of her, tugging the flimsy material down her thighs. Genna put up no fight, staring down at him as she lifted her feet so he could pull them off, his movements agonizingly slow, fingertips leaving searing trails along her skin. It never failed to mesmerize her how his simple touch ignited fire in her.

Standing back up, he held the lacy material up in front of her face. "Open wide."

Her lips parted, a seductive smirk curving her mouth as she leaned closer to him, whispering, "fuck you."

He didn't balk, mirroring her movement as he replied, "I think the deal was that *I* fuck *you*."

Squealing, Genna shoved away from him to duck out of his reach. Matty grabbed ahold of her, strong hands holding her there, playfully trying to turn her over as she shrieked and wiggled. The two wrestled, their laughter echoing through the apartment as she managed to sneakily slip away. He spun around fast, going after her, as she let out another squeal, her heart racing.

"Oh no you—"

Matty didn't have the chance to finish. '*Don't*' was halfway from his lips when the front door of the apartment abruptly swung open. Genna stalled, turning that way, her blood running cold. Matty stepped in front of her protectively, his stance suddenly defensive.

The vaguely familiar voice struck Genna seconds before she saw his face. *Enzo.*

"Yo, Matty, I saw your car parked downstairs and thought I'd—" Enzo stepped into the apartment, freezing, his words faltering and tone turning cold. "—say hey."

Enzo blinked rapidly, staring at her from a mere few feet away. Genna's vision blurred as the blood furiously pumped through her body, scorching her veins. Bile rose up, burning her throat, as she tried to swallow back the fear. She could only gape at him, wide-eyed, and Enzo stared back, purposely taking a step to the side to look past his brother, dead in her face.

From the corner of her eye, Genna saw Matty quickly slip her thong in his pocket as he took a proactive step toward his brother. The movement drew Enzo's attention. He forced his gaze away from Genna as he shifted back and forth between anger and disbelief, brow furrowing simultaneously as his nostrils flared.

"Calm down," Matty said, staring his brother straight in the eyes, before Enzo even said a word. The confusion faded from his expression, the anger winning.

Oh shit.

"What the fuck's going on here?" Enzo ground out, pointing at Genna. "Do you know who that girl is? Do you?"

"Yes, but—"

"Of course you do!" Enzo spat, clearly not interested in his brother's answer. "I remember *telling* you who she was! So why is she here? Huh? What the hell is that girl doing *here?*"

"I brought her here."

"You brought her here? *Her?* Why would you do that? What the fuck's wrong with you? Why would you even...? How would you...? When did you...?" Enzo's anger was overtaken by shock as his posture stiffened, his large hands grasping the side of his head, like the reality was dangerously close to blowing his mind. "Her? She's the one? God, please fucking tell me the girl you've been going on about isn't *her!*"

"Calm down."

That seemed to be answer enough for Enzo. All at once, he shifted his body toward Genna, taking a hasty step toward her, accusingly pointing. "*You.* I don't know what game you're playing here, but you've fucked up. Big time. Because I swear to Christ, Galante, I will—"

Genna's stomach lurched. This had been her worst fear. Seeing the revulsion in Enzo's eyes, hearing the threatening tone to his words, his voice so enraged it quivered... Genna wanted to evaporate from the room, out of sight. Fear like no other coated her insides. She felt like a wounded animal. *Fight or flight.* Her father always taught her to stand up for herself, but when it came to the Barsantis? Motherfucking *run.*

Before she could figure out a way out of the apartment—running past him and out the door, or a flying leap straight out of the closest window—Matty intervened, cutting Enzo off, an authoritative edge to his words as he snatched ahold of his brother's shirt collar and viciously yanked him toward him, pulling his attention momentarily away.

"Calm down." Matty's jaw clenched as he ground out the words. "Or get the hell out."

"Get out?" Enzo forced Matty's hands off his shirt and shoved him. "I *live* here. And you brought her here, to my home!"

"Our home," Matty corrected him. "I live here, too."

"Like that makes it any better!" Enzo threw his hands up in disbelief. "She's one of them!"

Matty sighed exasperatedly, running his hands through his hair. "Look, just... calm down, okay?"

"Calm down?" Enzo repeated. "Stop telling me to calm down! I'm fucking calm!"

He was the furthest thing from calm Genna had ever seen, his movements jerky as he waved all around, like he wasn't sure what the hell to focus on. His cheeks were growing red from agitation as sweat formed along his brow.

Carefully, Matty reached out toward Genna, and she didn't resist when he pulled her to him. His arms wrapped tightly around her as she stood in front of him, grasping his inked forearms so hard her nails dug into his skin, her knuckles bright white from the strain. Enzo's disapproving gaze burned through her.

"I told her she couldn't judge you because she'd never met you," Matty said evenly. "I told her you weren't the asshole she was raised to believe you were. Don't prove me wrong, En. Don't make her believe I lied."

Enzo closed his eyes briefly as he blew out a deep breath. Irritation still skirted his expression when he reopened his eyes, but his posture relaxed, his fists unclenching. "She should."

"Should what?" Matty asked.

"Should believe you lied. She should think I'm that asshole. She should judge me, because it's better that way. She ought to be afraid of me, ought to be scared of what I could do to her, what looking at her pretty little face makes me *want* to do." Enzo's gaze shifted to Genna, calmer, but there was no warmth in his expression. Genna shivered at the coldness of his words. "Because if she doesn't fear me, then she's a threat... to me, to you, to all of us. If she's not terrified, then *she's* the dangerous one."

"She's not a threat."

"How do you know?"

"I just do. Do you think I'd bring her here if she was?"

Enzo shook his head. "I don't know. I don't know why you brought her here. Maybe you forgot how things worked. Maybe you forgot what happened."

Matty's grip on Genna tightened, his muscles rigid. She winced at the pressure in her chest, her ribs pressing upon her lungs, constricting the flow of air. "You think I forgot? That I could just *forget?*"

"She's here, isn't she?"

"I'll never forget what happened," Matty spat, his voice with a hard edge Genna had never heard from him before. The menacing tone sent a chill down her spine. "I remember it better than anyone. I know what that family is capable of."

"Then why is *she* here?"

"Because I know what ours is capable of, too. I was fucked from *both* sides, Enzo, but maybe you forgot that. I can't blame her any more than I can blame you. Less, even, considering she has nothing to do with her father's dealings, but you?" Matty scoffed. "You're so far in the shit I'm surprised you don't stink."

He did, Genna thought. His cologne made her nose twitch.

The brothers stared at each other, locked in a mutual

irate glare, the air around them as silent as a graveyard. Genna remained still, her heart racing so hard she would be surprised if they couldn't hear it. She could, thump-thump-thumping away in her strained chest, echoing in her ears.

Enzo broke first, a fact that surprised Genna. He let out an exaggerated groan as he looked away, shaking his head. "You're playing with fire, Matty."

"Let me worry about that," Matty said, his hold on her loosening as he relaxed. He kept her close to him, never letting go, but she felt like she could finally breathe again at the casual tone of his voice. "If I get burned, I get burned."

"You'll get burned, alright," Enzo muttered, strolling right past them and plopping down on the couch. Matty spun them around to face him. "Pops finds out, he might burn you himself."

"He won't find out," Matty said. "Right?"

Enzo raised his hands defensively. "I'm certainly not going to tell him, if that's what you're worried about. But I don't see how you can keep it from him."

"He hasn't found out yet," Matty said. "And if he does, we'll deal with it then."

"When," Enzo corrected him. "When he finds out. Because he will. It's only a matter of time. And her father? When *he* finds out? That cold bastard is going to have your head chopped off. Probably display it on his fucking mantle like a trophy."

Genna's voice was meek as she instinctively spoke out. "He wouldn't."

Both boys laughed dryly as Enzo cast her an incredulous look. He clearly didn't like her. *At all.*

"He wouldn't," she said again, more insistent as she glared at him. "He's, well... he's not—"

"Don't," Matty said, the lips near her ear as he spoke the single word, brusque and firm, startling her into silence. "Just... don't."

"Nah, let her talk," Enzo said, his expression softening with amusement as he lounged back on the couch, stretching his arms out as he regarded her. "Come on, sweetheart. Tell us all about Primo and what he would or wouldn't do."

Genna tensed at those words.

Letting go of her, Matty sighed, slipping his arms from her grasp. He left her standing there, coldness washing through her without the comfort of his embrace. She remained in spot, stoic, as he strode toward the open kitchen. Without speaking, he grabbed a bottle of liquor, drinking straight from the bottle when he returned. He held it out to Genna, who took it without even looking, the bitter burn of alcohol scorching her throat.

She couldn't fight off the shudder.

"Genna, this is Enzo," Matty said, taking the bottle back from her and pointing it at his brother. "Enzo, this is Genna."

Neither one said anything. No warm greetings. No 'nice to meet you'. *Nothing*. Genna glowered at him for a moment before turning to Matty. "I've met him now."

Matty nodded. "And?"

"And he's even more of an asshole than I thought."

Matty just stared at her, but Enzo, surprisingly, burst into laughter, the animated sound drawing Genna's attention to him. He looked genuinely entertained by her assessment as he reached out, motioning for Matty to give him the bottle of liquor. Grasping it, he took a swig, trying to contain his amusement. "The feeling is mutual, sweetheart."

Genna grimaced at his condescending tone. That was the *second* time he'd called her that. "I'm not your sweetheart."

"I've got some other names I could call you, if you'd rather."

"What, like Medusa?" she asked, arching an eyebrow at him. "Ice Princess?"

Enzo's eyes flickered to Matty before focusing on her again. "I was thinking more like *bitch*, but whatever tickles your fancy, sweetheart."

Before she could bite back, Matty wrapped an arm around her again, tugging her toward him. "I should get you home."

"Don't leave on my account," Enzo said, standing up and thrusting the bottle of liquor right at Matty's chest as he strode toward the door. "Like I said, I just dropped in to say hey. I have work to do."

Matty sighed when Enzo left, the door slamming behind him. Leaning down, he pressed a light kiss on Genna's neck. "I'm sorry about him."

He was apologizing for his brother. A Barsanti, apologizing because another Barsanti was doing typical Barsanti things? Genna nearly laughed, but the reality of the situation kept her amusement at bay. "He took it all cooler than I expected."

"Yeah?"

"Yeah," Genna mumbled, leaning her head to the side as he kissed up toward her jawline. "Hell of a lot better than Dante would take it."

chapter TEN

Enzo sat in the passenger seat of the Lotus, scowling as he stared out the side window, watching the darkness whiz by. Matty sped through the Manhattan streets, heading southeast toward Little Italy. His skin felt too tight for his body, itching as if stretched too far, discomfort crawling across his flesh.

Enzo hadn't spoken to him in days. The strain, annoying at first, had grown concerning, to the point where Matty could physically feel it pressing upon him.

"You get all of last week's payments collected?" Matty asked, attempting conversation. The silence was too damn much.

"Don't I always by now?" Enzo asked, his tone clipped. He still didn't look at him. "I'll pay you when we get done today."

"I'm not concerned about the money."

"Then why are you asking about it?"

It was a great question, one that Matty couldn't answer. *Because you won't talk to me* sounded really fucking petulant, and he figured Enzo was being childish enough for the both of them. Strained silence infiltrated the car as he continued on, driving over to Mulberry Street. He swung his car in along the curb, parking in front of the old music store. Before he could even cut the engine, Enzo had opened the door and stepped out.

Turning off the car, Matty sighed and joined his brother on the sidewalk. He had resisted... and resisted... and resisted some more... but it was inevitable that he would eventually end up here, dragged into one of his father's many schemes.

Extortion.

Little Italy was notorious for being volatile, a fact that Roberto Barsanti decided to capitalize on. For a hundred dollars a week, he offered protection to the local businesses—an offer most of them were too terrified to refuse. It wasn't a new scheme, but they had never skirted in such a gray area with it, tiptoeing around the unwritten rules and pushing invisible boundaries, advancing on territory that had never quite been claimed.

But the Barsanti family wanted it.

Enzo, always first to step up, agreed to set it all in motion, but Matty couldn't just sit back while his brother took all the risk. So stupidly, he volunteered to play chaperone, a fact he was regretting as he stood there. The neighborhood was far from threatening, but this was outside of their box.

Sooner or later, he knew it would come back to haunt them.

Wordlessly he followed Enzo around the neighborhood, standing back silently while his brother did his thing. People hardly even looked at Matty, much less acknowledged him, a fact he had grown used to. Most had figured out who he was, but the unknowns terrified them. His absence had turned him into a legend of sorts, a scary bedtime story about the boy who may or may not be dead.

After a while he slipped away while Enzo chatted with an old friend. Matty made his way to *Casato*, the bell above the door jingling as he stepped inside the cafe. Instantly the man behind the counter looked up, grinning when he spotted him. "Matteo!"

"Uncle Johnny," he said, nodding in greeting.

Johnny propped himself up on his walking cane as he gazed at him. "What can I get for you, kid?"

"Nothing," he said. "I was just in the neighborhood and thought I'd drop by."

Johnny Amaro still oversaw business at his family's old cafe, despite being the head of the notorious and wealthy Amaro crime family. It was a matter of pride, he'd always told Matty. Of having something legitimate that had been built with hard work.

"Come, sit, eat something," Johnny insisted. "It's been too long."

Matty obliged and sat at a table, drinking espresso and picking apart a muffin. Enzo appeared a little while later, greeting their uncle coolly before motioning toward the door. "I'm done, so we can go."

Standing up, Matty tried to pay but Johnny refused his money, instead waving him away. "Don't be a stranger."

"I won't."

They walked out, and Enzo shot him daggers as soon as they were back on the street. "You're awfully friendly with the Amaros."

Matty's brow furrowed. "They're our family."

"Barely," Enzo said. "Besides, you know, when it

comes to *family*, blood doesn't matter as much as loyalty."

Matty ignored that, his head down as they strolled around the block, heading to where the Lotus was parked.

As soon as they turned the corner, Enzo's footsteps faltered and he cursed under his breath. "Fuck."

Matty glanced at him peculiarly, seeing the look of hatred on his face. He followed his brother's gaze, his stomach dropping. Down the street, lurking in front of the music store, were two guys, the nearby streetlight illuminating their shadowy figures and giving Matty flashes of one of their faces.

Dante Galante stood dead center of the sidewalk, blocking their path, his hands casually in his pockets, posture relaxed as he chatted with a guy in front of him. The other was short, five-feet-nothing with the build of the Pillsbury Dough Boy.

Enzo hardly balked, his footsteps picking back up as he strolled down the street right toward them.

"Well, well, well," Enzo drawled. "If it isn't the scum of the streets, clogging the sidewalk and being about as useless as a Galante is known for being."

Dante's shoulders stiffened but he kept his stance nonchalant. "Barsanti."

Matty skirted around them, stepping off the curb as he headed for the Lotus, but Enzo strode forward, right toward the men. He stepped between them, purposely walking slow, brushing against Dante as he glared at him, his expression imploring the boy to react. Dante maintained his stance, not backing down, feet cemented to the sidewalk.

Shaking his head, Enzo laughed bitterly under his breath as he stepped toward the car. Slowly, Dante turned around to watch, eyes narrowed at Enzo before drifting along the Lotus. His gaze caught Matty's after a moment. "Nice car."

Matty hesitated. A compliment? "Thanks."

"A Lotus, huh? What is it, an Elise?"

"Evora."

"Lotus Evora," Dante said. "Can't be too many of them around, huh? Thought I saw one in East Harlem one afternoon. Looked damn near identical to yours."

Shit. He knew he had seen him—Genna had confirmed it—but he had hoped it never went beyond that. He had tried to avoid lingering in the area since.

Before Matty could think of some response that didn't make him look so damn guilty or defensive, Enzo chimed in. "You accusing my brother of something, Galante?"

"Of course not," Dante said. "I'm just saying..."

"I know what you're saying," Enzo said. "And you can stop right where you started with that shit."

"Yeah, well, just remember," Dante quipped. "You stay on your side and we'll stay on ours."

"I don't need you to tell me what to do," Enzo said. "There isn't a damn thing we want in East Harlem."

Dante said nothing, but his suspicious expression told Matty he didn't believe that. *His sister* was in East Harlem, and that clearly worried Dante.

"We got better things to do than deal with you," Enzo muttered, turning away from Dante to get in the car. "Come on, Matty. Let's get the hell out of here."

Matty started to get in the car when Dante's voice rang out again, calling his name. "Matty."

He glanced at Dante, raising his eyebrows curiously. "What?"

"That's what they call you?" Dante asked. "*Matty?*"

Something about his tone stalled Matty from answering, but Enzo was quick to chime in. "That's his fucking name, isn't it?"

Dante ignored the hostile question, his eyes focused straight on Matty. "Just remember what we said here… stay out of our territory and away from what's ours. Ain't nothing there for you. *At all.*"

Matty didn't acknowledge the statement, getting right in the car and starting it up, revving the engine and speeding away from the curb before Enzo could even put his seatbelt on. Matty could feel his brother's gaze on him as he drove toward Soho, the judgment like daggers piercing through him.

"Never thought you'd do it, Matteo."

He glanced at his brother cautiously, knowing he was uncharacteristically furious. "Do what?"

"Be the one to catch pussy blindness," Enzo said, shaking his head. "Guess she fucked the common sense right out of you. Is it *that* good, brother?"

"En?"

"What?"

"I'm still not talking to you about my sex life."

"Yeah, well, you ought to," Enzo muttered, "considering I'm probably going to get fucked by all of this, too."

Genna leaned against the counter in the kitchen, watching the frozen dinner as it spun in circles on the tray in the microwave, the time on the clock steadily counting down.

Thirty seconds.

Twenty-nine.

Twenty-eight.

Twenty-seven.

Ugh, hurry the fuck up already.

"What are you doing?"

Genna glanced toward the doorway, seeing her brother standing there, staring at her incredulously. He was freshly showered and dressed impeccably in all black from head-to-toe. *Someone has plans tonight...*

"Trying to kill myself by overdosing on radiation," she said, motioning toward the microwave just as it beeped. *About damn time.* Five minutes felt like an eternity with your stomach growling. "Seriously, what does it *look* like I'm doing?"

"It looks like you're making food," Dante replied. "Genevieve Galante, in the kitchen, cooking something. One of these things just doesn't belong here."

She rolled her eyes, popping open the microwave door and pulling the container out—Salisbury steak, gravy, mashed potatoes, and corn. "It's a microwave meal thingy. I'd hardly call it cooking."

"Well, I'd still call it a miracle."

Genna removed the sheet of plastic from the flimsy white tray and grabbed a fork to poke at the food. She cut off a piece of meat and popped it in her mouth.

"Is it good?" Dante asked, expression laced with morbid amusement as he watched her struggle to chew.

"About as good as that shit I served everyone yesterday at the soup kitchen," she said. *Mystery Meatloaf.*

"So why are you eating it?"

"Because I'm hungry," she said, taking another bite.

"Because Dad's off God-knows-where, so there's no dinner tonight, so a bitch has gotta eat *something*."

Dante laughed, shaking his head. "You should come with me tonight."

Genna took a bite of corn. It had no taste at all, like she was chewing little yellow rubbery bits. "Where?"

"Out," he said, shrugging. "It's Saturday night."

She gazed at her brother skeptically, slowly taking a bite of potatoes and grimacing at the thin, grainy texture. *Gross.* Swallowing, she waved her fork at him. "This isn't, like, *work*, is it? You're not saying that because you wanna go out but Dad ordered you to stick around and watch me instead?"

"Nope," he said, shaking his head. "I'm off-duty."

"So it's guilt and not obligation."

"More like pity." Dante laughed at her when she forced down another mouthful of food. "Come on, I'll even buy you dinner."

Genna dropped her fork and shoved the tray of food aside before starting toward her brother. "I'll get changed."

"You look fine," he said, grabbing her arm to stop her when she tried to scoot past him.

Glancing down, she sighed—oversized gray shirt falling off her shoulder, ripped jeans, and a pair of black flats was certainly not going-out-on-Saturday-night *fine* in her world. "Seriously?"

"Yes, seriously."

Dante veered her straight out the door. Genna shrugged it off, climbing in the passenger seat of his car. She was only going for the food, anyway. She pulled her hair back, trying to tame the wild mess that she wasn't sure she had even brushed, as her brother set off toward Manhattan.

"Where are we going? Wait... can we go to that steakhouse again? Oh, no, how about the café down in Little Italy?"

"Negative," he said as he headed south. "We're going to a sport's bar tonight."

Her brow furrowed. "The Place?"

The words were from her lips, resonating in the air of the car before she had enough sense to restrain them or even realize what she was saying. She tensed when Dante cast her a curious look. *Shit.*

"What place?"

"The place you always go to," she said, trying to backtrack. "You know, whenever you go out. Your usual place."

"Oh, yeah, sure."

Genna blew out a breath, turning to look out the window. Maybe it was a genius name, after all. She said nothing else as they drove through the city, to a place riding the border between Little Italy and Nolita. Dante parked his car in an underground garage and led her into the bar from a back entrance. It looked similar to The Place but not quite as upscale, the interior worn and lighting dim. People packed the area, chatting and laughing, drinks covering tables as music blasted from speakers positioned in the corners. Above the sound of the rock song, Genna heard balls cracking from a game of pool in the back.

Dante headed straight to a booth and motioned for a waiter, who abandoned the customer he was helping to immediately attend to her brother. Genna involuntarily smiled at that, thinking of Matty. It was how they had treated him at The Place.

"Get me a beer—a Heineken," he said. "And get my sister a Coke."

"Just Coke?"

"Rum," Genna chimed in. "Rum and Coke."

"Rum and Coke, just without the liquor." Dante's voice had a hard edge to it, to stress his point. "You hear me?"

The waiter nodded. "Just Coke."

"Oh, and you got a menu?" Dante asked. "She's hungry."

"Absolutely." The waiter grabbed a menu, handing it over to Dante, before setting off to get their drinks.

Genna settled into the booth as she glanced at the menu, scanning through it for something to eat. The waiter returned with their drinks and stood there, patiently waiting to take their order.

"I'll have a burger," Dante said. "Rare, with everything on it."

"I'll have the same," Genna said, shrugging as she closed her menu. "Except I want mine actually cooked."

It didn't take long for their food to arrive, a few minutes at most. Genna scowled, picking the onions and pickles off of her burger, before diving in. Dante drank his beer as he ate before pushing his plate aside and motioning toward the back of the place. "You mind if I go hit a few balls?"

She shook her head. "Go ahead."

Dante smirked, tapping his fist against the table as he stood up to walk away. Genna finished her food in silence. She could see the pool tables from where she was sitting and watched as her brother slapped some money down on the nearest table. *Hustling*. Laughing, she glanced down at her plate and grabbed a fry, popping it in her mouth as she looked back up. Her expression fell instantly and she paused chewing, caught off guard when someone slipped into the booth across from her, blocking her view of the game.

He was no one she knew personally, although his face struck her as familiar, like she *should* know him from somewhere. Regardless, his sudden presence, uninvited at her table, made her hair bristle. She took stock of his chiseled jaw and clean-cut face... classically handsome, not the rough and tumble type, but his eyes told a deeper story. They were the color of steel, accentuated by his stark gray suit.

"Excuse me," she said defensively as she sat back in the booth, instinctively moving away from him. "But I was just trying to—"

"Genevieve, right?" He raised his eyebrows as he cut her off. "Genevieve Galante?"

That silenced her mid-thought. He knew her name. Her expression hardened as she stared at him, her thoughts already turning defensive. *Who the fuck?* "Depends on who's asking."

"You can call me Gavin."

"I'd rather not call you at all," she said. "Now if you'll excuse me, I was trying to eat."

He held his hands up. "Don't let me stop you."

She expected him to get up, to get a clue, but instead he remained in spot and motioned for the waiter. The man hesitantly approached, seeming surprised to see them sitting together.

I'm just as fucking surprised, buddy.

"Get me my usual," Gavin said. "And get Miss Galante a refill of whatever she's drinking."

"Rum and Coke," Genna muttered, picking up her glass as she laughed dryly. "Sans rum."

"Roman Coke," Gavin ordered, surprising Genna when he used that name. "*With* the rum this time."

"But..." The waiter slowly shook his head. "Mr.

Galante said not to."

"Well, *I* say give the girl some rum," Gavin argued. "So I guess what you do now depends on what outcome scares you more."

The waiter seemed torn, genuinely frightened, as he backed away from the table. Genna's eyes narrowed suspiciously as she gazed at the guy sitting across from her. "Gavin, you said? Do you have a last name?"

He nodded. "Amaro."

Amaro. Now that name she knew. The waiter's fearful expression made sense now. She relaxed back in the booth, waiting silently until their drinks were brought to them. She took a sip, grimacing at the bitterness of the liquor. It was *strong.*

"Nice to know I haven't lost my touch," Gavin said, noticing her expression.

"Well, thanks for the drink," she said, motioning toward him with the glass. "But really, I'm here with my brother, and I'm not so sure he'll be happy to see you talking to me, so you might want to... you know..."

"Go away?" he guessed.

Bingo.

"Your brother won't mind," Gavin said. "Besides, we're just talking."

"What do *we* have to talk about?"

Gavin picked up his drink and took a sip, not answering for a moment, his eyes leaving hers to scan the bar around them. "I'm surprised to see you here, Genevieve."

"Genna," she corrected him, "with a G."

"Genna with a G," he echoed. "Like I said, I'm surprised to see you here. I thought The Place in Soho was more your scene."

Panic bubbled up inside of Genna. His voice was nonchalant, but there was a deeper meaning in those words that twisted her stomach in knots. "I don't know what you're talking about."

"Don't you?" he asked, meeting her eyes again.

"No," she said. "Not at all."

He leaned across the table closer to her. "Liar."

Genna sat still, her gaze darting over Gavin's shoulder to where her brother played pool, oblivious to her visitor. She turned back to Gavin, trying to swallow back the alarm. "Look, I don't know what you want from me, but if you think you can intimidate me—"

Before she could finish, Gavin cut her off with an amused laugh. "You think I'm trying to threaten you?"

"I don't know what you're trying to do."

"I'm just trying to see what my cousin sees in you."

Shock washed through her as she gaped at him. Cousin? Before she could think of something to say, Gavin stood up and started walking away, heading straight back toward the pool tables. Genna snatched up her drink, gulping the rest of it down. *Dear God, give me strength to bust this motherfucker in the face if he doesn't keep his mouth closed.*

"Galante," Gavin hollered, his voice loud enough that Genna heard it over the music. She jumped to her feet and quickly started that way, her heart hammering in her chest. What was he doing? What the hell was wrong with him? Was he trying to start a fight?

Dante looked up from his game of pool, meeting Gavin's gaze. "Amaro."

"You stealing money from these fools again?" Gavin asked.

Dante stood up straight, leaning his cue stick against

225

the wall as he motioned for his opponent to take his turn. Slowly, he stepped toward Gavin as he shrugged. "Not my fault they're stupid enough to play me."

Gavin went straight for Dante. Genna gasped, her footsteps faltering when instead of throwing punches they grasped hands and did some sort of brutish boy-hug, fists pounding backs as both laughed, greeting one another like old friends.

What the hell?

"You'd think they'd learn by now," Gavin said.

"Yeah, well, I hope they never do," Dante said, grabbing his stick again to take his next turn.

Smirking, Gavin leaned against the far wall, his eyes shifting to Genna. She glared at him as she approached, finding no amusement as he winked playfully. Ugh, the smug bastard was *definitely* related to Matty. They both instinctively knew how to push her buttons.

Dante took notice of her presence and pointed at her. "Gavin, this is my little sister, Genna. Genna, this is Gavin Amaro, Johnny's son."

"Nice to meet you, Miss Galante," Gavin said politely, smirking. "I've heard a lot about you."

She said nothing in response to that, looking between him and Dante. "So you two are, what... friends?"

Dante shrugged. "You could say that."

Shaking her head, giving up on making sense of it, she strolled over and plopped down in a chair at a small table near where Gavin lingered.

Dante continued playing games, paying her no mind, as Gavin eventually took a seat across from her. He never once mentioned Matty's name, breathing not a word of what he knew, but she could see the knowing look in his eyes as he subtly teased her. Drinks flowed to their table, and Genna slowly grew intoxicated, the alcohol loosening her muscles and easing her tension. Dante strolled over between turns to chat, his pockets stuffed full of cash.

A few hours and just as many drinks later, Gavin stood up. "I should probably head home."

Dante leaned his cue stick against the wall, finishing a game, and glanced at his watch. "We ought to get going, too."

Gavin offered Genna his hand. She took it, wobbling when he yanked her to her feet. Before she could pull away from him, he brought her hand up to his mouth and pressed a kiss on the back of it, his gaze lingering on the watch she still wore, the one she'd hustled right off of Matty's wrist. "I think I might just see it, Genna with a G."

She stared at him, surprised, as he greeted her brother once more before strolling away. Dante took a few steps toward her, pausing beside her. "What's he seeing?"

"Uh…" She looked at her brother, seeing his eyebrows rose curiously. "A movie. I told him, you know, he should see this movie, and I guess he might."

"What movie?"

"Oceans 11." Jesus Christ. She cursed herself the moment she said it. *Really, Genna?* "And 12, too."

"He's never seen them?"

"No," she said quickly.

"And you have?"

"Yeah, sure… Julia Roberts is in them."

"And that's why you told him to watch them?"

She scoffed. "No. I told him to watch them because, you know, there's robberies in them, and since he's a…" She shook her head. She was a terrible liar when under the influence. "Whatever he is."

Dante stared at her, disbelieving. Genna was afraid to elaborate, knowing she was only digging herself in deeper. After a moment, her brother sighed. "Look, I respect Gavin. Despite the fact that he's close to *those* people, he's never given me reason to hate him. And I'm just asking you, Genna... I'm begging you... don't give me reason to hate him."

"Why would I do that?"

"You wouldn't intentionally, but I know how you are with guys. And while I like him, I'm not gonna like him touching my little sister."

"You think I... that we... me and him?" She scowled. "Seriously?"

"I'm just saying, don't start *seeing* him."

"Trust me," she said. "You do not have to worry about that."

chapter ELEVEN

The air in the house was frigid, angrily nipping at Matty's lungs as he took a deep breath. A chill crept up his spine when he stepped inside, not bothering to knock on the front door. They'd know he was there.

Subdued natural light streamed through the windows as dusk approached, the rooms dim and shrouded in shadows. Matty's back tingled uncomfortably as the hair at the nape of his neck bristled. Nothing was quite as aloof and unwelcoming as the Barsanti house without the sound of his mother's laughter. In fact, at that moment, the absence of it struck him hard. There was nothing peaceful about this silence.

It savagely screamed at him.

Soundlessly, Matty made his way upstairs, hearing shuffling and hushed voices from his father's study, the door wide open. Matty paused in the hallway right outside, glancing in at his brother and father standing around a wooden table. Weapons covered every inch of the surface—from the simplest .22 caliber pistols to the most high-tech assault rifles made by man.

Enzo clutched a 9MM revolver, studiously checking to make sure it was loaded. He glanced toward the doorway, doing a slight double take when he caught sight of Matty lurking there, but as expected, their father wasn't caught off guard in the least.

"Matteo," Roberto said, his firm voice as icy as the house. His back was to Matty as he ran his hand along an AK-47. He didn't even turn to look at him.

"Dad."

Enzo glanced between the two of them and blew out a deep breath as he slipped the gun into his waistband. He nodded once at their father, sending a wordless message Matty remained in the dark about, before striding from the room.

"She's resting," Roberto said quietly.

"Comfortably?"

"For now."

"What did the doctor say?"

"Same thing he always says," Roberto replied. *Hard to tell; no way to know.* "Doesn't matter, though, because *I* know. I don't need a doctor to say it. *I* can tell. It won't be long now."

Matty's chest tightened at those words. His lungs protested every intake of air. Roberto dropped his head low, letting out a sorrowful sigh.

Although he wasn't sure what to say, Matty felt the need to say *something*. Something, anything, to clear the air between them, to diffuse some of the frosty tension, to warm the house just a bit for his mother as she neared the end.

He didn't have the chance, though. The moment of understanding, the moment of mutual dread, faded away when Roberto opened his mouth again, grounding Matty back into their reality.

"Do you carry a gun, Matteo?"

"You know I don't."

Roberto nodded, finally turning to face him, his expression nothing more than a blank mask chiseled on his face. "After tonight, son, you might want to start."

The man strode out, leaving Matty there alone to listen to his heavy descent along the stairs, each footfall like a kick in the gut. There was nothing more dangerous in the world than a man with no foundation. Matty's mother was the cement that held them together. Without her, they were nothing more than fractured bricks and mortar, fragmented, giving the darkness easy access to sneak in as they fell to pieces.

And although Roberto looked as strong and sturdy as steel, Matty knew the loss they were about to suffer would be strong enough to bend even the toughest metal.

His eyes scanned the guns along the table briefly before he turned around and walked out of the study, quietly making his way further down the hall to the master bedroom. He lightly tapped on the door with his knuckles, merely out of respect, not in the least expecting a response, before stepping inside. His mother was fast asleep, a peaceful look on her face, her chest rattling with each breath she took.

Sighing, Matty sat down on the edge of the bed beside her. He remained there for a minute or so, listening to the sound of her breathing, before pulling his phone from his pocket.

He texted Genna. **Things aren't looking good for my mother.**

She replied right away. **I'm so sorry. Do you need anything?**

Did he need anything? He needed it all to be a dream, a vicious nightmare he could wake up from. **I need you to tell me she'll be okay.**

A lump formed in his throat even typing those words, his eyes glossing over with unshed tears. It was wishful thinking, the same mindset he'd sustained when he was just a child, refusing to believe someone he loved was actually gone forever. There was no way, he'd said. It was a joke, a *cruel* joke, a lie, the *worst* lie ever told. People didn't die. Not the people he loved, anyway.

Her response, once more, came instantly. **She'll be okay, Matty. She will. She might not be with you anymore, you might not see her, but she'll be okay. I promise you that.**

"So fucking unfair," he muttered to himself, typing a response to her as a tear broke through the corner of his eye and slid down his cheek. He brushed it away just as the bed shifted around him. Glancing over, he saw his mother stirring, her eyes drifting open to look at him.

A soft, sleepy smile curved her lips. "Hey, Sugar Cube."

Her voice was so frail. The ache in his chest deepened. "Hey, Mom."

"How long have you been here?"

"Just a few minutes."

"You should've woken me."

He scoffed. "You need your rest."

"I'll get plenty of rest soon enough," she said quietly, shifting around in the bed to get a better look at him. "I'm tired, Matty. So, so tired."

"I know, Mom." His voice cracked, despite his best effort to keep it steady.

She raised her arm toward him as he shifted around to face her, her fingertips brushing his cheek. "So handsome."

Her hand started to drop when he caught it, grasping hold of it and gripping gently as he held it in his lap. "That's because I came from someone as beautiful as you."

Her smile grew. "You keep that charm for that girl of yours."

"I will."

"You need to cherish her, to keep her safe," she continued. "If you get anything from your father, if you learn anything from him, I hope it's that. He was a good provider, a good protector, even if the way he went about it sometimes…"

"Not now, Mom," Matty said quietly, squeezing her hand. This was the last thing he wanted to talk about right now.

"Then when?" she asked, her voice earnest. "Now's all I have, Matty, and I want you to understand."

"Understand what?"

"That sometimes we do things that we regret, out of grief, out of anger, and it destroys people we love," she said. "Don't make that same mistake."

"I won't."

"And keep that girl safe."

Before Matty could respond, a throat cleared from the doorway before Roberto said, "what *girl* would that be?"

Glancing behind him, Matty eyed his father as the man strolled into the room, his footsteps heavy. He hadn't heard him come upstairs. He had intentionally snuck up on them. Enzo was with him, lurking in the doorway, hesitating before coming closer.

"Eavesdropping, Bobby?" Savina asked, eyeing her husband, her expression softening as she pulled her hand from Matty's to reach out once more. Roberto approached, grasping her hand, and leaned down to softly kiss her.

"Just merely overheard," he said. "Purely accidental."

"Yeah, yeah," she said. "And if you must know, I meant Matty's girl, much like I'm your girl."

"Ah." Roberto glanced between them curiously. "Keep her safe from what?"

"Life," she responded, hesitating before adding, "death."

"Impossible," Roberto said. "It's like swimming against a current. You fight, and fight, and fight, but you'll only get so far before it takes you under."

"But usually, it's the fighting that drags you down," she countered, her voice stronger now. "Sometimes it's better to just go with the flow."

Roberto stared at her for a moment, offering no retort.

"End it," she continued. "Please, Bobby. For me. For all of us. End this nonsense."

The feud. The fighting. The war with the Galantes. Matty had never heard his mother outright confront his father about it, had never heard her ask him such a thing, and based on Roberto's expression, his mask slipping as surprise shined through, she likely never had. She never asked for much at all, now that Matty thought of it.

Roberto let out a weary sigh as he raised her hand, pressing a kiss to the back of it. "Consider it ended."

The smile gracing her lips at that moment was radiant. She pulled her hand away from her husband, shifting position in bed to sit up, despite the protests from all three men for her to stay resting. Brushing them off, she patted the bed on both sides of her, asking them to sit.

Matty scooted toward the end of the bed, resting against the footboard, as Enzo and his father took spots right beside her. They chatted, relaxing, the world outside fading away, nothing else mattering in that moment except for her. She laughed at something Enzo said, some story he told, the sound washing through Matty and warming the air around him. He felt that laughter, felt it deep in his chest as it surrounded his heart, squeezing to the point it felt like it might burst. He smiled, tears once more swimming in his eyes, as he reveled in the sensation, the sound of her happiness.

Oh, how he wished it had been for him, but he would take it, nonetheless.

Minutes faded to hours, but in the grand scheme of things, it was no time at all. It wasn't enough. It *never* would've been enough. They could've sat there for days, weeks, months, and it never would have been enough time for any of them.

Sleep took her, despite her best attempts to stay awake, and not long after, death took her, too, despite her heart's determination to keep beating. Everything slowed, her last breath coming out gentle and shaky, as Matty watched her chest rise and fall for the very last time.

Nobody said anything for a moment. They didn't move; they hardly even breathed themselves. Eventually, Roberto let go of her hand and stood, backing away from the bed, his eyes still on his wife as he made the sign of the cross and bowed his head, uttering a quiet prayer. Afterward, he glanced between his sons, his gaze settling on Enzo. "I want you and the Civello brothers on Dante. Watch his every move; find his vulnerabilities. That sister of his, too. You're not going to get close to Primo, and I can't touch him, but his kids... *that's* how you get to him."

Matty's stomach dropped. Enzo's gaze shifted to him for a fraction of a second, as if worried about his reaction, before nodding and standing up. "Yes, sir."

"After the funeral," Roberto said, his gaze shifting back to his wife, "we strike."

Enzo stalked out, his head down. Roberto turned to leave as Matty watched him incredulously. "You said it was ended. The feud... you told her you would end it."

"I did, and I will." Roberto stalled briefly, right beside Matty, to stare him straight in the eyes. "It'll all be over soon."

After he was alone, Matty stood up from the end of the bed and straightened his clothes, once more fighting back tears. He took the few steps toward his mother, gently brushing her hair from her face, before pressing his lips to her forehead.

The *after*. He hadn't wanted to think about it before, life without his mother, but Genna had been right. He couldn't avoid it. It was all there was now.

Pulling his phone out again, he sent a text. **She's gone.**

Unsurprisingly, the response was almost instant. **How are you?**

How was he? Numb. Shocked. Heartbroken. If he were being truthful, he was downright fucking terrified. But instead of telling her that, he texted her one mere word... the one that seemed to linger most at that moment.

Alone.

Genna stood on the bottom of the stairs, staring at the lone word on the screen of her phone. *Alone.* It stalled her, her response slower than usual as she tried to think of something to say to him. What would make him feel better? *Nothing.*

You might feel lonely, Matty, but you'll never be alone.

As soon as she hit send, the front door opened and voices carried through the foyer. Glancing over, on edge, she saw her brother walk in, talking to someone right behind him. As soon as Dante stepped out of the way, Genna caught a glimpse of the face.

Ugh. Umberto Ricci.

"Hey, sis," Dante said, motioning toward his friend. "You remember Bert?"

Bert? Who the fuck willingly called themselves Bert? "Sure," she mumbled, turning her ringer to vibrate and slipping her phone in her pocket. "Bert and Ernie."

Dante laughed, nudging his friend. It didn't escape Genna's notice that Umberto's tanned cheeks flushed.

"Nice to see you again, Genevieve," he said quietly. "You look as beautiful as ever."

Her father stepped out of his office then, striding their direction. Primo faltered in the foyer, a grin lighting his face when he saw them standing there together.

"Umberto, I'm grateful you could join us for dinner," Primo said, greeting him warmly, shaking his hand firmly as he grasped his shoulder with his other hand.

"Thank you for the invitation," Umberto said. "It's an honor."

Genna scowled, watching as the two of them headed toward the dining room, her eyes narrowing at her brother as he lingered behind. Before she could even get out a scathing word, Dante held his hands up defensively. "Don't blame me. I was just as surprised as you."

This was the *last* thing she needed tonight. Groaning, she stepped off the steps and walked into the dining room. Only the usual place settings were put out, the normal five that adorned the table every night. Umberto took the one furthest from Primo—Genna's usual seat—and pulled out the chair beside it for her. She froze there, staring at the chair... her *mother's* chair.

Dante pulled out his own seat and hesitated, seeming to sense her dilemma, and started to speak out when Primo cleared his throat. "It's fine, Genevieve. Take the seat."

No. No. No. She shook her head instinctively, catching Dante's eye. He motioned toward the chair, his expression urging her not to make a big deal about it. Frowning, she slid into the chair, on edge even more now.

It felt all wrong.

Her skin crawled through the prayer as Umberto clutched her hand tightly, his palm sweaty. Nervous. Genna yanked her hand back away, wiping it on the leg of her pants under the table as the men immediately dove into dinner. Genna's stomach protested even the smell of the lasagna. Her appetite had been missing since the very first text Matty sent her that day.

As her thoughts drifted back to him, she felt her phone vibrating in her pocket. Carefully, she glanced around the table, making sure the others were preoccupied before sliding it out and concealing it in her lap, seeing a new message from Matty.

Is there any way I can see you?

The question sent her insides into total anarchy, her stomach clenching as her heart skipped a much-needed beat, making her momentarily dizzy. She stared at the question, her mind working fast, trying to think of a way to make it happen, when her father cleared his throat. "Put the phone away, Genevieve."

She cut her eyes at him, seeing he was watching her with disapproval. "Sorry," she mumbled, slipping the phone back in her pocket as she picked up her fork and stabbed at her food.

This was going to be one of the longest hours of her life.

"So how's the volunteer work going, Genevieve?" Umberto asked, reaching for conversation.

She took a small bite, so to give the illusion of eating. "Volunteer work?"

"Your father said you've been volunteering at the soup kitchen this summer," he clarified. "Such a wonderful thing you're doing there, you know, helping people who need help. What made do wanna do it?"

"My desire to stay out of jail," she said. "A jumpsuit would do nothing for my figure, not to mention the color orange washes me out."

Umberto's brow furrowed, not understanding, as Dante let out a laugh. "It's not so much volunteer work as it is community service."

"Ah." Umberto nodded, seeming to understand. "Point taken."

"Although, it's not so bad," she said, shrugging. "Could always be worse."

Primo hummed contemplatively. "Where'd you learn to look on the bright side of things?"

From a Barsanti boy. Instead of answering, she merely shrugged.

239

Again and again, as dinner wore on, they'd try to veer conversation toward her, and she'd deflect the best she could, having no interest in participating, all the while her phone continually vibrated with messages. The urge to read them nagged at her with every soft buzz, her leg bouncing under the table with anticipation for nine o'clock.

Dinner was always over then. He wouldn't keep her any later than that, right?

Oh God, he would.

A few minutes after nine, and Primo showed no sign of being ready to dismiss them. Genna was about to make up an excuse to slip away when an abrupt ringing shattered the air, silencing everyone.

The emergency line.

Primo instantly grabbed the phone, answering it with a brusque, "Talk."

Strained seconds passed as Primo listened on the line, finally ending the call without saying another word. He put it back away and picked up his fork to resume eating. He didn't appear distressed, a fact that relieved a bit of Genna's tension.

"So," Primo said after a moment. "Savina Barsanti is dead."

Genna froze. She knew it, had known it before any of them, but having her father announce it so casually, so coolly, was like a kick to her gut. Dante said not a word, not even looking up from his plate of food, as Umberto let out a low whistle. "Tough break. Always heard she was a good lady, you know, relatively speaking."

Primo scoffed. "The only good Barsanti is a dead Barsanti."

The only good Barsanti is a dead Barsanti. How many times had Genna heard her father say that? How many times had she *believed* it? The thought made her sick. A good woman was dead. A woman who had warmly welcomed Genna into her home.

She wasn't her last name.

Technically, she was a Brazzi, anyway.

The urge to say that was on the tip of her tongue, but her father continuing silenced her.

"We have the party this weekend, Friday night." An initiation party, Genna knew, although she scarcely got details. It had been planned long ago. "After that, we'll make our move."

"Our move?" Dante asked.

"Yeah, I think it's time we settle this once and for all," he replied. "And now that Matteo's back in town, it's the perfect opportunity to end them *all.*"

Genna dropped her fork when he said that, giving up the façade of eating, the clanking metal drawing her father's attention right to her seat.

"Can I be excused?" she asked, pushing her chair back to stand up without even awaiting his response. She felt like she was going to puke. She needed out of that room.

"Sure," he said, waving her away. "You probably shouldn't be around to hear this, anyway."

Genna walked out, turning the corner, her footsteps faltering in contemplation. She stepped to the side in the darkened foyer, leaning back against the wall near the dining room door, her heart beating erratically as she pulled out her phone, retrieving her messages.

Even just for a minute.

I just need to see you for a minute.

I don't want to be alone right now.

After that were two missed calls and one more message.

Please.

The word made her heart ache. It came over thirty minutes ago.

"How are we going to do it?" Dante asked in the dining room, his voice low. "Got a plan?"

"Not yet," Primo said. "But I'll come up with one."

Sighing, Genna pushed away from the wall and started upstairs, dialing Matty's number as she went. Two calls went straight to voicemail, followed by three texts to him that went unanswered.

Where are you?
I'm so sorry.
I'll try to get away.

She paced around her room, her mind racing, unable to relax or get her stomach to stop churning. She was at it for so long her legs grew tired, her head pounding as she worked herself into a panic. Eventually, she heard the taletell sound of her brother's car starting up outside and speeding away from the house as he rode off to do God knows what in the streets of Manhattan. Genna crept out into the hallway then, listening at the top of the stairs as her father shuffled around the house, dismissing the staff before settling into his office and shutting the door.

When she heard the lock click into place, she knew he would be in there all night, preoccupied.

Mind racing, frantic, she hardly gave it a second thought. She slid on a pair of shoes and put her phone in her pocket before quietly tiptoeing downstairs. She slipped out the back door, knowing from experience it was easier to escape undetected that way.

As soon as she was outside, she was gone, hailing a cab the second she encountered one. The cabbie looked at her in the rearview mirror, raising his eyebrows curiously. "Where to?"

"The Place," she said. "It's a bar. Do you know it?"

"Absolutely."

Thirty minutes later, she climbed out of the back of the cab, tossing the man a wad of money and telling him to keep the change. She glanced around the neighborhood cautiously, keeping her head down, as she ducked right by the bar and through the second door beside it.

As soon as she stepped inside, she caught sight of someone on the stairs, a pair of eyes meeting hers right away.

Enzo.

Wrong Barsanti.

He paused, halfway down the steps, and blinked a few times as if caught off guard by her presence. Genna just stood there, frozen, her heart racing as she stared up at him. She wasn't sure what to say, or what to do. He stared at her, judgment clouding his expression.

"Well, well," he said after a moment, slowly descending the steps toward her. "Caught yet again on the wrong side of the tracks."

"I, uh…" She willed her voice to stay steady. "I'm just looking for Matty."

Enzo stopped when he reached the bottom of the steps a few feet from her, so close Genna could smell his cologne. It made her head swim, her stomach churning harder than ever before. He stared at her, not even a fraction of the warmth coming from him that she felt from Matty.

"Tell me something, sweetheart," he said, his voice dropping low. "What is it *really* you're doing with my brother?"

"Excuse me?"

"What kind of games are you playing?" he asked. "What are you trying to get out of Matty?"

"Nothing," she said. "I'm not playing any games."

"Bullshit," he spat, taking an abrupt step toward her, the sudden movement making her balk. They stood toe-to-toe, so close Genna could see how bloodshot his eyes were, unshed tears swimming around the edges. Warning signs went off in her head, but there was little she could do at that point. He was unstable. Edgy. *Grieving.* "You might have swayed my brother, *seduced* my brother, but you'll never convince me. I know your kind, Galante."

"But you don't know *me*," she said, mentally cursing the quake in her voice. "And besides, I didn't even know he was... that he's..."

"Well, he is," Enzo said, seeming to know exactly where she was going with that. "He's one of us, and you're one of them, and this game you're playing is over. Time's up, sweetheart."

Her eyes narrowed. "What's that supposed to mean?"

"It means you have no business being here, and if you know what's good for you, you'll never come here again."

"I'm here for Matty."

"I heard you the first time," he said. "But Matty's not here, and you shouldn't be either."

Before Genna could respond, the door behind her started to open, unfamiliar male voices echoing through. She started to turn around when Enzo snatched a hold of her, throwing her against the wall into the darkened shadows. The air left her lungs in a whoosh, knocking the breath from her, as he shot her a stern look and held his hand out, wordlessly warning her to stay right there. She watched, stunned, as Enzo stepped into the doorway and blocked whoever was trying to come in.

"Hey, fellas," Enzo said, his voice casual. "I was just heading out."

"Your father told us to swing by," one of the guys replied. "Said we needed to come up with a plan for dealing with Galante's kids."

"Now's not the time," Enzo said. "I'll meet you in The Place in, say, an hour? We'll talk about it then."

Enzo stood there, continually blocking the doorway, until the guys conceded and walked away. Once they were gone, he turned back to her, his expression furious. "You Galantes certainly live up to your reputation... stupid as fuck."

"What are you up to?" she asked, her voice strained. "What was that about me and my brother?"

Enzo said nothing as he turned away from her, glancing out into the street, before grabbing her arm. "You need to get the hell out of here. *Now.*"

She wanted to protest, wanted to fight as he roughly pulled her out of the stairwell and into the street, but words were lost on her momentarily. He kept a painful grip on her as he hurried past The Place, toward the underground parking garage Matty always parked in. The red Lotus was nowhere to be seen, but Enzo pulled her toward a black Mercedes right beside the vacant spot.

"Get in," he demanded, opening the passenger door.

"What gives you the right to order me around?"

He glared at her. "Just get in the fucking car, Galante."

She hesitated naturally, frightened by what following his orders might mean, but a car abruptly swinging into the parking garage set her in motion. This was still enemy territory, and while the man glaring at her was undoubtedly dangerous, Matty had assured her *he* at least wouldn't harm her.

Besides, he had just protected her, hadn't he?

She slid into the cool leather seat, her heart racing, and flinched when Enzo slammed the door. She hoped she wasn't making a grave mistake.

"Where are you taking me?" she asked as soon as he got in beside her and started the car.

Enzo didn't answer right away, waiting until he was out of the parking garage and into traffic to address her. "I'm taking you home."

For some reason, that answer surprised her. "Home?"

"Yes, home, where you belong," he said. "It's not safe for you here, especially now."

"Why would you...?" She trailed off, stunned. "I don't understand why you'd do that for me, why you just shielded me back there. You *hate* me."

"I do," he admitted, not at all apologetic about that. "More than you even know. I hate everything about you, everything you stand for. I hate even having to breathe the same fucking air as you."

"Then why?"

"Because my brother doesn't." He cut his eyes angrily at her. "I don't trust you, I have no use for you, but for some godforsaken reason Matty says he does. And, well, we lost a lot tonight. I don't think he would take well to losing you on top of it. One death's enough to deal with."

"Thank you," she whispered.

"Don't thank me," he said sharply. "Thank my brother. If not for him, I would have killed you the second I saw your face. And fuck if I still don't wish I could."

From the tone of his voice, she believed those words.

They said nothing else as Enzo sped through the streets, the car never even slowing as he crossed into her father's territory. Not an ounce of fear showed in his expression, no apprehension. He must venture over there a lot, she thought.

That fact unnerved her. She always felt safe there, as naive as it may have been. These streets were theirs. Nothing could happen to her, nobody would ever dare touch her. But clearly, she'd banked too much on those invisible boundaries, acting as if they were bulletproof walls, physically repelling them from breeching the neighborhood. She had crossed the boundaries so easily, so carelessly... what made her think someone like Enzo Barsanti wouldn't be brazen enough to do the same?

He drove straight toward her house, just like Matty had, not needing any directions. He stopped a block over, though, swinging his car into a small alley and putting it in park. "I'm not going any closer, so you're going to have to walk the rest of the way."

She glanced at him, oddly having the urge to thank him again, but she swallowed back her gratitude, as bitter as it may have been. Her 'thank you' would never be met with a 'you're welcome'. "Where *is* Matty?"

Enzo glared at her. "Your guess is as good as mine. Probably better than mine."

"You don't know?" she asked hesitantly. "I came there tonight because he said he wanted to see me, that he *needed* to see me."

"Doesn't surprise me, but no, I don't know," he said, shaking his head as he laughed bitterly under his breath. "You ever seen my brother upset?"

"No."

"Let's just say I might not be the scariest Barsanti on the streets tonight."

Matty? Scary? *Hardly.* "He's always so calm."

"He is," he agreed. "But it's the calm ones you gotta worry about." Enzo reached over past her, grabbing the handle and thrusting the door open. "Now get out of my car before I change my mind and decide to kill you anyway."

He didn't have to tell her again. Genna climbed out, unable to stop the words "thank you" from escaping her lips that time. As she slammed the door closed, she heard Enzo groan with annoyance, shouting out, "you're not fucking welcome." He threw the car in reverse as she stood there, swinging it out of the alley and speeding away.

Genna ran the block home, breathing heavily by the time she reached the house. She snuck back inside, doing her best to not make a sound as she headed for the stairs, but someone startled her when she reached the second floor.

"Where have you been?"

Genna jumped, grasping her chest when Dante stepped out of his bedroom. "Downstairs."

"And before that?"

"Outside."

"Where?"

"Why?"

Dante's eyes narrowed suspiciously as he stepped toward her, circling her like a vulture. "Why do you smell like cheap cologne?"

"Why are you sniffing me?"

A smile cracked Dante's expression. "Why are you answering my questions with questions?"

"Why are you even questioning me?"

He seemed to have no response to that, merely shrugging a shoulder. Genna stood there, waiting for him to say something else, but she turned to head into her room when he remained silent.

"Hey, wait," he said, catching her arm. "I'm sorry."

"About?"

"Everything," he said. "Tonight, you know... Bert... what Dad tried to do. He just wants you to be with someone he can trust you with... someone that can keep you safe. Especially now."

Especially now. Those were the same words Enzo had used. Hearing them made her stomach drop. A storm was brewing, and she had a terrible feeling it was going to get ugly. "I don't need Bert to keep me safe. I have zero interest in him."

"I know you don't," he said, eyeing her peculiarly. "I'm just curious who you *do* have interest in."

"What do you mean?"

"Come on, Genna. I taught you everything you know. I know you better than anybody. Who is it?"

"It's, uh... nobody."

"Who were you with tonight?"

"Nobody."

"It's not Gavin, right?"

"What? Of course not!"

"Is it Jackson again?" Dante pressed.

"No."

"You can tell me, Genna," he said seriously. "I know Dad doesn't want you seeing him anymore, and I can't say I don't agree. I don't think he deserves even a second of your time, but I'm not going to rat you out. I never would. Just... *tell* me you're seeing Jackson again."

There was something in his voice, the pleading tone when he asked her to tell him, which suggested to Genna that he truly wanted to hear her say that. "Why?"

"Because you're seeing *somebody*," he replied. "Sneaking around, coming home smelling like cologne, being evasive... last week you had a hickey near your collarbone—don't think I didn't notice that. You're lucky Dad didn't spot it. So the point is there's someone, and I just... just tell me it's Jackson you're seeing and I'll leave you alone, but..."

He trailed off, and Genna heard the concern in his unspoken words. He was worried who else it might be. Was he on to her? She couldn't even fathom what he would think when he found out. This was the ultimate betrayal. She was consorting with the enemy.

But this was her brother, her best friend...

How could she ever choose between them?

"Fine," she muttered. "You're right."

Dante's expression instantly softened, relief shining through that made guilt nag at her. She hadn't exactly lied to him then... he was right, she *was* seeing someone... but she had misled him, letting him believe whatever he wanted to believe.

It was the only way.

"Just be careful, okay?" Dante said.

"I will," she replied, smiling softly. He was always concerned about her when there was so much more in life he needed to be worried about. "I promise."

She escaped to her room then, kicking her shoes off and flopping down on the bed as she pulled her phone from her pocket. No new messages. No missed calls. No sign of Matty.

She just hoped *he* was being careful, wherever he was.

TWELVE

Dark. *So fucking dark.*

The casket was the color of bitter chocolate, so brown it was almost black, matching the cars aligning the narrow pathway through the small cemetery. The air was dreary, cool and damp, clouds covering every inch of sky, not an ounce of sunshine breaking through anywhere.

Even the earth seemed to be mourning.

Splashes of color dotted the landscape as blood red roses covered the top of the casket. Roberto Barsanti stood front-and-center, Matty and Enzo at his side, all three dressed impeccably in pitch-black three-piece suits, while masses of bodies surrounded them, heads bowed, hands clasped in front of them. Hundreds had come out to pay their respects, so many connected men amassed in one place that it drew the attention of law enforcement.

Local cops were strategically positioned around the cemetery while FBI surveillance parked farther off, watching and waiting. It was probably the only time they appreciated the attention, given they were more vulnerable at that moment than they had ever been before.

Nobody came armed, out of respect for Savina.

She had wanted the violence to end.

It wouldn't, though. Matty could sense the storm brewing, the heaviness in the air about so much more than just one death.

It was about the ones to come.

"Eternal rest grant unto her, O Lord, and let perpetual light shine upon her," the priest said, making the sign of the cross over the casket. "May she rest in peace."

A chorus of "Amen" flowed through the crowd. Matty lowered his head and closed his eyes as the priest finished.

"May her soul, and the souls of *all* the faithful departed, through the mercy of God rest in peace."

The crowd dispersed then, scattering in different directions throughout the cemetery as the service ended. Dozens of people lined up, taking the chance to personally address the family. Matty kept his head down and his hands clasped in front of him as he listened to his father acknowledge their condolences. Nobody spoke to him, skipping right past as if he weren't there. He wasn't even sure they *saw* him.

He felt like a ghost.

When the last one had gone through, Matty turned to walk away when his father grasped his shoulder, squeezing so tightly Matty grimaced. "I expect you at the house, Matteo."

"Of course," Matty muttered. He would go, for his mother, but he had no desire to be around those people, and he ventured to guess most of them didn't care if he showed up anyway. "I'll be there."

He wandered through the graveyard, toward his

Lotus parked along the front, the bright red sports car sticking out like a sore thumb surrounded by the masses of dark sedans. He pulled his keys from his pocket, starting the engine from afar, and had almost reached it when someone called his name. "Yo, Matty, wait up!"

He slowed his steps as his brother jogged to catch up to him. He hadn't seen Enzo since that moment in his mother's bedroom when she'd taken her last breath. He had disappeared to handle whatever the family was planning, while Matty merely wandered around in a fog, getting lost in the darkness. "En."

Enzo slapped him on the back, breathing heavily as he said, "Where you been?"

"Around," Matty replied. "Why?"

"No reason." Enzo shook his head, his footsteps stalling. "Just haven't seen you. You haven't come home."

Matty knew he meant the apartment above The Place, but his words were contradictory. That wasn't his home. He didn't have one, not really, not anymore... if he had even ever had one. The closest he got was the house in New Jersey, and that was exactly where he had gone.

At least he could *think* there.

Sighing, Matty opened the driver's side door of his car and paused, not intending to entertain his brother with an explanation. He turned to Enzo, eyeing him curiously. "You need a ride?"

"I, uh..." Enzo glanced around, shrugging a shoulder. "Yeah, sure."

They didn't speak during the drive, the music so loud it hindered any chance of conversation. Matty struggled to find parking at the Barsanti house, pulling past the waiting sedans, and leaving the Lotus down the block. He expected to slip into the house undetected, to continually fly under the radar, but he was accosted the second he stepped through the door. Someone stepped right in front of him, someone Matty only vaguely recognized as one of his father's associates.

The man, with deep gray hair and leathery skin, immediately grasped Matty's hand and firmly shook it. "Matteo Barsanti, it's an honor to finally meet you."

Matty was taken aback.

"You don't know how long we've waited for you to come back," the man continued, clutching his hand tightly, showing no sign of letting go anytime soon. "How long we waited for you to take your place."

Matty's stomach sunk. "I wouldn't say I—"

Before he could finish his sentence, they were interrupted by a group of men, others butting into the conversation to introduce themselves to him. Matty shook their hands, names evading him, forgotten the second they were given. An overwhelming tension overtook his body, his hair bristling at the attention. He tried to take it in stride, to brush it off and slip away, but it became clear to him quickly that it wasn't fleeting.

It was just beginning.

Glancing across the room, he saw his father standing along the wall, sipping from a glass of scotch, his lips twitching as he watched them. And he knew it then, taking in his smug expression, the look that spoke of countless expectations.

He'd orchestrated this.

Enzo slipped through the crowd, interrupting to pull a baffled Matty aside.

"The books opened today," Enzo explained quietly, keeping his stance nonchalant but there was a caution to his words. "I wanted to warn you, I was going to tell you on the way here, but..."

But Enzo wasn't supposed to. Matty sighed, running his hand through his hair. "He's using this as a meet-and-greet, isn't he? He's going to try to nominate me."

"Not *try*," Enzo said. "The old man is going to do it, whether you like it or not."

"And if I decline?"

Enzo shrugged. "Beats me. Nobody's ever refused him before."

Matty glanced around, surveying the crowd. He hadn't thought it possible, but the worst day of his life had suddenly gotten even worse. "I'm gonna need a drink."

Enzo slapped him on the back. "I'll get you one."

"Make it strong," Matty said.

If he had to do it, there was no way he could do it sober.

Rambunctious chatter and loud music trailed Genna as she trudged upstairs, head down, eyes fixed on her pink-polished toes. Her shoes swung in her hand and her shoulders sagged. Relief washed through her as she escaped the festivities, but it wasn't nearly strong enough to overshadow her sorrow. Now that she was alone, away from prying eyes, it shone brightly in her features, worry etched in the too-deep lines on her young face. She was worried.

Really fucking worried.

She hadn't heard from Matty in days, ever since he had sent the string of desperate text messages.

She strode quietly down the hall and slipped into her back bedroom, shutting and locking the door behind her.

She dropped her shoes on the floor and leaned back against the wooden door, closing her eyes. This night had been the longest of her life, the most trying of her patience. So many times she had been close to flipping, to snapping, all of her frustrations and grievances perched on the tip of her tongue, but she continually swallowed them back as she plastered on a smile to save face. So they wouldn't know... so they wouldn't see.

So they wouldn't realize she felt differently.

All night long, over and over, she had heard the name, spat in scathing, disgust-filled voices. *Barsanti.*

Sighing, she pushed away from the door and glanced around. Her dress was too tight, the air too stifling. She felt like she was suffocating as the sounds from below reached even in here. Frustrated, she walked to the sliding glass door and unlocked it, shoving the curtains aside to open it. A rush of cool, damp air assaulted her. She inhaled deeply, breathing it in, welcoming it as she stepped out onto the small terrace. Her feet seemed to slide against the wood from the drizzling rain. Despite summer being upon them, the nights were still chilly. Not a star could be seen tonight, the moon shrouded in a thick blanket of gray clouds, casting a hazy gloominess upon everything.

She propped herself on the wooden railing as the wind whipped around her, rustling the blooming trees and blowing her long hair into her face. It was such a tumultuous night, her thoughts distracting her so much that she nearly missed the movement in the yard below. The form blended into the shadows around the trees just below the balcony until a blast of silent lightening flashed, illuminating the area. Although it made no sound, Genna jolted as if a crack of thunder had struck right beside her. Startled, she grasped her chest as she stared at the figure.

"Matty?" she gasped.

He stood there in the yard, his fitted black suit somehow looking too big, like he was drowning in the material. The top buttons of the shirt were undone as it hung half-tucked into his pants, the tie knotted loosely around his neck as he tugged on it.

Suffocating. He was suffocating, too.

"What are you doing here?" she asked, heart thumping erratically in her chest. He was there, in her backyard. That was the last place he should *ever* be.

His words slurred together as he said, "I needed to see you."

"You couldn't have just called?"

"*See* you," he stressed. "I had to see you, Genna."

"Skype?" she suggested, leaning over the railing as she gaped at him, rain starting to fall harder on them as more lightning flashed. "Facetime? Something?"

"It's not the same."

It wasn't, she knew, but he shouldn't have come there. Her eyes darted around nervously as her stomach clenched. "Jesus, Matty, you can't be here. Someone could see you. It's not safe. You know that."

"It doesn't matter." He stepped forward, staggering as he tugged on his tie some more.

"It does matter! Do you know what they'd do if they saw you here?"

"Kill me." His response was impassive. "I don't care."

"You should."

"Why?" He gazed up at her, raindrops splattering his face and dripping from his washed-out skin. "What do I have to live for?"

"Me," she said right away. "Live for *me*."

Agony crossed his expression, his eyes leaving hers as his gaze drifted toward the backdoor of the house. Just yards from him, the biggest and most powerful members of the Galante crime family gathered. Every single man down there knew who he was and wanted nothing more than to see him and everyone he loved destroyed. Nothing but wood, and brick, and glass separated him from his demise, yet he just stood there, statuesque, like he wasn't afraid to see his end.

It terrified her, though. God, did it scare her.

"You can't be here," she said in a panicked whisper. "You have to leave, Matty."

"I can't." His voice cracked as his eyes met hers again. "I have nowhere to go."

The torment in his voice struck deep inside of her, squeezing her heart and making her chest ache. Stupid, stupid boy. Her eyes darted around again in shock that he hadn't yet been discovered. It was only a matter of time, though. She had to do something—fast.

"The shed," she said, motioning toward the small building along the back of the property.

His eyes darted that way, his brow furrowing. "You want me to hide in your shed?"

"No, you fool," she hissed. "There's a ladder in the shed."

It seemed to dawn on him what she was getting at. He started that way as she called out to him. "Make it fast! And for God's sake, *be quiet*!"

Her words fell on deaf ears... or maybe just drunk ones. His steps were slow and awkward, and Genna's heart viciously pounded as he made a ruckus dragging the ladder away. It clanked and clattered as he heaved it toward her, and Genna grimaced when it thumped against the side of the house.

He climbed it, his shiny black dress shoes sliding on the slippery metal rungs. As soon as he was close enough for Genna to reach, she grasped his arm and helped yank him over the railing. She stared at the ladder, contemplating.

Ugh. Hadn't really thought that through.

She considered lugging it up with them, but instead just gave it a push and knocked it into the backyard. *Maybe nobody will notice.*

Matty stared down as it landed in the grass. "Guess I'm staying."

Sighing dramatically, Genna tugged him into her bedroom and out of the rain. She left the sliding glass door open, the cool breeze following them as Matty pulled her into his arms. An odor clung to him, an echo of a bottle of liquor, slightly overshadowed by the strong peppermint melting on his tongue.

"You're drunk," she said, her earlier worries not at all eased with him there. If anything, it confirmed her suspicions. He was a wreck. "Please tell me you didn't drive like this."

"I didn't," he said. "I'm not stupid, Genna."

"Not stupid?" She scoffed. "You couldn't be *more* stupid! You showed up at my house while they're all--"

"Celebrating." His voice shook as he bitterly forced out the word. "I'm grieving, and these people—they're *celebrating.*"

"They're... not," she said, knowing it was a lie the moment she said it. They certainly weren't distraught about the turn of events. They would never tell her any of their plans, would never bring her into the business, but she heard the whisperings and insinuations all night long. Now that the Barsantis were distracted, the perfect moment to make a move was upon them. They were going to eliminate the enemy before the enemy even knew war had been declared. If Genna's father had his way, this was only the beginning of the desolation for Matty. They were going to take down his entire family, pick them off one-by-one.

She ran her hand along his jawline, feeling the scruff scratching at her palm. His eyes looked so hollow, red-rimmed and glossed over with unshed tears. Seeing him in so much agony stirred up the same feelings within her. She felt betrayed... but not by him. Not by them. Not the Barsantis. Her own father, her own family, caused this anguish, and she wasn't sure there was any way to cure that pain. The sense of loyalty that had been embedded in her since birth sealed her lips and silenced her tongue from spilling the things she knew.

"I'm so sorry," she whispered, brushing her fingers across his chapped lips, wondering what sort of secrets he, too, swallowed back. "So, so sorry. I wish I could've been there for you. I wanted to be there for you. I *tried*."

He grabbed her hand, holding it there as he kissed her fingertips. "You're here now."

"I am," she said. "Whatever you need."

"I need you." He pulled her hand away from his mouth, no hesitation as his lips met hers in a fiery kiss. She gasped, wrapping her arms around his neck as his hands drifted to her hips. He shoved her dress up, hands slipping beneath the fabric as he cupped her ass, squeezing the cheeks and pressing her flush against him. She moaned into his mouth, heat igniting in her gut when she felt his erection straining the fabric of his pants.

He walked her over to her unmade bed as he fumbled with their clothes, breaking the kiss long enough to pull her dress off and toss it away. She gazed at him in the darkness, biting down on her bottom lip, watching as he made work of his clothes.

"Now?" she asked as he unbuckled his pants and let them drop to the floor, leaving him in nothing but a pair of black boxer briefs. "My dad's here... and my brother..."

"So?"

"They could hear."

"Not if you're quiet… if that's possible for you."

She dramatically rolled her eyes, unable to keep the blush from staining her cheeks. Quiet? With him? Unlikely. Matty pulled her down on her bed. She lay back on it, her heart feverishly pounding in her chest as he hovered over her, kissing her deeply. Her lips tingled from the force of his, the taste of peppermint coating her tongue as she, too, grew intoxicated, but from lust. He awakened every part of her, igniting every nerve ending, as her body instinctively welcomed him in.

He kissed and caressed her exposed skin as she closed her eyes, relaxing into the soft satin sheets. His hands explored before he roughly grasped her side, startling her as he pushed her over onto her stomach. Her eyes opened, questions on the tip of her tongue, but they were halted the moment she felt him settle between her legs. He stroked her thighs, parting her legs and raising her bottom half off the bed just enough for him to thrust inside of her from behind. She cried out, fisting the bed sheets as he filled her. He trailed kisses along her spine before lying down on top of her, his warm chest flat against her back, covering her, enveloping her in his embrace. One arm snaked around her chest as he held her tightly, his hand resting at the base of her throat, as his other hand rubbed her hip before slipping beneath. His fingertips stroked her clit, eliciting a loud gasp from her lips.

"Shhhh," he whispered as he kissed the shell of her ear, covering her body completely with his own. "Quiet, remember?"

"I'm trying," she gasped as he pulled out and slowly pushed back in. "It's hard."

"It is, isn't it?" he whispered. "It's all for you. Only you."

Her eyes rolled back into her head as he increased his pace, each thrust just a little bit harder, a little bit deeper. He held her so tightly she could hardly breathe, but she relished the sensation, savoring the burn in her chest and the heat encasing her. It was smothering, and overpowering, as she let go, handing control over to him, tension and worry evaporating from her body. Sweat coated her, small patches of goose bumps trailing her skin from the cool breeze drifting in through the open outside door whenever he shifted position.

He said nothing else—neither of them did. There was nothing more to say. Genna buried herself into the sheets, choking back her cries of pleasure as he gave himself to her. She could feel it in every thrust, in every forceful slam of his hips into her, every strangled grunt that escaped his throat as he nuzzled into her neck. This wasn't lust. It was something else, something greater. This wasn't want; this was *need*, more so than she had ever felt before. It was despair, a drowning man desperate for air, a starving man scrounging for scraps to sustain him. He clung to her, like he held on for dear life, afraid of drifting away.

No, not lust. This was love.

And she knew, when his breathing grew ragged, his body shuddering, his grip somehow tightening even more, that it wasn't pleasure that drove him close to the edge. This was that agony he so desperately tried to hold back purging from beneath his skin. He cried out as he came, his tears sliding from his cheeks and hitting her damp skin, mingling with their sweat. Genna could feel it as he spilled inside of her, feel remnants of it running down her thighs as he stilled his movements. He violently shook, his arms beneath her trembling so hard it felt like an earthquake shook the bed. And she almost felt it in that moment, her oh-so-stable ground quaking and knocking her off her feet, taking both of them down together.

"I love you," she whispered, wishing there was something more she could do for him, something to ease his suffering.

How long had he been suffering, she wondered?

How much of it was her family's fault?

He barely restrained a sob at the sound of her words, inhaling deeply. His body shifted as he pulled out, loosening his hold on her. Genna rolled over onto her back beneath his body and looked up at him in the darkness. The second their eyes connected he looked away, dipping his head to avoid her gaze. Hiding from her.

Reaching up, she grasped his face and turned it toward her. Fingertips brushed his cheeks before he leaned down to lightly kiss her. The salty taste of tears lingered on his lips.

Something stirred inside of her then as she stared into his bloodshot, watery eyes, an ominous heaviness in the pit of her stomach. It had been there since that day on the street when she heard his name spoken for the first time.

He was a Barsanti...

...but maybe the Barsantis weren't the enemy.

His expression remained serious for a moment before softening, a small smile on his lips. "You really love me?"

"I do."

"I love you, too."

Her heart fluttered, skipping a beat at those words, before she let out a light laugh. "We're so fucking cliché."

"You think?"

"Yes," she said. "The first time we say it's during sex."

"Technically it's *after* sex."

"Same difference." She rolled her eyes. "Next thing you know you'll be running through an airport trying to stop me from leaving you, and then we'll kiss in the rain."

"But not before we break out into song, right?"

Her brow furrowed. "What?"

He shrugged. "They do that shit in movies all the time. They did it in *My Best Friend's Wedding*."

She gaped at him. "Disturbing."

"What?"

"Your knowledge of Julia Roberts movies."

Chuckling, Matty pulled away from her and stood up beside the bed, swaying a bit on his feet, still inebriated. The moonlight streaming through the open glass door cast a soft glow upon his naked flesh. Genna lay there, admiring him in the light as he turned to face her, cocking at eyebrow. He started to speak when a loud bang silenced him. Panicked, Genna's eyes darted toward the door as the knob jiggled and someone knocked, Dante's voice carrying through the flimsy wood.

"Genna, open up!" he hollered.

Her heart thudded like a bass drum in her chest as

she sprung to her feet in alarm. Snatching her dress from the floor, she quickly pulled it on as she shouted, "hold on, one second!"

"Hurry the hell up," he said, banging on the door.

Genna started gathering up Matty's clothes, thrusting them in his arms before pushing him toward her walk-in closet. "Hide."

He started to protest, but she silenced him with a quick kiss before launching his shoes toward him. She shut the closet door, concealing him inside, and paused to take a deep breath just as Dante started knocking again. Her hurried footsteps rushed toward the bedroom door as she smoothed out her hair and yanked on her dress. Unlocking it, she swung the door open, halting in the doorway to block her brother from stepping inside.

"What?" she barked, clutching tightly to the door, trying to force a look of annoyance on her face to keep him from seeing her panic.

Dante shoved her out the way to step into the room.

"Don't *what* me," he said, striding past. "You disappeared from the party."

"Well, here I am," she said, shrugging it off as she opened the door even wider, hoping he would take it as an invitation to leave as quickly as he had shown up. "Do you need something?"

"Nah," he said. "Dad was just wondering where you ran off to. I told him I'd come check on you."

Slowly, Genna stepped over to her bed and sat down on it, eyeing her brother peculiarly as he moseyed through her room, glancing around. His gaze shifted to the open sliding door and he headed that way, pushing it open further to step out on the balcony. Genna tensed, holding her breath as he approached the railing. *Please don't look down.*

"Uh, Genna?" Dante said, looking straight down. *Fuck.* "Why's there a ladder outside your window?"

"I don't know," she said. "Maybe the gardener left it out or something. You know I don't do yard work."

Dante shook his head as he strode back inside, brushing the raindrops from his hair while grumbling about incompetent workers. He nudged her as he strode past. "I'll tell Dad you've gone to sleep so he'll leave you be."

"Thanks," she muttered as he started for the door to leave. She watched his back, breathing a short-lived sigh of relief. As soon as he made it to the doorway, a loud thump echoed through the room. Genna inhaled sharply as Dante's footsteps faltered. He turned back around, eyes narrowed at her briefly before turning straight to the closet where the noise had come from. Seemed she wasn't the only one who struggled being quiet. "Are you alone?"

"Of course."

Dante's gaze bounced between her and the closet door, skeptical. "Is it Jackson? Jesus, Genna, tell me it's not Jackson, that you didn't sneak that idiot in here with Dad home."

"It's not," she said quickly as he stepped right back into the room. "It's nobody."

Dante walked straight toward the closet when Genna jumped to her feet. She darted toward her brother to stop him, but he shrugged her off, grasping the knob. She felt queasy as she frantically tried to pull her brother away, but he was undeterred.

Please be hiding, she thought. *Up on a shelf, in a fucking trunk, piled high with clothes... something. Anything. Don't let my brother see you.*

She chanted it in her head those few seconds when Dante hesitated, hoping Matty was smart enough to be out of sight, but her hope exploded when Dante flung the closet door open. Right in front of the doorway, barefooted and only half-dressed, his hair askew, stood Matty, his expression severe and shoulders squared as if preparing for a fight. Dante froze a mere few feet in front of him and blinked rapidly, momentarily stunned into silence, like he couldn't believe his eyes. Strained seconds passed, each one accented by the beat of Genna's terrified heart, as the two men who meant the most to her—her brother, and the one she had so willingly given her heart to—stared each other down with bitter hatred as if the world had been put on pause.

All at once, the impasse came to an end. Swiftly, in the blink of an eye, Dante reached into his waistband and whipped out the pistol he always carried. Genna let out a startled yep, tears stinging her eyes, as Matty slowly raised his hands in immediate surrender. Sober now, his eyes betrayed his stern expression, fear shining through as his panicked gaze flickered to hers.

"Dante, please," Genna pleaded, grabbing her brother's arm, but he seemed to hardly even register her presence. "Let me explain."

"Dad!" Dante shouted, so loud his voice cracked. Genna cringed, her ears ringing. Her panic intensified. "Get up here, Dad! Quick!"

No, no, no. "Please," she pleaded, shoving past Dante to wedge between the guys. She held her arms out defensively as she stood in front of Matty, her wide-eyes imploring her brother. "Please, Dante. Don't do this!"

"Move, Genna," Dante ground out, aiming right over her left shoulder… right at Matty's heart. "I don't want you to get hurt."

"I'm already hurt!"

That drove Dante's attention to her. "He hurt you?"

"No, *you're* hurting me," she said frantically, stepping to the side, her face lined straight up with the muzzle of her brother's gun. If he planned to shoot Matty, he would have to go through her first. "Please stop this, Dante. Don't do this!"

Dante's expression shifted, rage clouding his face. His free hand snatched ahold of Genna's arm so tightly she winced. Dante yanked her away, shoving her behind him, before he stepped toward Matty, gripping his pistol with both hands. Matty instinctively took a few steps back as Dante cornered him in the closet, trapping him. "I don't know what your plan here is, Barsanti, but it isn't going to work. You think you can poison my sister against us, that you can use her to get to us?"

"Dante!" Genna cried out, trying to stop him again, but he hardly wavered. He sounded just like Enzo. "Please, stop, for me!"

"You don't know what you're asking, Genna," Dante ground out before raising his voice once more. "He's one of *them*."

"You don't understand," Genna cried out, tears burning her eyes and streaming down her cheeks. "I love him, Dante! I *love* him!"

Those words caught Dante off guard for the second time that night. He faltered, turning his head slightly to gape at her. "You love him?"

"I do," she cried. "Don't do this, please. Please. You owe me."

"I *owe* you?"

"You said you owed me, that anything I needed, all I had to do was ask," she said. "So I'm asking... I'm begging... *please* don't do this."

Dante hesitated as the sound of footsteps neared, ascending the stairs.

"Dante?" their father called out. "Where are you?"

"Please," Genna whispered, her voice quaking. "For me."

Dante took a step back, eyeing Matty hard for a moment before looking away and lowering the gun. "In Genna's room, Dad."

Before Genna could protest, Dante stepped out of the closet and shut the door with Matty still inside. Genna wiped her face, shaking as their father's footsteps hurried down the hall. He stepped into the doorway, pausing as he assessed his children. "What's going on in here?"

"It was just a mistake," Dante said. "Thought I saw a rat."

Primo's brow furrowed. "A rat?"

"Yeah, a rat."

Primo stared at him briefly before his eyes turned to the gun in his hand. "And you were going to what? Shoot it?"

Dante forced out a laugh as he slipped the gun back away. "Force of habit. Like I said, though, it was a mistake. Right, Genna?"

"Yes," she whispered. "A big mistake."

"Ah." Primo glanced between them, his gaze settling on Genna. "You okay, sweetheart? You're flushed."

"I'm not feeling well," she said. At least it wasn't a lie. Bile burned her chest. She wanted to throw up.

"Well, get some sleep," Primo said. "I'll tell the men you said goodnight. And I'll call an exterminator tomorrow, you know, to make sure there aren't any rats. I fucking hate them."

"Thanks," she said, closing her eyes with relief when her father walked away. Nobody said anything, the attention focused on the sound of footsteps as they descended the stairs again. Once he was gone, Dante reopened the closet door and stood between Genna and Matty, severe eyes bouncing between them, scolding, judging.

"You get him the hell out of here," Dante spat. "And don't you ever ask me to do that again, Genna. I'd do anything for you—you know that—but you can't ask me to do this. You can't ask me to *accept* this."

"I'm sorry," she whispered as her brother started walking away.

"You will be," he said, matter-of-fact. "If you don't stay away from him, Genna, you *will* be sorry."

"Don't threaten her." Matty's voice made Genna flinch as he stepped out of the closet, protectively wrapping an arm around her waist and pulling her to him.

"I'm not threatening her," Dante said angrily, eyes narrowed at Matty. "The only threat to her here is *you*, Barsanti."

"I'd never hurt her," Matty said.

"Maybe not," Dante said. "But that doesn't mean you wouldn't *get* her hurt. I dare you to deny that. I dare you to fucking deny that being with you won't get her hurt."

"I'll protect her."

"Maybe you believe that," Dante said, "but I learned long ago not to trust my family's safety around a Barsanti, and I'm not going to ignore that now, no matter how much my sister begs me."

Dante stormed out, not even looking at Genna again.

She stood there for a moment, trying to get her heart to slow down, as she seemed to melt back into Matty's embrace.

"This is going to get us killed, isn't it?" she whispered.

Matty let out an exasperated sigh as he held her tighter. She hoped he'd contradict her, say something to set her mind at ease, but instead he mumbled a response that made her stomach sink.

"Probably."

chapter THIRTEEN

Before Savina Barsanti was even lowered into the ground that dreary summer afternoon, plans were set into motion, sparking flames of animosity that had been smoldering for years. After nightfall, as Matty sought support in Genna's embrace, found solace in her warm flesh, the fight between their families violently rekindled as both sides crossed borders under the cloak of darkness, sneaking and scheming, stealing and stalking.

Slaughtering.

Come morning, when the smoke cleared from that first night of destruction, leaving usually quiet parts of Manhattan suddenly tainted by violence, the first blood had already been spilled.

Two Galante soldiers lay dead on the grungy asphalt in Soho, just a few blocks from The Place, gunned down as they crossed the street. Nobody knew where they were going, or what they were doing on that side of town. They'd been killed on sight, no questions asked, for merely venturing into enemy territory.

War had been declared.

Trucks were hijacked and stores were broken into, people assaulted and others robbed. It went on, night after night, no corner safe from murder and mayhem.

Matty sat at his usual table in The Place a few weeks later, eyes peeled on his notebook as he worked out the statistics in the margin of the paper, ensuring he was still ahead of the game. The Blackberry on the table in front of him rang and rang, but he ignored it, just as he ignored the men gathered around the tables and along the bar, waiting for their chance to place a bet for the weekend.

It was half past ten... he was already thirty minutes behind.

"Are you going to answer that?" Enzo asked exasperatedly from the seat across from him, motioning toward the still ringing Blackberry.

"No."

Enzo stared at him, his gaze piercing. "Are you almost done?"

"No."

"Are you ever going to get around to taking bets tonight?"

The word "no" was on the tip of Matty's tongue, but he swallowed it back. He would... eventually. Just not now.

"You've been slacking off lately," Enzo said, picking up his beer and taking a sip of it. "Dad's not happy about it."

"Yeah, well, instead of the unwanted promotion, I'm hoping he'll send me a pink slip."

Enzo laughed dryly. "Dad's pink slips come in the form of bullets to the brain."

"I know," Matty muttered, tossing his pen down and glancing around the bar, skimming right over the studious waiting eyes to look for the waitress. He spotted her, motioning for her to bring him a drink, before turning to his brother. "It's a twenty-cent line again this week."

Enzo guzzled the last of his beer. "You can count me out."

"Why?" Matty asked. "Afraid you'll lose?"

"Hell yeah," Enzo said. "And if there's anything I've learned, it's that I hate losing a hell of a lot more than I enjoy winning."

Shrugging, Matty reached for the Blackberry, picking up the ringing phone as Enzo stood up and walked away. Matty answered the phone with an exasperated sigh. "Yeah?"

There was no small talk. The men blurted out their bets and Matty jotted them down, knowing names the second he heard their voices. In between calls, others from the bar came by, making bets in person, handing their money over for Enzo to keep. It was methodic and tedious, Matty's mind wandering as he kept tallies of the bets and the running totals in case he needed to adjust his figures.

A few minutes before midnight, he shut it down, tearing out the page of bets and slipping it across the table to Enzo. The waitress sauntered over, bringing him another drink without him having to order one as his brother scanned the list.

"Start late, end early." Enzo folded the paper and put it in his pocket for safekeeping. "Your heart's just not into it anymore, is it?"

It never was, Matty thought, sipping his drink. "Too much else on my mind."

Enzo nodded knowingly, his cautious gaze shifting around the bar. "Nobody knows yet, if that's what you're worried about."

Yet. The key word, one that made Matty's head hurt

just acknowledging it. Nobody around there had figured out
about him and Genna yet, but it was only a matter of time
before the wrong person caught wind of it. They had
intentionally stayed away from each other the past few weeks,
knowing it was too dangerous to risk being caught together
again right now, but it was wearing on his nerves,
uncomfortably burrowing under his skin. Some short, vague
text messages and a few whispered, rushed phone calls did
nothing to satiate him when he needed *her*.

But he couldn't have her, not now, not when their
families were on guard, watching their every move in an
attempt to protect them, and he was starting to wonder if he
could truly have her *ever*.

*Not as long as our families are dead-set on killing each
other.*

"I can tell you haven't seen her," Enzo said.

"How?"

"You're more of a tightass than usual," Enzo
muttered. "I'm starting to see why you like each other.
You're both moody bitches."

"En," Matty warned, glaring at him. "Don't start."

"I'm just saying, you've been mopey as hell, and I get
it... it fucking sucks, bro. Trust me. I don't like this shit,
either. But you're getting on my nerves with this *poor me*
attitude."

"Trade places with me and see how you deal."

Enzo laughed dryly. "First of all, I wouldn't be in
your shoes, because I wouldn't be stupid enough to fall for
Medusa."

"En..."

He held his hands up. "She's ballsy, I'll give her that,
and I wasn't lying when I said she was badass. But the fact

remains… she's a Galante. And maybe you enjoy this whole star-crossed Shakespearian bullshit romance, maybe that appeals to you. To each their own. But don't dive headfirst in it and then try that *poor me* bullshit out on me. They call it tragedy for a reason. It can't end well. I know it, you know it, everyone fucking knows it, so start acting like it."

"What the hell am I supposed to do?" Matty ground out, gripping his glass so tightly his knuckles hurt from the strain.

"Something," Enzo said. "Anything."

"That's easy for you to say."

"Yeah, *easy*." Enzo shook his head as he stood up to leave. "It's real fucking easy, helping to break my brother's heart by taking from him what he loves… *again*. No sweat off my fucking back, right?"

Genna stirred the corn chowder around in the massive pot, ladling what was left of the goopy, puke-colored mixture into the disposable cups and sending them down the line. It was nearing seven o'clock, but she was in no rush to leave, no rush to go home.

She couldn't see outside the community center from where she stood behind the partition, but she knew what was out there, awaiting her. Dante would be lingering, parked right out front, leaning against the passenger side of his car to take her straight home for dinner.

And he wouldn't be alone. Others were positioned around the neighborhood, human shields, guarding the area from any unwanted visitors. Her father was having her followed, people watching her like a hawk every time she stepped foot outside of the house. He'd gone so far as to try to have her punishment lifted, her community service signed off on so she wouldn't have to venture away from the house anymore, but she insisted on going anyway.

Maybe it was stubbornness. Maybe it was to piss her father off.

Or maybe it was because, foolishly, she hoped Matty would find a way to come by undetected.

Seven o'clock rolled around, the food already gone for the day. Genna untied her apron and pulled it off, tossing it in the hamper. Instead of heading for the door, however, she grabbed the empty pot and lugged it back into the kitchen.

"Heading out?" the coordinator asked.

Genna shook her head. "I'd rather stick around."

"You don't have to."

"I know."

Truth was, as much as she used to look forward to hanging out with her brother, as much as she used to cherish their time together, just the few minutes in the car with him now was practically unbearable. The strain between them was suffocating, ever since Dante had discovered her secret. When he looked at her, she could see the judgment in his eyes, the disgust, the lack of comprehension of how she could love someone like *that*, someone like Matteo Barsanti.

You don't know him, Genna thought every time her brother looked at her that way, but she never said it. He wouldn't understand. He couldn't. His animosity ran deep, cemented inside of him by the thickened scars on his chest.

She washed dishes and wiped down tables, helping out every way possible, until she was out of excuses to stick around. It neared ten o'clock when she finally strolled toward the door and stepped outside, her eyes immediately drawn to Dante. He still stood there, pacing the sidewalk in front of his car, the streetlight shining down on him. He was on his phone talking to someone, his voice quiet yet firm.

Turning, he caught sight of Genna standing there and paused, opening the passenger door for her to get in the car as he continued his call. Once she was inside, he slammed the door and climbed in behind the wheel.

"No, don't worry about it," he said into the phone, his voice strained. "I'm sure… I'll head over now and handle it."

He hung up, letting out an annoyed groan as he tossed the phone aside and started up the car.

"Problem?" Genna asked hesitantly.

"You could say that," he muttered, swinging the car around in traffic. "I need to go to Little Italy."

"You can drop me off at home first."

"Nobody's at home."

"So?"

"So," he said, "I'm not dropping you off there alone."

"Are you kidding me? I can't even be home by myself?"

"Not right now, no. It's not safe."

"You're being paranoid."

"And you're *way* too fucking trusting, Genna." He cut his eyes at her, that familiar abhorrence in his expression. "For all I know, this could just be a diversion, their way to get you alone, to isolate you, so they can get to you without one of us being around."

Genna rolled her eyes and crossed her arms over her chest, a small part of her wishing that were so. At least then she would know it was possible to see Matty again. It had been so long—*too* long.

Dante sped through the streets, heading south to Little Italy. Despite it being dark out and most places closed for the night, the neighborhood was alive with action. People hung out on the corners, buildings lit up, music blaring and cars whizzing around the streets. Dante sped past the little café and turned onto Mulberry Street, pulling the car into the first parking spot along the street that he came to.

"Wait here," Dante said, his tone serious. "Whatever you do, Genna, do not get out of this car."

She didn't humor him with a response as she slouched down in the seat, mock saluting him instead. Dante got out, slamming the door, using his keys to lock the doors behind him. Genna laid her head back and closed her eyes, letting out a deep sigh. She felt like a little kid with the way her family was treating her. *Ridiculous.*

A few minutes passed before there was a commotion outside, raised voices down the block. Opening her eyes, Genna glanced out the windshield, vaguely making out her brother shouting at someone. She sat up, suddenly alert, as Dante shoved someone in front of the music store. The man stumbled backward a few steps from the unexpected strike, and Genna caught sight of a face in the glow of the streetlight.

Enzo.

"Oh, shit."

The moment Genna breathed those words, chaos erupted. Dante stepped forward, still shouting, prepared to strike again, but Enzo was ready that time. He swung, his fist connecting with Dante's jaw and sending him stumbling. Before he could get his footing again, before he could counter, Enzo pounced at him, brutally knocking Dante to the sidewalk and landing on top of him, pounding him with his fists.

Genna's heart stalled a beat, momentarily freezing her in her seat, but the moment it kicked back in gear, hammering hard in her chest, she was *gone*. She swung the passenger door open, not even thinking twice, and jumped right out of the car into the street. A horn blared, a car swerving as it sped past her, narrowly missing taking off the car door and hitting her. She slammed the door and ran up onto the sidewalk, out of harm's way as tires squealed. A car skidded to an abrupt stop, and Genna stared at it, her vision blurring as she blinked rapidly at the sight of the familiar red Lotus.

It idled in the middle of the street, the driver's side door opening. Matty jumped out and sprinted onto the sidewalk, heading right for where their brothers rolled on the ground, scuffling.

No. No. God, please, don't get involved.

A small crowd quickly gathered, people nearby hearing the ruckus and coming to investigate. Dante managed to get the upper hand long enough to punch Enzo in the face, the force knocking him into someone from the crowd, who backed up a few steps. Dante climbed to his feet and lunged then, striking at Enzo feverishly, just as Matty forced his way through the onlookers to reach the two of them. He tried to jump between them, taking a blow to the cheek from Dante's swinging fists, but Enzo blocked his brother in an attempt to fight back. The two went at it, undeterred, despite Matty's attempts at intervening.

"Stop it!" Genna shouted, squeezing through the crowd. "Stop!"

The sound of her voice distracted her brother, who instinctively glanced her way. "Get back in the car, Genna."

Before he even had the sentence completely out, Enzo attacked, taking advantage of her interference. He hit Dante so hard blood flew, a sickening crunch echoing through the crowd from Dante's nose. He stumbled, hitting the ground hard, as Enzo landed on top of him again.

Genna cursed, shoving people out of her way, but before she could reach them someone grabbed her from behind. She screamed, trying to fight off the arms wrapping around her, until the soft voice whispered in her ear. "Calm down, princess."

Matty.

"Stop them," she cried, tears stinging her eyes. "Do something!"

"I am doing something," Matty said, pulling her away from the horde. "I'm getting you out of here."

Those words didn't quite strike her until he dragged her into the street, not loosening his hold as they approached the Lotus. She tried to fight him off again then. What was he doing? "No, wait, stop! We have to stop *them*!"

"There is no stopping them," he said, opening the passenger door of his car and pushing her inside. She struggled, but he was stronger, forcing her into the seat and slamming the door. She reopened it to get back out as he climbed in beside her, but before she could get a foot out, he threw the car in gear and sped away. Startled, Genna slammed the door again and gaped at him. "What are you doing? Why are we leaving?"

"I need to get you out of here."

"What? Why?"

"Really, Genna? Why? You're seriously asking me *why*?"

"But we have to stop them!" Why wasn't he grasping

that fact? "They'll kill each other!"

"No, they won't" Matty said, sighing with frustration as he sped west through Little Italy. "There are way too many witnesses for that to happen. They'll just beat the hell out of each other until they get tired."

She stared at Matty, horrified, a sense of disbelief settling over her. She watched as he rubbed his jaw, swelling from Dante's punch. She felt dizzy, the surge of adrenalin nauseating her.

"I'm gonna be sick," she said, covering her mouth as the bile burned her throat. Matty cut his eyes at her before pulling the car along the side of the road and throwing it in park. She opened the door, barely having time to lean out before she lost it, purging everything from her stomach.

"You okay?" he asked when she closed the door again and settled back into the seat. She nodded, putting the window down and taking a deep breath, the smell of leather overwhelming her. Tears blurred her vision as she shook, trying to get herself under control. Matty glanced at her, frowning, and reached over to wipe the tears from her cheeks. "It'll be fine, Genna. I promise."

She reached up, placing her hand over his as his fingertips brushed against her skin. It felt like she hadn't seen him in forever, much less felt his touch. Matty gave her a soft smile, sympathy darkening his eyes in the dim car.

He drove straight to Soho, parking in his reserved spot in the garage, and grabbed her hand as he helped her out of the car. They hurried past The Place and he led her straight up to his apartment, not letting go of her until they were safely inside. Genna was shaking as she started pacing around the living room, Matty's words rushing over her but not sinking in. She just kept picturing Dante hitting the ground, seeing the blood fly, and hearing the crack of bone from Enzo's vicious fist. Again and again, over and over.

"They're going to kill each other," she kept repeating, running her hands down her face before gripping tightly to her hair in frustration. "Those two are going to fucking kill each other, Matty."

"No, they won't," he reassured her, holding out a bottle of water and encouraging her to drink. "Not tonight, anyway."

She scoffed, shoving his hand away as she ignored the drink. *Reassuring.*

Time moved in a blur, each tick of the clock agonizing as she continually watched the time. Mere minutes had passed, but it felt like an eternity as she waited. What was she waiting for? She wasn't sure…

…until the apartment door swung open.

Genna gasped as Enzo strolled in, his lip busted and nose bleeding, his jaw swelling and eye starting to bruise. He was alive. Oh God, was Dante? Queasiness rushed through her, her stomach violently twisting. "I'm gonna be sick again."

Matty shoved his bedroom door open, motioning inside. Genna ran into the room, looking around frantically, and made it to the connecting bathroom just in time. She dropped to her knees on the floor and violently heaved, over and over, until her stomach painfully cramped and she felt like she might pass out.

Matty gave her a few minutes before strolling into the bathroom and crouching down beside her. He brushed the hair from her face and she blinked rapidly, the smell of his cologne washing over her and making her dizzy.

"You're awfully pale," he said, cupping her chin as he

eyed her intently.

"Yeah, well, your cologne's strong," she muttered. "What did you do, bathe in it?"

His expression softened as he stared in her eyes, once more offering her the bottle of water. She took it that time, sitting on the bathroom floor, and slowly sipped the cold liquid. It soothed her throat, washing the bitterness from her mouth.

"So, uh," she mumbled. "I guess your brother survived."

"He did," Matty agreed. "Yours did, too."

"Did he?"

"Yes," he replied. "They both survived... just like I said they would."

"So, he's okay? Dante?"

"Well, he's about as okay as Enzo is."

"He looked kinda fucked up."

"He is," he agreed. "They beat the hell out of each other... just like I said they would."

"Yeah, yeah," Genna said, waving him off as she took another sip of the water. "I get it—you know everything."

Matty laughed dryly at that. "I wish that were true. Then I'd know what to do now."

"You mean what to do about me?"

"Exactly," he replied. "What am I gonna do about you, princess?"

She gazed at him, her stomach finally settling down as she inhaled through her mouth and exhaled through her nose, taking slow and steady breaths. "Love me," she whispered.

Matty smiled, reaching over and brushing the back of his hand along her flushed cheek. "I already do."

He started to lean toward her but Genna balked, moving away as she quickly held her hands up to stop him. Matty froze, brow furrowing at her reaction.

"Ugh," she said, motioning toward her mouth as she made a face. "Trust me, you don't want to kiss this mouth right now. It's disgusting."

He stood up and grabbed her hand to help her up off the bathroom floor. "Brush your teeth if it'll make you feel better."

"I don't have a toothbrush."

"Use mine."

"Ugh, gross."

"You can kiss me, but you can't use my toothbrush?"

"I *kiss* you, not pick the food from your teeth."

He laughed as he stepped by her, rooting around in a drawer until he pulled out some brand new toothbrushes. He held them up. "Blue, green, or orange?"

She stared at them. "Uh, blue."

He tossed the other two back into the drawer and held the blue one out to her. "There you go."

"Why do you have so many spare toothbrushes?" she asked, gazing at it.

"I like to buy things in bulk."

"What else do you buy in bulk, Mr. Thrifty?"

"Everything."

"Like?"

"Like tissues, bottled water, toothpaste... condoms."

She looked at him peculiarly. "Use a lot of condoms, do you?"

"Seems that way."

"Huh. You use many this past month and some change?"

He stared at her, the amusement gone from his eyes. "Not a single one. Haven't used one since, well... since the last time we used one."

She felt silly standing there, her insecurities stirring up at such a moment, but she couldn't help herself. She had to ask, had to know, without coming out and asking him directly. They'd never exactly talked about it before, choosing to live in the moment instead of dwelling on the past or trying to figure out the future. Did they have a future, she wondered? Did he want one?

"What *are* you going to do about me, Matty?" she asked, surprised by the vulnerability in her voice.

"Brush your teeth," he said quietly, taking a step back, "then come find out."

He stepped out of the bathroom, shutting the door behind him to give her some privacy. Genna brushed her teeth, trying to pull herself together, before glancing at her reflection. Her eyes were bloodshot, her face puffy from crying, every stitch of makeup wiped off or smeared. Sighing, she splashed water on her face, washing the rest of it away, and dried off with a towel before heading into Matty's bedroom.

He stood beside his bed, wearing nothing but a pair of black boxer briefs. Instinctively, Genna's gaze scanned him, taking in every inch of his body with her eyes. He wasn't overly strong, but he wasn't at all weak, his body formed just right—not too soft, not too hard. It was a body that made her feel secure, yet a body that made her so susceptible. When he held her, she felt as tall as a mountain, a force of nature, unstoppable and undeniable, yet a mere look from him made her feel as fragile as tissue paper, like the simplest wrong touch could tear her to pieces.

Matty held his arms out to her, and Genna didn't even hesitate, sliding right into his embrace.

"I've missed you," she said quietly.

"I missed you, too," he replied, kissing the top of her head. "It's been killing me, not seeing you... not knowing when I'd be able to see you again."

"My father's had me on lockdown."

"I know." Matty tilted her chin and softly kissed her lips, pulling back after a second and grimacing. "You're right."

Her expression fell. "What?"

"You taste like mint. *Disgusting.*"

Genna rolled her eyes, elbowing him as he laughed. "Funny."

"You want something to sleep in?" he asked, loosing his hold on her to motion toward his large dresser along the side. "I'm sure there's something in there you can wear."

"Sleep?" she asked hesitantly. "That's what you plan to do with me?"

He nodded. "I plan to do everything with you, actually, and one thing we've yet to do is *sleep* together."

As much as she loved hearing those words, her heart dropped at what sleeping together meant. There was a reason they hadn't done it, why they'd never been able to spend an entire night together before. "My family... they'll be looking for me."

"I don't doubt it."

"Dante will know exactly where to look," she said. "He knows about you... about *us.* He'll know I'm with you."

"I don't doubt that, either."

"He might tell." She believed Dante wouldn't tell on her just to tell—that wasn't his nature, at all—but if he thought she was in danger, if he thought her life was on the line, he would certainly spill what he knew. "You know, tell my father."

"Wouldn't surprise me a bit."

"So we shouldn't... I mean, we can't..."

"You're right that we shouldn't. But I won't agree that we *can't*. We can, and I want to. I want to, because I want *you*, and I'm tired of not having you. I'm tired of staying away from you, of *avoiding* you. You're the last person I want to avoid." Sighing, Matty sat down on the end of his bed and grabbed Genna's hips, pulling her toward him. She stood between his legs, looking down at him as he gazed up at her, his expression serious. "Look, Genna, I'm giving you a choice... I'll take you home right now, make sure you're warm in your own bed tonight, where I'm sure your family will do everything in their power to protect you. I'll do that if that's what you want."

"Or?"

"Or you can stay here," he said. "Stay with me tonight, sleep in my bed, be with *me*. And I guarantee you, if you stay, *I'll* keep you safe. I'll protect you, no matter what. I won't let anything happen to you. But I can't be with you, Genna, and not be *with* you anymore."

"But who's going to protect you?" she asked. "Who's going to keep *you* safe?"

"You stepped in front of me when I had a loaded gun pointed at my chest," he said. "I think I'll be just fine."

She pondered over that as she gazed at him. He meant every word of it. She could tell, believed it deep down in her soul, and although it terrified her still, what staying with him meant for her... for him... for *them*, she knew there wasn't really a choice to make. Staying with him meant choosing him.

Hadn't she'd already chosen him?

"I don't need any clothes to sleep," she said, leaning down to softly kiss him.

"No?"

"No," she whispered against his lips. "I like to sleep naked."

He chuckled, grasping her hips tighter as he pulled her closer to him. "You'll hear no complaints from me."

Genna grasped the hem of her shirt and pulled it over her head, tossing it on the floor by her feet. Matty leaned over, trailing soft kisses along her stomach as his hands shifted forward, slowly unbuttoning her pants and sliding the zipper down. He tugged on the pants, pulling them down, and Genna kicked them off along with her shoes, leaving her in nothing but her black bra and lacy underwear. His hands roamed her skin, exploring, caressing, as he gazed at her soft flesh under the bright lights. He stared at her as if he were memorizing every curve, studying every mark, and line, and goose bump that coated her body, leaving no inch of her unexplored.

Without another word, Matty tugged her onto the bed with him.

chapter FOURTEEN

Genna's heart painfully hammered in her chest, feverishly racing and banging against her ribcage to the rhythm of the music vibrating the car's speakers.

Thump-thump. Thump-thump. Thump-thump.

Matty drove through Manhattan, flowing with traffic as he headed north. She had never seen him go the speed limit before.

Didn't think the Lotus went this damn slow.

He was nervous, distractedly drumming his fingers against the steering wheel as he obsessively checked his mirrors, monitoring the cars around them. Genna could feel the tension radiating from him, although he kept his expression blank, his shoulders relaxed so not to alarm her.

Senseless, really. She was on edge. Nothing would calm her down.

"You don't have to do this," she said quietly, once again trying to give him the chance to back out.

"I'm not afraid, Genna," he replied.

You ought to be, she thought. *I sure as hell am.*

As if he could somehow sense her thoughts, Matty

reached over and grasped her hand, gently squeezing it in an attempt to reassure her.

Genna stared out the side window as the streets became more familiar to her, ones she ventured on day in and day out, the Lotus creeping through the core of Galante territory. Her heart somehow managed to pound even harder then, thrashing in her ears, the heated flow of blood making her feel sick.

Ugh, please don't puke again.

She pinched the bridge of her nose as she closed her eyes, trying to ease the sensation.

"It's going to be okay," Matty said. He sounded like he really believed it. "Trust me."

"I do."

Genna reopened her eyes as they headed into Westchester County, heading straight for the Galante residence. The Lotus slowed even more, pausing in the street for a few seconds before turning onto the driveway that led to her house. Dante's car was right near the front door, parked crookedly as if hastily abandoned.

Matty stopped a few yards away, putting the Lotus in park and turning to her. Silence surrounded them as they sat there for a moment, the engine purring as the car idled.

"Do you need me to walk you in?"

She scoffed. "Definitely not. I should, you know… face them alone. They're going to be upset enough, but maybe I can calm them down if, you know…"

"If they don't have to look at my face."

"Exactly."

As gorgeous as she found that face, she knew the sight of it would send her family into a rage.

"Well, call me if you need me," he said, staring at the

front door of the house as it opened. Dante stepped out onto the porch. "If you need *anything*. I'll come get you, okay? Anytime, day or night. I mean it."

"I will," she said, leaning over and quickly kissing him before getting out. She walked toward the front door, her arms nervously wrapped around her chest. She could sense Matty's concerned gaze on her from behind, while Dante's fierce stare burned through her from the porch.

Slowly, the Lotus backed away before disappearing down the street. Genna stepped up onto the porch, avoiding looking at her brother, and tried to waltz right past him when he stepped in her path. Glancing up, she froze when her eyes connected with Dante's.

He looked *rough*. Cuts and bruises marred his tanned skin, his nose badly swollen. The sight of his obvious injuries made her chest ache. "Dante, I—"

Before she could get the words out, to tell him she was sorry if she worried him, to tell him she didn't want to fight, to tell him she loved him and never meant to hurt him with any of this, he snatched a hold of her and yanked her to him, hugging her tightly as he let out a deep breath. "Fuck, Genna, don't scare me like that."

"I'm fine," she insisted, hugging him, lightly rubbing his back. "I was, uh..."

"You were with him," Dante said. "I told you to wait in the car and instead you ran off with *him*."

"I just..." She was at a loss for words, unable to force out a complete thought. "Did you...? Is Dad...?"

"He's in his office," Dante said. "Hasn't been to sleep, was up all night waiting for some sign from you."

Genna sighed, pulling away. "You told him."

There was no accusation in her tone. It was merely

matter of fact, and she had expected no less.

"I was worried," he said, his voice low.

"I know," she whispered. "I'm fine, though."

For now.

Genna headed inside, hesitating in the foyer. Part of her wanted to rush upstairs, to camp out in her bedroom and hide beneath her covers for the rest of eternity, but she knew the longer she put it off, the worse it would be. She had to face her father. She had to face reality.

Taking a deep breath to steady herself, she walked to his office and knocked on the door before pushing it open. Her father sat on the couch right inside and looked up at her as she entered, his expression so harsh, so *unforgiving*, it was as if his face had been chiseled from a block of rigid stone.

"Matteo Barsanti," he said coldly.

"Matty," she said, her voice hardly above a whisper.

"Matty," he growled. "*That's* your Matty?"

"Yes."

He stared at her in silence, not softening a bit, intense rage focused straight on her as she stood there, fidgeting.

"Do you hate me, Genevieve?" he asked finally, his voice dropping a pitch, low and menacing. "Do you hate our family that much?"

"No." She shook her head. "I don't hate you at all."

"You must, to turn your back on us," he said. "To turn your back on me, on your brother... your *brothers*. All of us! That family... they killed Joey. My Joey, my boy! They stole him from me, from *us*, and you're in cahoots with them! With the enemy!"

"I'm not!" she said. "I'm not in cahoots with anybody."

"Don't lie to me, girl!" Primo stood up, pointing his

finger at her, his face twitching from the anger surging through him. The sight of it made Genna instinctively step back. Her father was a dangerous man. She wasn't at all in the dark about that. "I know you've been with that boy, that you've had secret meetings with him, that you've sought him out behind our backs. You've betrayed us!"

"This isn't about you! It has nothing to do with you, or this family, or their family! This is about me, about him."

"He's one of *them*!"

She threw her hands up in frustration. "Oh, who gives a fuck?"

"I do!" He moved toward her quickly, eliciting another retreat from Genna. "And if you cared anything about this family, it would matter to you, too. He's no good... he's poison! And you're drinking it, you're letting him infect you!"

"I love him!" she shouted, the words tearing from her chest, unable to be contained. They seemed to echo through the room and hit her father so hard he flinched. "And I'm sorry if that upsets you... if that hurts you... but I do. I love him, and nothing you say or do can change that."

"You're wrong."

Genna's blood seemed to run cold at his words, his voice suddenly dropping low again.

"You're playing a game of Russian Roulette with that boy," he continued, staring at her. "You might get lucky, you might come out unscathed a few times, but the odds are never *always* in your favor. All it takes is once... one time... for your finger to be on that trigger when that bullet is in the chamber. And then you won't come home anymore."

"Maybe so," she said. "But given that this isn't *my* war, I guess it was *you* who loaded the gun in the first place."

He glared at her, his rage never lessening. After a moment he looked away with a grimace, like he couldn't stomach the sight of her anymore, and pointed toward the ceiling. "Go to your room."

"I'm not one of your men," she said. "You can't boss me around."

"You're my daughter."

"I'm an adult."

"As long as you live under my roof, Genevieve, you'll follow my rules."

"Then maybe it's time for me to move out."

He cut his eyes at her again and there, past the anger and resentment, she finally saw something else shining through. *Fear.* She had never quite seen her father afraid before. The sight of it startled her.

"Go to your room," he said again, running his hands down his face, his voice hedging on pleading.

Genna backed out of the room, turning around to head for the stairs, and nearly ran straight into Dante. He had been lurking behind her, listening. He said nothing, stepping out of the way to let her pass, before taking her place in their father's office and gently closing the door.

Matty strolled into The Place, ordering a Roman Coke from the bartender before heading for the back of the bar, where Enzo sat, studiously counting money from the week's take. Tens, twenties, fifties, hundreds… stacks of cash covered the table in front of him, crinkled and worn.

Blood money.

Matty slid into the seat across from him, sighing as he

sipped his drink. Enzo cut his eyes at him briefly, never losing his place, continuing counting even as he addressed his brother. "Where have you been?"

Matty shrugged. "Dropped Genna off at home."

"At home."

"Yeah," Matty said. "Home."

Enzo shook his head, turning to another stack to count. "You really do have a death wish, don't you?"

"I wouldn't call it a wish," Matty said. "It's more of a disinterest."

"Disinterest."

"Yes."

"I hate to break it to you, bro, but you ain't gotta be *interested* in death for it to find you."

"Death has been after me since I was young," Matty said. "It doesn't matter what I do... when it's ready to find me, it will."

"Yeah, well, you don't have to draw it a fucking *map*."

Despite himself, Matty laughed at that, picking his glass up and taking another sip. Enzo continued counting, sorting out bills in silence, arranging them in different stacks before shoving them in envelopes. He pushed one across the table toward Matty, who picked it up and stuck it in his back pocket.

"I still owe you about a grand," Enzo said, collecting the rest of the envelopes before standing up. "Have a few people that still need to pay up. I'll get to them later today, but first I have to head up north for a bit."

North. Galante territory. "Why?"

"*Why* is never a good question to ask," Enzo said, slapping his brother on the back as he walked past. "You'll never get the answer you want to hear."

"Why?"

Enzo laughed, glancing over his shoulder at him. "Trust me, you don't want to know."

He didn't. He was smart enough to realize that. Whatever they were up to, he wanted nothing more than to stay out of it, and to keep Genna far, far away from the danger.

Sighing, he set his glass down and pulled out his phone, glancing at the screen. She hadn't called yet, so that was promising. If she didn't need him, she must be okay.

I hope, anyway.

After finishing what was left of his drink, he stood back up and headed for the door. As soon as he stepped outside, the sound of his brother's voice captured his attention as he spoke animatedly to someone along the curb. Matty glanced over, surprised that Enzo hadn't left the neighborhood yet, and froze when he caught a familiar gaze.

His father.

"Matteo," Roberto said, stalling Enzo mid-sentence as he diverted the attention straight to Matty. Others surrounded them, some Matty didn't know, with the Civello brothers lingering off to the side, waiting.

Without speaking, Matty nodded at his father in greeting, not having much to say to the man. They hadn't shared more than a handful of words in over a month, not since the night of his mother's funeral. She had been their connection, their last tendril of true relationship, and without her they felt like nothing more than strangers who happened to share a name.

"I heard something fascinating this morning," Roberto said. "Something about the Galante girl."

"Yeah?" Matty feigned ignorance as he kept his expression blank. "What's that?"

"Why don't you tell me, son?"

Matty shook his head. "Nothing to tell."

"Ah, so you're *not* seeing her?"

A frigid silence followed that question as everyone within earshot stiffened, questioning gazes darting straight to Matty, awaiting his response. He stood there on the sidewalk, staring right at his father as sweat beaded along his forehead at the intensity of which he stared back.

"So what if I am?"

Matty's shoulders squared, his muscles tensing as he prepared for an argument, prepared to defend himself to his father, to defend *Genna*, but instead of lashing out, Roberto's expression lit up, a smirk tugging his lips that he didn't even bother containing. Within a matter of seconds, he full on grinned, a light chuckle escaping.

Matty's blood ran cold. He would have preferred fury. This was a man tickled with amusement, like it was nothing more than a big joke to him. "I don't see what the hell is so funny."

"Funny, no," Roberto said, "but definitely interesting."

He turned away from Matty, his attention going back to Enzo as he motioned with his head for him to leave. Enzo nodded, acknowledging their silent conversation, as Roberto walked away to get in a waiting car. The others scattered as Enzo lingered there, waiting until everyone else was gone before sighing. "I swear I didn't tell. The Civello brothers heard it on the streets… Galante had word out last night, looking for his daughter. Spread like wildfire that she was somewhere with you."

"It doesn't matter," Matty said, eyeing his brother peculiarly. "Why are you heading up north, En?"

"Thought we covered this," Enzo said.

"We did, but I changed my mind," Matty said. "I wanna know now."

Enzo pulled out his keys, dangling them up so they jangled. "Come along and find out then."

chapter FIFTEEN

The smell of marinara hung in the air, infiltrating Genna's lungs and making her stomach growl with every breath she took. It was late, well after nine o'clock, everything from dinner cleaned up and the staff gone for the day.

She hadn't come down for dinner, figuring it was best to just stay in her room, and her father hadn't sent Dante after her. But it got to be too much after a while, her hunger getting the best of her. She had breakfast that morning with Matty, then had lunch with him that afternoon before he brought her home, yet she felt like she hadn't eaten in days.

Strolling into the quiet kitchen, she opened the refrigerator and peered inside, shifting some containers around, seeking out whatever they'd had tonight. "Ugh, why isn't there anything to eat?"

"There's plenty to eat."

She startled at the interruption and looked across the kitchen at Dante in the doorway. "Where did you come from?"

"Same place you did," he said. "Mom."

Genna rolled her eyes. *Smartass.* "Where are all the leftovers from tonight?"

"Ah, there are none."

"What?" She gaped at him. *Nothing* left? "You ate all the food?"

"No, Dad told the cook to get rid of whatever was left," he replied. "Said if you wanted some, if you were hungry, you would've brought your ass downstairs at dinnertime."

"That's foul."

"You know how he is."

Stubborn as fuck. Genna turned back to the refrigerator and started pulling out the other containers, glancing inside of them. She found an almost empty container of chicken salad and grabbed a fork, leaning back against the counter as she ate. When it was all gone, she tossed the container in the sink and went right back to the refrigerator, seeking out more. "He in his office?"

"Yeah," Dante replied quietly. "He's fast asleep, already snoring."

When was the last time he slept in his bed? Probably years, Genna thought. Probably since the last time her mother slept in it with him.

Sighing, Genna grabbed a jar of pickles and pulled one out, taking a bite of it as she glanced back at her brother. He was still standing in the doorway, watching her, and making no move to come any closer.

"You know," she said, pointing the pickle at him. "I only went with him last night because he didn't want me to get hurt."

"I would've kept you safe."

She scoffed, taking another bite of the pickle as she

glanced back into the refrigerator and looked around some more, finding a pack of ham. She grabbed some slices and wrapped them around her pickle before taking another bite. "You were a little, uh, preoccupied getting your ass kicked."

Dante scowled as he finally broke his stance, taking a few steps toward her. He didn't humor her with a response, his attention on her food. "What the hell are you eating?"

She shrugged, leaning back against the counter. "Food."

Dante fixed himself a drink as she finished off her snack, the last bite not settling well on her stomach. It started churning again, dizziness making her head fuzzy, as bile burned her chest. She swallowed thickly, trying to push it back, but it was too much.

Too sudden.

Too *strong*.

Genna dove for the trashcan, barely making it in time before she lost everything she had just eaten. Her stomach painfully heaved, purging everything inside of it.

Dante cursed and stepped back from her.

"Call the priest," she gasped, trying to catch her breath. "We need an exorcism."

"You all right?" he asked hesitantly.

"Yeah," she said, sitting back on her knees in front of the trashcan as her stomach settled back down. "Just haven't been feeling well. Think I got a virus or something."

"You're not pregnant, are you?"

His voice was playful as he nudged her, handing over his drink. She took it, scoffing as she took a sip of the cold water. *Pregnant?* "Of course not. I..."

Genna trailed off as that thought settled into her. *No fucking way.* She couldn't be. Jumping to her feet, knocking into Dante and spilling the water, she bolted across the room for the calendar on the wall and flipped back through it, counting the weeks.

No. No. No. Please, God, No.

Five weeks since that night with Matty in her room. Time had passed in such a blur, life delving into chaos, that she hadn't even noticed she missed her period. "Oh, God."

"Relax, sis, I'm just fucking with you," Dante said, laughing. Genna swung around to look at him, swallowing thickly, suddenly feeling like she was going to be sick again. Dante stared at her, his expression falling, his eyes widening. "You're not."

"It's just the stress," she said. "Stress does that, right? Because I've been under *a lot* of stress."

"Please tell me it's not even fucking possible, Genna," Dante said, stepping toward her. "Tell me you're smarter than that, that you've been safe."

"I, uh… it's not possible. It's just not. It can't be." She blinked rapidly. "Oh, God, please don't let it be."

Pregnant?

As that sunk in, Dante stormed out, heading straight for the front door and leaving the house, slamming the door as he left. Genna heard his car start up outside as she headed out to the foyer.

She went upstairs to her room, leaving the door wide open as she plopped down on the bed. She was in a daze, the word continually running through her head.

Pregnant?

In what seemed like no time at all, Dante reappeared, springing up in the doorway in front of her, clutching a bag from the nearby drugstore. He thrust it at her. "Do it."

She glanced inside the bag, seeing a pregnancy test.

"I, uh…"

"Do it," he said again, his voice firmer. "Now."

Genna stood up, her legs shaking as she strode into the bathroom. *Impossible*, she thought. *It just can't be.*

Five minutes later, she stared at the two bright pink lines that told her it could be… that told her it was so. She stumbled out of the bathroom, seeking out her brother in her bedroom. Dante sat on the edge of her bed and slowly stood up, regarding her warily.

She said nothing. What could she say? Words evaded her, abandoning her when she needed them. She stared at him, shell-shocked.

Dante's face paled. She needn't say anything, anyway. He knew. He ran his hands through his hair, lacing his fingers together on the top of his head as he started for the door. "Guess we might need that priest, after all."

Her voice shook as she whispered, "Where are you going?"

"To do what I always do, Genna," he muttered. "Watch out for you."

The night was clear, the full moon glowing bright, high in the pitch-black sky. It neared midnight, another day almost upon them… another day of much the same.

Matty sat in the passenger seat of Enzo's Mercedes, his eyes focused out the window as the streets flew by in a blur. They were back in Soho, having survived the trip north.

Guns, it turned out. The Barsantis were stockpiling guns in a storage unit in East Harlem, ones they had stolen right under the Galantes noses in their territory. Matty had stood in the parking lot and watched a truck of freshly acquired weapons being unloaded. It left a bad taste in his mouth, bitterness he couldn't quite get rid of. All those guns, all that ammunition... they were preparing for something big.

Something he wanted far away from.

"You're tense," Enzo said, cutting his eyes at him. "I don't like it."

"Thought you said I was always tense."

"You are, but not like this. Usually you're like a coil, you know, ready to spring at any moment, but tonight you're like a thread... like if you get pulled any tighter you might finally break."

He felt that way. Fuck, did he feel that way. He wasn't sure how much more he could take, and he didn't want to stick around and find out. He had come for his mother, but now that she was gone, why was he even still there? "I'm tired of waiting around for that pink slip... think I might hand in my resignation instead."

"Think Dad will *accept* your resignation?"

"He won't really have a choice," Matty said. "By the time he realizes I quit, I'll be far away from here."

Enzo hesitated. "Alone?"

"I hope not," he said. "I hope she'll go with me."

"I hope she goes, too."

"You do?"

"Yeah." Enzo frowned, gazing at him, his voice earnest as he said, "I don't wanna see her hurt. I couldn't care less about the girl, but she's yours... she's your girl... and you're my brother."

He didn't say it outright, but Matty heard the full truth in those words. If they stuck around, if Genna stuck around, Enzo knew he might someday be the one to have to hurt her.

Neither spoke anymore as Enzo navigated the streets of Soho. He pulled the car into the lot near The Place and they climbed out, heading out of the parking garage.

They rounded the corner, heading for the apartment, when someone behind them shouted, "Barsanti!"

They turned around, stopping in the middle of the sidewalk. Dante Galante. Enzo immediately braced himself for a fight, both brothers expecting Dante to lunge for him, but instead he hastily stepped right toward Matty. Another guy flanked him, a short, stocky guy—the same one that had been with him on the street that day in Little Italy.

"What the fuck are you doing here, Galante?" Enzo spat, taking a step forward, but Dante quickly sidestepped him. Matty tried to react, to back up, his hands up defensively, but Dante was right in front of him within seconds, swinging.

Dante's fist connected with Matty's jaw, brutally knocking his head to the side, pain tearing down his spine as he stumbled a few steps, stunned. Before he could even get his footing, Dante snatched ahold of his collar, glaring angrily. "This is for my sister."

He swung again, back to back, his fists frantically pounding Matty's face, blackening his eye and busting his nose. Blood spewed down his face as he stumbled backward, all sense of logic disintegrating in the blast of blinding pain. Without even thinking, he struck back, clocking Dante upside the head. The punch ignited a brawl as Enzo fought off the second guy, leaving Matty to defend himself alone.

Matty unleashed every ounce of anger he could conjure, trying to keep him at bay, but he had nothing compared to Dante's fury. His fists packed venom that Matty couldn't match.

Dante knocked him to the ground, hauling his foot back and brutally kicking him. Pain split Matty's side, knocking the breath from his lungs. He could hear the crack and feel the agony from the force of the foot battering his ribcage, again and again. He tried to shield himself, snatching ahold of Dante's foot and yanking on it, trying to throw him to the ground, but Dante merely kicked himself loose.

"Fuck!" Matty cried, seconds before he saw the foot coming straight for his face. He tried to move, to block himself from the attack, but he barely had time to blink before he stomped his face. Pain exploded in his skull, so intense, so overwhelming, he momentarily blacked out.

As soon as everything came back into focus, Dante stepped away. Enzo's voice echoed around them, bitter and full of malice. "Back away from my fucking brother before I kill you."

Matty sat up, his vision blurred, warm blood pouring down the side of his face and staining his clothes. Through the haze he saw the gun, the shiny silver automatic Smith and Wesson revolver in his brother's steady hand, pointed right at Dante.

"En," Matty yelled, frantic, his voice cracking as he painfully forced it from his throat, but it was too late. *Too fucking late.* In the blink of an eye, Dante reached into his waistband, pulling his own gun and aiming.

A single gunshot tore through the night. It sounded like an explosion going off beside Matty, the street around them lighting up for a fraction of a second, as the lone bullet shattered every hope of the two families *ever* finding peace again.

chapter SIXTEEN

Dust tickled Genna's nose, the attic smelling strongly of mothballs and mildew, the air stifling and stale from being locked up for years. Genna hadn't stepped foot in the room since her fifteenth birthday, but she had the overwhelming urge, at that moment, to head up those stairs.

It was the closest she'd ever come to seeing her mother again.

Genna tiptoed along the creaky wooden floor and pulled the string on the hanging overhead bulb. Light instantly surrounded her for a few seconds before flickering and vanishing with a loud pop.

She shrugged it off and sat down on the dirty floor, drawing her knees up to her chest as she wrapped her arms around them. Her body practically folded in on itself then, disappearing in the darkness, disintegrating into thin air, despite the heaviness in her limbs that made her feel like she was made of lead. Her mother's things surrounded her, a thick layer of dust coating it all, blankets of soil on the boxes, her old wedding dress tinged gray from neglect.

It felt like a lifetime ago that any of it had seen the

light of day. A lifetime that Genna found herself longing for again, a life of simplicity, where the world made perfect sense. Things had been black and white then. Her family was everything, the good in her life, the heroes of her story, whereas the Barsantis were all that was wrong with the universe.

Sighing, Genna spread her legs out in front of her and lay back on the floor, her head landing on a pile of her mother's old summer dresses, mere rags now. She stared up at the ceiling, her hands drifting to her stomach as she lay there in silence.

What was she going to do?

What were *they* going to do?

How was she going to tell him?

Would he feel how she felt?

How the hell do I even feel? She was in total disbelief, numbness coating her body. She felt detached from the world, like she had slipped into an alternate reality where a Galante and a Barsanti could somehow be one family.

Certainly wasn't any reality she had ever lived in before.

Terrified, she decided. *I'm fucking terrified.*

She lay there for a while before closing her eyes, exhausted, but sleep evaded her. Eventually she heard a clatter downstairs in the house, noise she shrugged off at first as merely her imagination, until she heard doors slam and feet scurrying about. Curious, and not wanting her father to catch her up here, Genna headed out of the attic, hearing the commotion. She quietly tiptoed downstairs, finding Umberto standing in the foyer alone. His expression was grim, his face freshly battered. He'd taken a beating tonight.

Oh, God. Another fight.

She stepped right by him without speaking. He hardly looked at her, in a daze as he gazed off toward the kitchen. Genna walked that way, hearing hushed, frantic voices inside. She paused in the doorway, seeing her brother in a pair of boxer shorts, his white socks splattered with flecks of red. The rest of his clothes were in a heap on the floor, discarded, as Dante paced around them. His body trembled as he shook his hands, as if trying to get feeling back in them. "This is fucked... *I'm* fucked."

"You'll be fine, son," Primo said, pulling out a black trash bag to gather up his clothes as he motioned toward his feet. "Give me those socks."

Dante tore them off, nearly losing his balance, and tossed the socks into the bag before continuing to pace. His hands ran down his face as he muttered to himself, frenzied. "I swear I didn't mean to do it. I just... *he* drew first. The stupid fuck drew a gun on me. What else was I supposed to do?"

Genna's stomach sunk, her eyes widening in horror.

"You don't have to explain yourself," Primo said. "It was premature, yes, and you shouldn't have done it in Soho, but I'm not going to get *upset* that a Barsanti boy is dead."

Dead. Genna gasped at the word, drawing their attention straight to her. Dante's expression flickered, whatever bit of calm he had been struggling to maintain slipping away as his face contorted, almost as if he fought back tears. Genna frantically shook her head, those words pounding through her like a jackhammer.

Barsanti boy. Dead.

"Oh, God," she gasped. "What did you do?"

"Go to your room, Genevieve," Primo barked. "Now!"

She ignored him as she stepped further into the

kitchen, her focus on her brother. "Dante, please... tell me."

"Genevieve!"

"Tell me!" she yelled frantically. "What did you do, Dante?"

"He drew on me," Dante said, his voice shaking. "Enzo pulled his gun. I had no choice. I *had* to shoot him."

Relief washed through Genna, so intense that her knees buckled. She had to grasp the wall to keep from hitting the floor. It wasn't Matty. Matty wasn't dead.

But that relief was short-lived. Matty may not be dead, but his brother was, killed at the hands of *her* brother. Dante—passive, protective Dante—was a murderer. The knowledge made the ground quake beneath her feet.

"Why were you there?" she asked desperately, trying to make sense of it. "Why were you even in Soho tonight?"

Primo spoke up again, stepping between his children. "Genevieve, you know better than to meddle in business."

"Business?" She glared at her father. "This isn't just *business*, Dad. This is personal, and you know it! A boy is dead, and why? For what?"

"Because he's one of them," Primo growled. "And if this works out like it's supposed to, they'll *all* end up that way. I won't be satisfied until every single drop of Barsanti blood is spilled."

As soon as those words struck Genna, her hands instinctively clutched her stomach. She backed away, shaking her head as tears stung her eyes. Turning, she ran from the room, heading straight for the front door.

She couldn't be there. She couldn't be with them.

The trek to Soho felt like it took hours in the back of a cab. Genna fidgeted, repeatedly trying to call Matty but getting no answer again and again. The cabbie had to drop her off a block away from The Place, the neighborhood blocked off by police. Genna sprinted past the gathered onlookers, ducking right under the yellow crime scene tape, ignoring the protests when an officer tried to stop her.

"Matty?" she hollered, looking around desperately and freezing when she spotted him sitting along the curb across the street. His clothes were soiled, bloodstained and filthy, while dried blood caked the side of his swollen face. A medic hovered over him, trying to bandage his head. Genna started toward him when he looked up, his expression harsh. He shoved the medic away, refusing treatment, as his eyes met hers.

"Matty," she said frantically, crouching down in front of him and grasping his cheeks as she surveyed his battered face. "Oh God, look at you!"

"I'm fine." His voice was hardly a whisper as he covered her hands with his own, pulling them away from his face. "What are you doing here?"

"I know... I mean, I *heard*..." Tears spilled down her cheeks, despite how hard she fought to contain them. "Enzo."

Matty flinched at his name, his gaze darting across the street toward The Place. "They already took him away."

"Was he really...? I mean, is he...?"

She couldn't even say the word. *Dead.*

"It's not safe for you here," Matty said quietly, not answering her question, but the truth was there, swimming in his bloodshot eyes. "You need to go home."

"I can't." She shook her head. "How can you even say that? I can't be there with them. Not now. Not *after*..."

"I have to deal with this," Matty said, brushing the tears from her cheeks. "When it's over, I'll come for you, and we'll leave. We'll get the hell out of New York and never look back."

"You promise?"

"I swear it, but until then, home is the safest place for you." Before she could argue, Matty grabbed a hold of an officer as the man strode past. "I need someone to escort Miss Galante home right away. She shouldn't be out here."

The officer nodded, surveying her. "I'll handle it."

"Thank you."

Matty gazed at Genna for a moment before pulling her toward him and pressing a soft kiss to her forehead. "I love you."

"I love you, too," she whispered. "I'm so, so sorry."

"Yeah," he mumbled, looking away from her as she stood up to follow the officer to a waiting car. "I'm sorry, too."

The Barsanti residence appeared abandoned, a shell of a once-loving household, now shrouded in shadows and doused with coldness. Matty parked right out front and sat in his car for a moment, staring at the front door. It was quiet and dark, all except for a subtle glow of light coming from a room on the second floor.

His father's study.

The police hadn't come by to make the official notification yet and probably wouldn't for a few more hours, but Matty wasn't a fool—he knew his father would know by now. Roberto likely knew the second Enzo took his last shaky breath.

Roberto hadn't gone to the hospital, though, and he

hadn't shown up at the scene. That subtle glow streaming through the curtains upstairs told Matty he hadn't gone anywhere. He sat tight, and waited... and waited... and waited...

But for what?

Matty wasn't sure he wanted to know.

Pushing his apprehension aside, he climbed out of the car and headed up onto the porch, using the spare key his mother had given him to go inside. Quietly, he ascended the stairs, his feet sounding like steel against the wooden floor, the sound bouncing off the white walls, as he made his way straight to the study.

The door was wide-open. Roberto sat in his plush leather chair, his gaze trained on the top of his barren desk. He didn't look up when Matty entered, didn't speak, although the subtle slumping of his shoulders as he let out a deep breath told Matty he knew he was there.

Slowly, Matty stepped into the room, his gaze shifting from his father to the table of weapons right inside. He trailed his fingers along the long barrel of a rifle, the metal cool against his fingertips. Every muscle in his body ached, pain stabbing at his chest every time he breathed deeply, but it was nothing compared to the mental anguish going on inside of him.

Nothing compared to the fresh sting of the memory.

"They killed him." Roberto was quiet, although a restrained quiver accented his words as he fought to keep his voice steady. "He's dead."

Matty sighed, wincing at the discomfort in his chest. He fought back tears, keeping his mouth closed so not to inadvertently let a sob loose. Instead, he nodded, despite knowing his father still wasn't looking at him.

"They killed my boy," Roberto said again, his voice cracking that time, his grip slipping as grief shined through. "They took him from me."

Matty's hand skimmed overtop of a box of ammunition before his fingertips grazed the ridged grip of a pistol. He picked it up, grasping it tightly and gazing at it clenched in his hand. After a moment, he slid it into his pocket, concealing it, and grabbed the box of ammunition.

Without uttering a single word, he turned around and left.

Matty was in a daze as he sped through Manhattan, weaving in and out of the streets, no clear destination in mind. Lines were a blur to him, neighborhoods meaning nothing anymore. Eventually, he ended up cruising out of Manhattan, heading north, telling himself he was just going to look. He was just going to watch. He was just going to *see…*

He parked the Lotus along the street, not far from the Galante residence, giving him a view of the house. It was dark, almost as dark as his family's house had been, only a few dim lights on in the sprawling mansion. Were they sleeping, he wondered? Resting soundly in their beds, not a care in the world, no sweat off their backs.

How callous, how *cruel*, could people be?

Getting out of the car, curiosity getting the best of him, he crept toward the house. He felt a twinge of guilt that he had sent Genna back here, that he had insisted she go home, but it wasn't safe for her elsewhere. If Roberto Barsanti caught wind that she was in the vicinity, if he even thought she might be within arm's reach, they would certainly snatch her.

There was no doubt about it.

Matty walked around the outside of the house, slipping into the backyard and glancing up at Genna's room. The lights were off, the balcony door wide open to let air filter through. He could climb up there, he thought, and slip into her room, spend the night with her, hold her in his arms, find the comfort he so desperately sought, but doing so meant breathing their same air. It meant being in that house, with those people.

He knew what she meant about not being able to come back here after everything. Just the air around the house felt poisoned.

He was surprised they weren't celebrating.

Sighing, he strolled back away, heading toward his car. There was nothing here for him tonight, nothing he could do to change what happened. He had nearly made it back to the street when the porch light flicked on and the front door of the house opened. Matty's footsteps stalled as he turned back around, watching as someone strolled outside. It wasn't a Galante, but it was close enough—the boy from earlier that had been with Dante.

He paused there on the porch, the door wide open behind him, as he waited for something… or *someone*. Matty took a few steps back into the shadows, watching, his blood running cold when Dante stepped outside behind the boy.

Dante had showered and changed clothes, wiped clean of all evidence of anything ever happening. The men talked quietly as they stepped off the porch, strolling toward a car parked along the curb.

The other boy climbed into it after a moment and drove away while Dante just stood there, his eyes studiously scanning the neighborhood. It didn't take long for him to catch sight of the Lotus, his gaze locking on it as he tensed, his shoulders squaring. After a second he swung around, on guard, but Matty was faster than him.

His mind blanked, rational thought fading away as he sprung at Dante. This boy—this *monster*—had attacked them, killing his brother in cold blood before running off like a coward, leaving Matty there to pick up the pieces. Before Dante could react, Matty hit him, knocking him to the ground, before savagely railing on him. Dante tried to fight him off, to thwart the attack, but Matty was too far gone to be deterred.

Gasping, Dante lay on his back on the ground, blood spewing from his mouth, as Matty stood over him. He pulled the gun from his pocket, cocking it and aiming it right at Dante's head. His finger loosely touched the trigger, trembling from pent-up rage, as he stared into the eyes of the one who had stolen his brother from him just hours ago.

"Why?" The question came out forceful and full of so much venom that Matty hardly recognized his own voice. "I want to know *why*."

'Why is never a good question to ask,' Enzo had warned him just the day before. *'You'll never get the answer you want to hear.'*

"You gave me no choice," Dante growled. "Because of *you*, my sister's as good as dead."

Before Matty could process that, the front door of the house opened again. Hearing it, Dante sat up as Matty backed away, lowering the gun. The moment he caught sight of Genna's alarmed face in the doorway, his senses came back to him.

He'd watched his brother die tonight.

He couldn't put Genna through the same.

chapter SEVENTEEN

Last week of community service finally arrived.

Genna punctually showed up to the soup kitchen for dinner duty, going through the motions as she cooked and served, helping clean up as much as she could in between, in order to be out the door at exactly seven o'clock. There was no staying late anymore, despite how much she wished she could stick around and lose herself in the work.

But every day, Dante would be parked out front, waiting for her, even though they all knew he had a target on his back. He risked exposure to make sure she was delivered home safe and sound, a fact that she both appreciated and loathed. Their drives were even more strained, so much so that she didn't think they would ever get what they once had back. Too much had happened. It had gone too far for everything to be forgotten.

She felt it weighing on her, heavy in the air those thirty minutes they were confined in his car together. She wanted to say something, to come up with some way to lessen the tension just a bit to make it easier to breathe around him, but she wasn't sure what to say.

One thing she was certain of, though: she yearned for her best friend again.

Friday afternoon arrived, and Genna slouched in the passenger seat, staring out the window as Dante drove north toward East Harlem. Sunlight blasted them through the tinted windows of his car, the afternoon warm and breezy. She'd say it was a beautiful day, normally, but it still felt drab.

Dante swung his car in along the curb just down from the community center and put it in park as he let out a deep sigh. "Last day, huh?"

She was surprised he'd even attempt conversation. He hadn't bothered all week long. "Yeah."

"Gotta tell you, sis, I didn't think you'd do it," he said, "but you saw it through to the very end."

"Yeah," she said. "I did."

"I'm proud of you."

Those words startled her. Blinking rapidly, she turned to Dante, seeing the soft smile tugging his lips. "What?"

"I'm proud of you," he said again, no sarcasm in his voice. "Dad would never say it, but well... I'm proud as hell. Proud that you didn't give up, that you stuck with it, no matter what."

She was taken aback. "Thanks."

"I have a hard time accepting that you've grown up," he continued. "I know I'm not much older than you, but I've always felt responsible for you. And I know you resent me sometimes for it, but—"

"I don't resent you," she said, cutting him off.

He closed his eyes briefly before continuing just where he had left off. "But I just tried to look out for you, the only way I knew how."

"I know."

Raising his eyebrows, he glanced at her curiously. "Have you told him yet?"

Her cheeks heated at the question. "I haven't had the chance."

"Are you happy, at least?"

The honesty of his question surprised her. "I, uh... yeah. Well, I mean, I was... as happy as I could possibly ever be under the circumstances, anyway. It sucks, being who we are, but..."

"But he's different," Dante said quietly. "That's what you told me that day. You said he was different."

"He is."

Dante ran his hands down his face. "I can't help you anymore, Genna. I can't watch out for you... not like I always have before. You're on your own with this, and I don't think it can end well."

"I know."

A smile slowly returned to Dante's lips. "But you proved me wrong last time I doubted you. Maybe you'll do it again."

Genna returned his smile. "I will."

Reaching over, Genna hugged her brother, feeling his arms wrap around her tightly. He turned away as he let go, his attention focusing out of the windshield. "Seven o'clock?"

"Seven o'clock," she confirmed.

She got out of the car and headed inside of the community center, pausing there and watching as Dante merged into traffic and sped away. Sighing, she glanced around. *Last day.*

Dinner was a breeze, with more than enough food to

go around. Come seven o'clock Genna was pulling her apron off and tossing it into the hamper for the last time when the coordinator approached, waving around a piece of paper as he grinned. "You know what this is?"

"What?"

"Your discharge papers."

"Huh." Genna took it, reading the glowing remarks the coordinator had written about her. "Thanks."

She headed for the door, still skimming through the paper as she stepped out onto the sidewalk. Looking up, she expected to see Dante's car waiting for her, front and center as usual, but an old Toyota was parked in that spot instead. She glanced around, scanning the neighborhood, thinking maybe he couldn't get a close spot, but his car was nowhere to be found.

She reached into her pocket for her phone, cursing when she didn't find it. She must have left it in Dante's car.

Shrugging it off, forcing back the feeling of dread her brother's absence conjured up, she strolled down the block toward the train. He must've lost track of time, she figured. There was no telling what he was out there doing.

She glanced both ways, making sure nothing was coming, before jogging across the street. She stepped up onto the sidewalk, folding the paper and slipping it into her pocket, when someone called out to her. "Galante."

Genna's blood ran cold. The voice was unfamiliar and lacked all warmth. Glancing behind her, she immediately saw two vaguely familiar faces—guys who used to hang around Enzo. Tweedledum and Tweedledee, Dante had called them. They stood close, a mere few feet between her and them. Alarmed, she took a step away. "What do you want?"

The grin that crossed one of their faces spoke louder than any words. *You*, it said. *We want you.*

She didn't hesitate, turning around and sprinting, running as fast as her legs could carry her down the block. They immediately gave chase, keeping up with her pace. Frenzied, she ran down into the train station, shoving people out of the way, ignoring their shouts as she tried to move through the crowd. She continually looked behind her as she ran, trying to catch glimpses of them, but she lost them somewhere along the way.

Heart erratically pounding, she dodged onto the first train that came along, instantly taking a seat as she nervously fidgeted, turning to the side to watch outside. Someone took the seat beside her, brushing against her, and she jumped, yelping. Turning toward them, she started to apologize for her startled reaction but froze when she caught his eye.

Tweedledum. Or Tweedledee.

She didn't know which one it was, but that didn't matter. One of them had caught up to her. He sat back in the seat as Genna shifted away from him as far as she could, her vision hazy as tears of panic sprung to her eyes. "I'll scream."

"No, you won't. Besides, I'm not here to hurt you."

"Then why are you here?"

"What?" He raised his eyebrows, feigning innocence. "A guy can't take the train?"

"I know you want something," she pressed, hands trembling. "So tell me what you want."

"To pass along a message."

"What message?"

He didn't respond, relaxing back in the seat as he glanced around nonchalantly. The train stopped after a minute, the doors opening and passengers filtering out.

Calmly, the man stood. "Exodus 21:24."

"Excuse me?"

"Exodus 21:24," he said again, reaching into his pocket and pulling out something, tossing it onto Genna's lap. She snatched ahold of it before it hit the floor, seeing it was a wallet. "Tell your father Bobby Barsanti sends his regards."

Before she could process it, the man was gone, the doors closing and train moving on. Carefully, Genna opened the leather wallet, hoping against logic it wasn't what she thought it was, but there, right inside the plastic on the inside, was her brother's smiling face on his driver's license.

She took another train before hailing a cab, sprinting home when it dropped her off a block from her house. Out of breath, she shoved her way through the front door.

"Dad! Where are you, Dad?"

"What's with the shouting?" he called from his office, stepping into the doorway, his brow furrowing as he looked at her. "Where's your brother?"

Immediately, she ran toward him, shoving Dante's wallet at him as her mouth frantically moved, words spewing out in an attempt to explain what had happened. She made little sense to even herself, and she could tell he had no idea what she was saying from his confused look.

"Slow down, Genevieve, and tell me what happened."

"Dante didn't show up tonight," she said, trying to calm down. "I was taking the train home and I saw one of them... one of *them*... and they gave me this wallet and told me to give you a message."

Primo's expression hardened as he did exactly what Genna had done: opened the wallet to look at the driver's license. "What message?"

"Uh, Exodus... 21:24."

Genna's eyes darted to where the plaque bearing that scripture hung on the wall. She was mentally cursing herself for not paying attention in Sunday school as a kid, for never cracking open that crisp new bible her mother had bought her before she died. Although she had been baptized Catholic, and her father liked to claim they were a righteous family, religion had never been a big part of her life. The commandments? She could probably name them, thanks to the Charlton Hesston flick her father watched every godforsaken Easter, but beyond that?

Nothing.

Primo stood still for a moment, staring at Dante's driver's license. "Did he say anything else?"

"No." She shook her head, hesitating. "Just that Bobby Barsanti sends his regards."

Primo nodded, saying not a word as he turned around and went straight back into his office. Genna followed, lingering in the doorway, watching incredulously as he took a seat on the couch.

"So?" she asked, fidgeting anxiously as she waited for some kind of reaction from him. "What does it mean?"

Primo fiddled with the wallet, opening it and closing it again and again, his expression strained. "Exodus 21:24."

"Yes," she said. "What is it?"

Sighing, he closed the wallet for the final time before setting it aside, his gaze meeting hers. "An eye for an eye... a tooth for a tooth... a hand for a hand... a foot for a foot..."

Genna's hand covered her mouth as the implication of that sunk in, washing all hope from her system, leaving her left with nothing but bitter sickness.

A son for a son.

EIGHTEEN

Peace.

It didn't happen often, not to the extent that settled over Manhattan that weekend. Both sides willfully retreated in an unspoken cease-fire, crossing back into their own territory, those invisible walls that divided the city locking back into place to keep the families apart, but the damage had already been done.

Their worlds were fractured by a misery that moments of strained peace couldn't begin to mend.

Nothing happened for days—no violence, no theft, no brutality. No blood spilled into the desolate streets. Dante's car was recovered not far from home, the driver's side door wide open and the keys still dangling in the ignition. There was no sign of him, the interior splattered with blood. Her phone had been found lying on the passenger floorboard, the front of it cracked from an apparent scuffle.

Genna wallowed, mourning, holed up in her house, not even stepping outside on the porch to face the sun. She didn't want to see it shining, didn't want to see the world continuing to turn. Days passed as a blur of hours... minutes... seconds...

She went through the motions, looking but not seeing, touching but not feeling. She was there, but she felt so far away.

"Are you okay?" Matty asked quietly over the phone one night, their communication the two weeks since Enzo's death little more than a string of missed calls and text messages. She had so much to say to him, so much to tell him, to ask him, to beg of him, but their words were lost in a haze of grief. *Are you okay?* It was a question she'd asked him more than once, but it felt like a slap to the face when wielded in return.

Of course I'm fucking not okay.

"It doesn't feel real," she whispered, her voice strained. She lay on her bed in the darkness, her phone on the pillow beside her on speakerphone. His voice surrounded her, so close, yet too distant. If she closed her eyes, it almost... *almost*... felt like he was right there. "It's like, if I don't see it... how can it be real?"

No body, no funeral. Although Dante was presumed dead by the family, the assumption didn't offer any closure, didn't comfort her, when without *him* it just didn't feel real. There one minute and gone the next... but gone where?

Logically, she knew she would likely never know. Dante had warned her of that once before. It felt like a lifetime ago when they had stood in Little Italy and he warned her that if the Barsantis got ahold of one of them, there would be nothing left to identify.

"You know, I tried to go to Joey's funeral," Matty said. "I almost did. I got dressed and went downstairs and said I was going. I didn't ask... I *told*. My father forbid it, but

I stood up to him."

"What stopped you?"

"He did, of course. Locked me in my bedroom until it was over. He said it wasn't safe, and he was right—it wasn't. It *still* isn't. It'll never be safe for me in this city. But still, to this day, I regret not going. Without closure, it's hard for a wound to heal."

"Will it?" she asked. "Will it get better? Will it ever *heal*?"

"I don't know," he replied. "I was only eight when I lost my best friend, and it hasn't healed yet."

"Yeah, well, I'm eighteen, and my best friend's gone now, and I don't think I'll ever be okay again."

"You'll be okay." Matty's voice was barely a whisper. "We both will be."

Genna closed her eyes, tears streaming from the corner of them and running down her cheeks. Wiping them away, she let out a shaky breath. Would they be okay? She so desperately wanted to believe that.

"Matty, there's something I need to tell you," she said, her voice shaking. "Something you should know."

"What is it?" Before she could respond, there was a shuffling on the line, and Matty cursed under his breath. "Hold that thought. My father's here."

Immediately, the phone beeped as Matty ended the call, silence overcoming her bedroom again. She continued to lay there, in no mood to move, in no mood to do *anything*. Time passed again, darkness falling over the room, before a chime rang out with a new message from Matty.

Tomorrow

Tomorrow... *Monday*. She knew they were planning to finally bury Enzo then, to put him to rest.

She replied right away. **What about it?**

His answer was prompt. **Tomorrow we leave.**

Genna stared at those words. He had promised her they'd go, that they'd leave and never look back. That they'd start over new somewhere. Matty told her he lived in the present, that he took things as they came, but somewhere along the line that had changed. He was preparing for the future now.

A future for them *together*.

Tomorrow, she thought, closing her eyes again, her hands drifting to her stomach instinctively. *Just one more day and we're out of here.*

For the second time that summer, Matty found himself standing in the middle of the Catholic cemetery, in nearly the same exact spot both times—the Barsanti family plot.

Weeks ago it had been vacant, just a grassy knoll, perfectly kempt and waiting for the day it would be needed. But now a headstone stuck up from the ground, bearing the name Savina Brazzi-Barsanti, the grass just feet from it freshly disturbed as they said goodbye to yet another one.

Enzo. Matty felt the void, the space beside his father where his brother had always stood now nothing but air, nobody daring to step foot there. Sighing, Matty kept his head down, hands clasped in front of him, until the final "Amen" was spoken from the grieving crowd.

Within seconds he was walking away, not bothering to stick around for the customary *'pay your respects to the family'* bullshit, and approached his cousin Gavin. Subtly, Gavin nodded in greeting, his voice quiet as he said, "I'll be in touch."

Matty returned the nod before he strolled through the cemetery, away from the crowd, off toward the other side where he had never ventured before.

It took him a while—ten, maybe fifteen minutes—before he caught sight of what he was looking for. The headstones were worn, having been here for years... one more faded than the other.

Joseph Galante

Below his name, below the too short dates spanning his life bore the words *'forever young'*. He was buried beside his mother, her headstone larger to someday accommodate Primo on the same marble marker. His name was there, etched in the stone, his day of death left blank.

The callous bastard was still breathing.

Around them were empty plots Matty suspected were reserved for the other Galante children, but neither would ever be buried there. Dante, because he had vanished, and Genna, because Matty was getting her the hell out of there. She wouldn't be around to see the end of it, to see the bitter conclusion of the long-standing rivalry.

Neither of them would be there.

Because Matty knew, deep down inside, that it wasn't over. They were merely standing in the eye of the hurricane... and it only stayed calm for so long.

"Soon."

The gruff voice behind Matty made the hair at the nape of his neck bristle. He hadn't heard his father approach. Slowly turning his head, he eyed the man. "Soon?"

"Soon that headstone will have a date," Roberto said, glaring at the worn marble displaying Primo's name. "And then I'll finally be satisfied."

"Will you?" Matty asked quietly, turning away from his father. "Will you really be *satisfied*?"

Instead of being offended by the question, Roberto let out a light laugh, slapping his son on the back before roughly squeezing his shoulder. "As satisfied as a man like me can be."

Not satisfied at all.

Roberto let go of him and took a step away. "You coming back to the house?"

"No, I have some things to take care of," Matty said.

"Family business?" Roberto asked.

"Yes," Matty said quietly. "Family."

Nodding, Roberto walked away without saying another word. Matty stood there for a few minutes longer before glancing at his watch. Six o'clock. He was picking Genna up a little after nine, after her father went to sleep.

That gave him three hours.

Strolling back through the trail of headstones, he headed toward his Lotus parked along the road, pressing the button a few feet away to unlock the doors and start the engine. As soon as he was inside, he sped away, giving only a brief glance back at the cemetery.

He drove to The Place, ordering a Roman Coke from the bartender and taking a seat at his usual table out of pure habit. He sat there, staring at the empty seat across from him as he nursed his drink, trying to gather the courage to go upstairs. Enzo's things were scattered all over the apartment, exactly where he had left them, and Matty didn't have the heart to face it.

When his drink was finished, he ordered another.

And another.

And another.

Time faded away, darkness falling outside before his phone chimed with a message from a familiar number. **Meet me at Casato.**

Matty stood back up and strolled through The Place as he glanced at his watch again. It was already pushing eight. Instead of going upstairs, instead of packing his things like he had planned, he merely walked away. He had just enough time to swing by Little Italy before claiming his girl and getting the hell out of Manhattan, the hell out of New York, the hell away from the Galantes, and the Barsantis, and everything.

"Not working tonight?" the bartender asked when he strolled toward the door.

"No," Matty said. *Not working ever again.*

He drove to Little Italy, parking the Lotus in a spot just past his destination. He strolled toward Casato, his hands in his pockets, his head down. The café was quiet at this hour as they were closing up for the night. Matty stepped inside, the bell above the door jingling. Johnny wasn't working tonight, a young woman behind the counter casting him a curious look. "We're closing in five minutes."

"Yeah, I'm just looking for somebody," Matty said. "Gavin Amaro?"

As if on cue, the door to the kitchen swung open and Gavin stepped out, his attention on his phone as he dialed a number. He brought it to his ear but hesitated when he looked up, his expression brightening. He laughed as he ended his call and slipped his phone back away. "I was just calling you."

"Here I am," Matty said.

Gavin turned toward the girl working. "You can go ahead and leave. I'll finish closing up."

She said her thanks and jetted out the door. Once she was gone, Gavin pulled a manila envelope from his suit coat and slapped it down on the nearest table. "Everything you asked for—two brand new identities, totally legit, complete with birth certificates and driver's licenses."

"And the person you got it from...?"

"No problem," Gavin said. "Called in a favor out of Chicago. He'll never utter a word about it."

"Ah." Matty picked it up, clutching the envelope tightly. "Thanks."

"Don't mention it," Gavin said, waving him off. "That's what family's for, right?"

Matty smiled. "Right."

chapter

NINETEEN

"Nope... definitely not... no way... ugh, what the fuck is that?"

Genna shifted through the clothes in her closet, shoving hangers aside. A black duffel bag sat on the floor by her bare feet, completely empty. She was supposed to be packing but had no idea what to take. It would help if she knew where they were going, but Matty had given her no clue.

Sighing, Genna kicked the bag aside, discarding it in the corner. *Fuck it. Who needs things, anyway?* Slipping on a pair of shoes, she headed back into her bedroom and glanced at the clock.

A few minutes past eight.

Adrenaline, fueled by anticipation, scorched through her veins. She was nothing more than a tangled ball of nerves, so wound tight and jumbled up that she couldn't settle down. Giving up, she strode out of the room and headed downstairs, taking the stairs slowly as she headed toward the dining room. Primo sat in his usual spot at the head of the table, the food in front of him completely untouched. Four empty place settings surrounded him, a sight that made Genna pause to take in.

"Joining me tonight?" Primo asked, his voice emotionless as he picked up his glass of wine and took a sip. "You haven't come down for dinner in days."

"Yeah, I, uh... I thought..." What *was* she thinking? Guilt nagged at her chest, twisting her stomach and taking away the last shred of hunger she had even felt. "Just thought it would be nice to eat together again... you know... like old times."

Unshed tears stung her eyes as she stammered through those words. *Ugh, fucking hormones.* The fact that it could very well be the last time she saw her father—the last time she sat at this table, at this dinner, inside of this house— stirred up a bitter pang of longing inside of her.

"Sit," Primo said, motioning toward her chair before calling for the staff to bring her dinner. They set a plate of pork roast in front of Genna before disappearing back into the kitchen, preparing to leave for the night.

As soon as her plate was in front of her, Primo held his hand out toward her. Carefully, she took it, his strong hand dwarfing hers as he squeezed it, bowing his head to pray. "Forgive us, Father, for our sins," he said. "We thank you for our many blessings."

Genna pulled her hand back away as soon as he let go and grabbed her fork, poking at the food on her plate. It was quiet, neither of them eating. It was bittersweet, as Genna's gaze kept shifting to the spot directly across from her, the chair Dante had sat in every day. She had avoided it all weekend, had avoided the reality, but there it was, staring her in the face... the tangible truth, a glaring reminder that he was gone.

Unable to stop it, a tear rolled down Genna's cheek. She tried to brush it away, to hide the evidence of her distress before her father saw, but nothing escaped his notice. Without even looking at her, he let out a deep sigh. "Your brother loved you."

"I know he did," she whispered.

"It won't be the same without him."

"It won't," she agreed.

Nothing would ever again be the same.

Dinner was silent after that, neither one seeming to have any more to say. Genna's gaze kept bouncing toward the clock, counting down the minutes as it slowly approached nine o'clock. The silence was so thick, permeating every corner of the dining room that Genna startled when a phone ringing shattered it. Dropping her fork, she grasped her chest as Primo snatched up the emergency line, barking the word "talk" into the phone.

Strained seconds passed.

"He's there?" Primo asked, his voice void of all sentiment. "Do it now."

He hung up the phone then, glancing at Genna again just as she wiped away another wayward tear.

"Don't fret," he said. "They won't get away with it."

Genna cut her eyes at her father suspiciously. "What?"

"They'll get what's coming to them."

"They already have." She shook her head exasperatedly. Was he so blinded by his hatred that he couldn't see the fact that *both* families had already paid with blood? Young blood—*innocent* blood—that had been underhandedly drawn into the rivalry. "They lost a son."

"I lost *two*."

Those words hitting Genna was like an ice bucket of water being dumped over her head. Unable to stop herself, she violently shivered.

The phone rang again. Primo snatched it up to answer, ignoring the worried look that his daughter cast him. "Talk."

More icy silence.

"It's set?" Primo asked. "Good."

"Is *what* set?" Genna asked when he hung up the phone. "What are you up to?"

Primo cut his eyes at her. There, in the deep brown of his gaze, Genna saw the hatred. She saw the bitterness, the anger, and the need for vengeance. But nowhere, in the look he offered her, did she see any compassion. No understanding. No regard for the fact that she was in love with one of them, no regard for what they may be going through.

The Barsantis called her father callous. For the first time in her life, Genna saw it.

"What did you do?" Her voice shook, a terrified whisper. "Tell me."

"An eye for an eye," he replied. "A life for a life."

"A son for a son," she whispered.

"A car for a car." Primo let out a short laugh, his attention on his glass of wine. "The sky in Little Italy will be lit up once again."

Genna's stomach sunk, the breath knocked from her lungs at those words.

The Lotus.

Shoving her chair back, Genna was on her feet without another word. Terror propelled her, pushing her toward the door as she ignored her father calling after her.

She snatched her keys from the ring by the door before bounding out onto the porch, glancing around in frenzy, debating what to do as she pulled out her phone. She dialed Matty's number as she set out through the yard, straight toward where her car had been parked for the past two months, not driven.

The phone rang... and rang... and rang.

No answer.

Panicked, she jumped into the car and sped away from the house, distractedly weaving through traffic as she headed into Manhattan and toward Little Italy, dialing Matty's number again and again, hanging up as soon as she reached his voicemail before dialing it yet again. She refused to think it was too late... that she was too late. It couldn't be.

It fucking couldn't be.

She sped through the streets, passing cars illegally, not caring who she ran off the road. Anxiously, she ran straight through a red light, smashing the gas in an attempt to get through unscathed, the close blaring of a horn distracting her. She glanced back, terrified, and saw the car narrowly missing her rear end.

Genna breathed a sigh of relief, but it was short-lived. The moment she turned back around, she saw the glow of a pair of taillights right in front of her. Cursing, she slammed the brakes, but she hadn't been fast enough. The phone dropped from her hand, hitting the floor of her car, as she braced herself for impact.

Her body lurched, and she winced, slamming into the steering wheel as she skidded right into the back end of a car, nearly knocking it into an intersection. Heart hammering in her chest, she flung the door open to climb out, dizziness overwhelming her momentarily. The driver of the other car started to get out, but Genna was already gone.

She ran.

She ran until her legs burned and her chest felt like it was going to burst. She ran faster than she had ever run before, along streets she vaguely knew, past the music store and the old movie theater, Italian flags flapping in the night breeze above her head.

She ran, and she ran, and she ran some more.

But she didn't run fast enough.

The moment she turned the corner off Mulberry Street, a flash of shiny red caught her eye. The Lotus was parked just down from her favorite small café. Genna's breath hitched, her feet taking a few hurried steps that direction before she was brutally knocked backward by the blast.

BOOM

She felt it before she saw it, the vibration ripping through her before the loud bang tore through the neighborhood. The air was knocked straight from her lungs as she stumbled, the fireball shooting straight up in the air. The car exploded, disappearing in a mass of smoke and flames, metal flying as debris scattered, windows shattering in the vicinity.

The heat was so intense Genna's skin felt like it was ablaze half a block away. Inhaling sharply, excruciatingly, she let out a shriek of agony, the sound resonating deep down in her soul, unable to be contained within her body. She screamed his name, her voice painfully cracking, as the explosion consumed the car and ignited others surrounding it.

The streets erupted in chaos, the world around her in fast-forward while she was stricken by slow motion. Crying, tears coating her face, she dropped to her knees on the sidewalk and clutched onto her hair, eyes peeled on the blazing inferno where Matty's car used to be. People ran past her, knocking into her, moving around her as if she weren't even there. But Genna couldn't move. She couldn't speak. She couldn't breathe.

All she could do was stare.

Suddenly, abruptly, as a crowd descended upon the scene, Genna was grabbed from behind. Arms snaked around her waist, violently yanking her to her feet. Startled, her voice cracked as she shrieked and fought them away, but their grip was strong.

Breath tickled the back of her neck as their voice trembled, whispering to her. "Calm down, princess."

The voice washed through her, simultaneously sustaining her, while stealing away the last bit of her strength. Her body went limp, her head dropping as her hands clutched tightly to the arms around her. Her knuckles, bright white with strain, stood out strikingly compared to the dark ink coloring his forearms. "Matty."

He dragged her down the street, away from the madness, and straight into the café. The windows had been blown out, the restaurant deserted except for the two of them. As soon as they were inside, he let go of her. Genna turned, blinking rapidly as she took in the sight of his face, marked only by the remnants of past trouble. Hurriedly, frantically, she grasped him, feeling on his chest, assessing him to make sure he wasn't hurt. "You... you're here... you're okay! How? I saw it... the Lotus... I just saw it..." She frantically shook her head, so wildly her vision blurred. "I *saw* it!"

"Genna." His voice was strong as his hands firmly

grasped her cheeks, holding her there, forcing her to look at him. "Calm down."

She stared at him, her thoughts frantically racing. "But... how?"

"Remote start," he said, raising his eyebrows. "Remember?"

Remote start. She'd picked on him about how unnecessary it was, having a button on his keys to start his car from far away. *Pretentious bastard and his flashy gadgets.* "Thank fuck you're so goddamn lazy."

Before he could respond, she threw herself at him, wrapping her arms around him. He hugged her back, holding her tightly and smoothing her hair. "My best friend died from turning a key in an ignition. I try to do that as little as possible."

Tears streamed down Genna's cheeks as he held her. "You're okay."

"Well... I'm *alive.*"

She let out a shaky breath. "That'll do."

The adrenaline inside of her, shielding her from the pain, keeping her in shock, slowly started to wane. Every muscle in her body was tense, strained, her stomach cramping.

"We need to get out of here," Matty said quietly, letting go of her. "First we need to find a car and head for Jersey... then we'll take it from there."

Genna took a step back, wincing as her stomach clenched. Her alarm spiked again. "Wait, I have to tell you something."

"Can't it wait?" he asked.

She shook her head. "I don't think so. You should know. Before we do this... you should know."

"What is it?"

"I'm, uh…" She inhaled sharply, eyes wide. "I'm pregnant."

She wasn't sure how he would react, especially now— especially *then*—but she certainly didn't expect stone-cold silence. He stood there, a mere few feet in front of her, his expression blank, and said not a single word in response.

She eyed him warily. "Matty?"

He still said nothing.

"Oh God," she groaned. "Did I break you? Matty, for fuck's sake, talk to me, please."

"You're *pregnant*."

"Yeah."

"Are you…? I mean, you know…" He waved toward her stomach. "Is it…?"

"Is it… *yours*? Is that what you're asking me?"

"No." He blew out a deep breath. "I'm asking if you're okay."

"Oh." She clutched her stomach. "I *think* so."

"Okay then," he said, nodding. "Change of plans. First, we find a car, then we find a doctor… *then* we hit the road and never look back."

EPILOGUE

This is where the story ends, back where it began, lingering in a cloud of thick black smoke, heavy with the weight of misery.

Roberto Barsanti never believed he was to blame for anything that happened. He was merely protecting his family, avenging an attack that had been perpetrated against them on his oldest son's eighth birthday. A few times he had felt shame for certain unfortunate circumstances, although never strong enough to stop his quest for retaliation. His anger was too deep, the betrayal too serious, for him to just back away and forget about everything.

But standing on the corner in Little Italy that summer night, staring through the hazy air at the mangled frame of Matteo's car, he finally felt what had been missing all along.

Remorse.

The explosion had been felt for miles around in the form of a small quake, a vibration beneath their feet. Roberto would have been shocked had it not registered on the Richter scale with the way it seemed to rock his universe, shaking his last bit of stable ground.

He had nothing left. *Nothing.* Through it all, he had told himself it was for his family, for the Barsantis, but what was left of them now?

Nobody except for *him.*

He had no way to truly know, as he stood there, if Matteo had been in the car when it exploded. Fragments of it were scattered throughout the neighborhood, the sleek sports car resembling an aluminum can someone had carelessly crushed. Even if he had been inside, they may *never* know. But at that moment, all he could think was that God was punishing him for his sins, had stolen his boy from him in exchange for the one he had taken this very same way so many years ago.

A son for a son, indeed.

Roberto never believed in karma. It was why he had always been so quick to act, so quick to seek vengeance. He couldn't rely on the universe for retribution. He needed to go out there and get it himself. But he believed now.

He believed, and he *grieved.*

As Roberto watched all that was left of his world burn, a lone voice broke through the haze, dense with the same heartache that he felt constricting his chest. The desolate sound drew his gaze away from the inferno as the familiar man ran right past him, oblivious to his presence.

Primo Galante.

"Genevieve!" he shouted, frantically shoving his way through the crowd. "Where are you? Oh God! *Genevieve!*"

His voice broke, cracking the last time that he screamed her name. Roberto watched as officers tried to restrain the man, subduing Primo before he could break through the barrier surrounding the scene. He shoved them away, shaking, as he frantically looked around, still shouting her name, looking for her.

Their eyes met after a moment from where they stood, a few yards away from each other on the sidewalk. They had seen each other over the years, had sat in the same room a few times while dealing with business with the five families, but it was the first time he had actually looked his old friend in the eyes in over a decade, since their children were knee-high and still innocent to all of it.

Their children. Roberto saw the same fear he felt reflected back at him in Primo's eyes as they stared at one another in silence.

Unable to handle it, Roberto's gaze shifted past his old friend, down the frenzied block. Gavin Amaro, only son of the Amaro crime family, stood right in front of his family's café, a stunned expression on his face as he watched them. Gavin regarded the man warily as a lone question touched Roberto's lips, barely a whisper of words. "My son."

Slowly, hesitantly, Gavin nodded once before lowering his eyes, his gaze flickering toward the flames. He hadn't heart him, but he knew, and it was all the confirmation Roberto needed. He turned back to the demolished car, the heat from the raging fire lapping at him even from afar, making it feel as if his skin were melting. Numbness coated him, the shock washing away every shred of anger. He felt a strange connection with Primo Galante again, the man he had once considered his best friend, and then his mortal enemy. He would never forgive him, just as he would never forgive himself now, but it was over, as far as he was concerned. It had to be. Death was too good for Primo, just as he knew it wouldn't yet come for him.

They would have to live with their choices.

Someone approached Roberto then. He glanced beside him, seeing one of the Civello brothers, a look of sick shock on the kid's face as he viewed the chaos around Little Italy. He paused there, after a moment meeting Roberto's eyes. "Is that...? Was that...?"

Roberto didn't respond right away, turning his gaze back to the burning vehicle as the fire department tried to battle the intense flames. Somehow, that was crueler than actually *seeing* your child dead. And all of Primo's children had been taken that way.

"We need to discuss Dante," Roberto said, his gaze once more seeking out his former friend as the man struggled, still screaming for his Genevieve.

Was she with Matteo?

Had the man killed his own daughter?

"What about him?" the Civello boy asked.

Roberto closed his eyes, his chest heavy from the regret building inside of him. "I'm considering delivering him back to his father."

There was a moment of odd quiet as the blood-curdling screams of desperation stopped. Reopening his eyes, Roberto watched as Primo dropped to his knees, his face a blank mask as shock seemed to set in.

"Whatever you want, boss. You want him delivered back, we'll deliver him." The boy hesitated before adding, "just one question, though."

Roberto turned away from the fire, away from the chaos, and regarded him. "What?"

"Should we actually kill him first?"

Acknowledgements

First and foremost, I want to thank a man I've never met before... a man by the name of Chris Baty. You see, years ago Chris founded National Novel Writing Month, and this story right here? This was my NaNoWriMo book of 2013. So, on behalf of the countless writers out there, foregoing sleep and sanity to crank out a book in thirty days, I thank you for inspiring us and giving us the motivation we sometimes need.

Sarah Anderson, who was there from the very first word of this book, trusting me not to destroy her *too* much when I told her I was totally gonna *Romeo & Juliet* this shit... you deserve a gold medal for your patience and positivity when I try to flounce my own work. You're a brilliant writer. Never forget that, my friend.

Nicki Bullard, my best friend for more years than I'm willing to add up because it makes me feel super old... without you, I'd probably end up on a primetime TV special, the crazy cat lady that everyone thought was dead because she hasn't left her house in forever. Thank you for being my partner-in-crime and going on these crazy adventures with me. Love you to pieces, bitch.

I guess I should also thank Tony, the waiter at Chili's, who helped inspire a scene in this book when I asked for a ten-inch steak and he just would *not* let it go.

To my dad, for reading everything I've ever written, even when it was totally not his thing... thank you for being my biggest fan, even if I know you'll always prefer Stephen King. I love you. To my mama, the strongest person I've ever known... man, I wish you were here for all of this. I miss you terribly. To the rest of my family... my spawn, my brother, my sister-in-law, my niece/nephew, my aunts/uncles, all of you... I'm blessed to have been born into a family full of so many kickass people. I love you all.

Special thanks to Scott Hoover for the spectacular photo on the cover, and to Hollis Chambers for lending his gorgeously photogenic face, and to Ellie at Love N Books for making it all possible. Thanks to my amazing agent, Frank Weimann, for never forgetting about me, even when I'm off doing my own thing.

Much respect goes to Shakespeare, who didn't invent the concept of forbidden love, but who certainly wrote the most notorious star-crossed lovers of all time. (He did however coin the name "Jessica", which I happen to think is the best name of all time... not that I'm biased or anything).

Last, but certainly not least, thank *you*. Every single one of you reading this. Without bloggers and readers, none of this would even be possible. Because of you, I'm following my dreams. I'm eternally grateful for you taking a chance on my words.

Made in the USA
Lexington, KY
25 February 2015